THE IKON

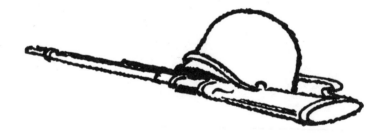

THE IKON

A Novel by
CLAYTON C. BARBEAU

Ikon Press
San Francisco, Ca.

Library of Congress Catalog Card Number: 61-6838

ISBN: 0-9633157-0-6

Printed in the United States of America
Ikon Press
842 Clayton Street
San Francisco, Ca. 94117-4424

To

MYRA ELLEN BARBEAU

A Token for My Lady

"Our souls are made or unmade by the quality of our response to being and the trials of bodily life."
JAMES COLLINS: *The Existentialists*

*H*IS hair powdered with the warm silt, his nose itching from it and from the putrid, stomach-tangling stench of human fertilizer, Warren walked from his tent down to the small river that bordered one edge of the replacement compound. Careful not to drop any of the clothing he carried in his arms, he picked his way through the men who squatted or lay on the sandy bank. Across the river a crazy quilt of brackish rice paddies ran into and up the slopes of the hills. The hills, at least, imposed some sense of order upon the paddies, forming them into giant stairs that diminished as they rose upwards. On the summit of the nearest hill, stone markers looked over the property that had once belonged to the men beneath them. Korean children—grandchildren, perhaps, of those deceased patriarchs—ran among the naked and the half-naked, the sunbathers, waders, cardplayers, and swimmers. Two children were busily scrubbing clothes while a sprawled GI kept an eye on the progress. Warren wondered what the kids charged. Probably a dollar. A GI is always good for a dollar. A ring for a dollar, dirty pictures for a dollar, laundry for a dollar, a woman's body for a dollar.

"Washee, washee," a kid tugged vigorously at his elbow.

"How much?"

"One dollah."

"Fifty cents." Warren decided to barter.

"One dollah." The child was about six years old, Warren guessed.

"Sixty cents."

The boy brushed past Warren and rushed up to another dogface with a bundle.

"Sure, kid, how much?"

"Two dollah."

"Go to it, kid."

The boy threw a disdainful glance at Warren before grabbing the clothes and hurrying to the edge of the stream.

Warren stripped, piled his fatigues on the sand, and stepped into the icy water. Taking his dirty clothes, he squatted and began to scrub, remembering peasant women along the green streams of France.

"I help, Joe."

"How much?" Warren looked at the thin boy already busily scrubbing a tee shirt. The boy's head was large for his tiny body, his black hair was thick and ran far down his neck.

"You no payee, Joe. I help you." The deep-set eyes burned brightly. "I like GI, Joe. Other boys, they no like. They like money. They sons of bitches, eh, Joe?" The

8

slender arms continued to work furiously at the clothes, while the large head and dark eyes swerved from the work to Warren's face. "War kill mother, sister, father. We live North. War very bad. Communists kill. Americans kill too."

Warren nodded.

"My brother he come with me. GI they bring us here. My brother he die last winter. It very cold. This winter I die. I hang your clothes on fence."

Warren watched the child, the wet burden almost too heavy for him, pick his way out of the water. While the boy hung the clothes on the already burdened barbed wire fence, Warren left the water and stretched naked on his towel. When the boy had finished and returned, tiptoeing over the sand and rocks and through the sprawled forms to lie down beside him, Warren said: "I die this winter, too."

He looked at the boy who had provoked the admission. The boy's eyes, deep-sunk in his misshapen skull, glowed like black marbles. "I think so," he smiled.

"Where do you live?" Warren asked.

"No place, everyplace," the boy said rapidly. "Sometime I live same place with boy, other time I live no place. I no like live with many boy, Joe. They do many bad thing. You no changee money with boy, Joe. Boy takee money, give you paper. Boy alla time steal. Cut pocket like this," the skinny hand drew a line around the pocket of Warren's fatigue pants which lay folded before them. "Takee money, wallet, everything. Bad. You no keep wallet there, Joe."

"Where do you live now?" Warren asked.

"No place, everyplace." The boy shrugged his bone-thin shoulders.

Taking his wallet out of his jacket pocket, Warren handed the boy five dollars in military currency.

9

"No," the boy shook his head. "You friend. I no takee money."

"Yes. You're my brother. Take it."

The boy took the money and folded it carefully before putting it into his pocket. The two lay quietly, side by side, for many minutes. Warren felt the sun soaking his body, applying a gentle warm pressure on his flesh. Some vague tenderness within him encompassed the little body beside him, as if they shared the same thoughts. Warren was thinking about the Main Line of Resistance. He had no curiosity about the M.L.R.; it was as if he had already seen it. When he had gone to France, it had been the same; he had never escaped the sensation that he was returning to a place he had left long ago rather than viewing a new land. Nothing ever seemed to surprise him.

Not even Jean. He had been startled by her, but on their first evening together it was as if they had known one another since childhood.

"Joe," the child spoke to him with a tentative softness. The words partook of the warmth that surrounded the two of them.

"Yes?"

"How you know you die this winter?"

"Samo-samo as you."

"No," the boy shook his head. He was not smiling. "Me, no food, very cold, I die. GI, lots of food, very warm, not samo-samo as boy. How you know, Joe?"

No, it was not the same, Warren realized. Death was a fact of life for the boy. Death was the reason for the persistence of the little boys in Pusan who grabbed your sleeves, saying: "You want woman, GI? Nice woman— number one—four dollar—real good woman—follow me, GI. If no like, no take. Okay, GI, follow me, GI. Nice woman—young—nineteen, fifteen—good—do anything— follow me, GI." It was death that would not let them stop until threatened by force. Even then they did not

10

desist without a last attempt: "Changee money, GI? Good deal." As one turned away, another would grab the sleeve. No matter where Warren walked that free afternoon in Pusan, he had his little companion: a seven-to-twelve-year-old child who held off death by becoming a pimp and black marketeer.

Warren sat up and the boy imitated his movement. "You see," Warren said, "I had a vision. You know what a vision is?" The boy's expression stopped him. "Let's call it a dream. You know the word dream?"

Again the boy stared intently at Warren's lips, his face screwed up painfully. "Dlem," he said.

"No, no. Dream. Dre-eem."

"Dre-eem," the boy repeated. "Yes, yes, go on."

"Do you know what it means?"

"No." The boy's face registered his sense of failure.

"Well, let's say that I saw it happen."

But the child did not understand and Warren felt their communion shattered by his attempts at explanation. He looked across the river, beyond the crazy quilt of the stinking paddies, up the steps of the hills to the carved stone markers that thrust their pagoda tops into the blue sky. "We are brothers, though, eh?" he said, touching the boy's hair.

"Yes, yes, Joe," the boy said eagerly.

Warren got up and dressed while the boy watched, his face beaming. They strolled to the gate that led through the barbed wire fence into the replacement enclosure and there shook hands solemnly while the ROK sentry eyed the boy menacingly.

Later, Warren sat in his tent, cleaned the dust from his equipment, and smoked a cigarette. In the States it was yesterday. He was now living in Jean's tomorrow.

Perhaps he should have told her what he had tried to tell the boy. With her there would have been no difficulty about the words—but would *she* have understood? Did

11

he himself fully understand what had occurred that wintry evening as the Metro screeched its way out of Paris toward Sceaux?

——The train shot upward, out of the white-tiled tubes under Paris into the world above: the world of suburbs and road crossings where pedestrians, cyclists, and autos waited patiently in the November shower for the train to pass them by. Foot weary, Warren slouched in his seat and gazed out of the window as the images flashed before him: shopkeepers folding their shutters; women, their purchases bulging in cloth sacks, scurrying along the glistening sidewalks; children hugging long loaves of bread under their coats; men cupping a match to the cigarette at their lips, spotlighting their intent faces. The play of lights and shadows distorted by the rain fascinated him as they streamed through his reflection on the windowpane. In the glass he could see the reflections of the other passengers projected out into the rain itself like disembodied souls illuminated in the night. Untouched by the rain, they were rushed through the world out there as if carried by a strong wind. To Warren, the world of the reflected passengers became more real than the passengers themselves. He stared in fascination as that outer world was penetrated by telegraph lines, lamp posts, fences and yet remained intact.

He saw himself out there, a person distinct from the onlooker, an individual with thin face and thick hair looking as tired as the rest of the people around him. Others must see him as he now saw himself, he thought, just another member of a group of wan specters imprisoned in a fleeting moment of their lives, caught alone in the crowd of fellow humans. At his shoulder a young St. Cyr officer with a blond mustache half-dozed over a copy of *L'humanité,* while opposite him a round-faced man peered through thick glasses at a sheaf of papers on which were written entries and amounts. Warren saw that his lapel

12

carried the little red rosette of the Legion of Honor. Beside the businessman, a middle-aged woman wearing a worn wool coat and balancing an enormous black purse on her lap turned the pages of *Paris-Match* with a puffy finger, moistening the finger tip each time by applying it to her pursed lips. Her wedding band was thin and worn. She was not reading, but looking at the pictures. Her sagging, tired face never changed expression. Above and around them were students, laborers, more soldiers, more women, all pushed together in enforced intimacy, filling the car with their warm human odors. Their eyes shifted, peered into one another's ears, into the hairs of the next head, or apparently stared at nothing.

Even as he watched, the scene faded then reappeared and faded again as if obscured by the mist of the rain. He shook his head slightly, placed his brow on the cool windowpane and the scene came into focus again. He found himself peering into his own eyes in close contact. The train was on a trestle now and the sky had darkened. The eyes in the window faded, and he watched a man crawling along the earth in painful slow motion.

As he watched, the man's long legs were brought forward and the figure thrust upward. He was wearing a uniform and holding an object in his hand; his arm went back in readiness, the object was sputtering. Thin whips of light flashed from the direction the soldier faced and even as his arm shot forward, the figure stiffened, was lifted imperceptibly from the ground and thrown backwards and down. Warren felt some fiery thing tear into himself, a series of dull thuds clocked his own descent into darkness even as he saw the face on the fallen figure and knew the man for himself.

He must have cried out, for turning he saw the St. Cyr officer rousing himself to look curiously at him. The housewife's wide eyes surveyed him with an air of shocked self-righteousness. The businessman leaned down, his bald

13

head nearly touching Warren's knees, to pick up some of his papers, and Warren realized that he must have caused the papers to fall. Too embarrassed to look beyond this immediate circle to see whether others in the car were watching him, Warren gazed down at the man's bald head until the other righted himself and began to rearrange his papers.

"Pardon, monsieur," Warren said. "Je songeais."

"Je comprends," the man muttered.

The man may have understood, but Warren did not.——

"Beer ration's come!" someone yelled into his tent.

Warren walked out into the glare again and waited his turn in line for the three cans of beer.

"Never cared much for beer," the man ahead of him turned around, "but here it sure tastes good." They got their beer and the fellow walked beside Warren back to the tent area. "This place makes you appreciate things," he said. "Like Marge, that's my wife. I never appreciated her, not really, until now." He wagged his head. "Well, see ya," he said entering a tent.

Back on his cot Warren propped himself against his duffle bag and drank his beer. The tent was still deserted. The other men were along the river bank or in the tents of buddies. He wondered where White was. From a nearby tent he could hear a voice . . .

"So there I am, crawling under that damned barbed wire and this runt of a gook pimp is trying to help me through when the gook guard comes by waving his arms and shouting and pointing that sawed-off shotgun. I says to him, 'Point that damned thing at me and I'll break your head open.' The guard drops his weapon and begins pulling at my legs. He's shouting away and I'm shouting right back and the pimp on the other side of the wire is tugging at me and shouting and . . ." The voice rolled on . . . Warren dozed.

"Warren. Come on, slob, wake up." The voice came

14

from far off. "Hey, boy, rise and shine." The insistent words penetrated the warm restful area of his sleep and he fought against them, turning to push his face into the blanket upon which he lay. "Up, man, you've got a visitor." Feeling the hand on his shoulder, pushing at him, Warren slowly came out of sleep into the drugged heat of the tent. The voice irritated by its cheerfulness. Reluctantly, Warren opened his eyes.

Robert Lesley, his soft body parked on the neighboring cot, was grinning at him. He looks like a pig, Warren thought, focusing his gaze upon Lesley—those plump cheeks, that nose turned back exposing the nostrils. A snout, that was what it was, a snout separating two little pig's eyes. But who ever heard of a smiling pig?

"Well, fellow," the pig's face leered at him, "how'd you make out? Where they sending you?"

"To the line, I hope."

"You're a fool. I can get you out of it."

"You?"

"Sure. You gotta work the deals. Look at me. I got here two days ago and I'm already assigned. Guess where?"

"Right here."

"That's right, boy. You gotta watch out for number one, nobody else will."

"What are you doing?"

"Special Services. Told 'em about my theatrical background and here I am, Special Services."

"Your theatrical background? You've got no more theatrical background than I have."

"That's it, lad, but not too loud. Now I've already told the sergeant in charge of my office that you were coming through and he wants to talk to you."

"I don't want to talk to him."

"Look, now, you've got more sense than that. Here's a deal all ready-made for you and you can't turn it down." The smile was on the face still; it was a leer to which

15

Warren could not accustom himself. It seemed to imply a dirty joke. "Come on." Lesley took his arm, "Up with you. The sergeant's waiting."

"I'm not going anywhere." Warren jerked his arm away.

"But you've gotta. I told the sarge all about you. He wants to meet you. You'll be leaving me in the lurch on the first day of my new job. Now, come on, for old time's sake."

"Okay, but I'm not taking any offers."

"That's all right by me. I just want you to meet this guy, a real swell fellow, good to work with—"

"You know that after one day?"

"Sure."

Sitting on the edge of the cot, Warren tried to clear the fuzziness out of his head. Sleep was the only escape from the enervating heat, but sleep took the marrow out of the bones. He did not want to go with Lesley, but his resistance had been sapped. He picked up his fatigue cap. "Let's go."

"I knew you'd come through," Lesley was suddenly all eagerness. Warren could not get the image of a pig out of his head.

Lesley led him through the dusty company area, one hand resting, cowboy fashion, on the butt of his forty-five which was slung low on his buttocks. They entered a quonset hut. "Some office, huh? Beats bunker life, I'll bet."

There was no one in the office. "Probably out to the can," Lesley said. "Three desks and right now only two of us here. That would be your desk there, but look around."

A woven matting covered the floor. The desks were well set apart, each in a corner, while in the fourth corner there was a bar. Warren walked over to examine it. The front was made of bamboo poles and a sign above it read "R & R Special." On its smooth surface a large electric

16

fan moved its benevolent head back and forth. Warren felt the cool air pushing the sweat from his face.

"Pretty nice, eh?" Lesley slapped the bar counter. "No liquor yet, but it decorates the office fine. We put out the Rest and Recuperation flights. You know, see who's eligible for five days of brothel life in Japan. But c'mon back here and see . . ."

The quonset hut was cut by a partition and it was through the separating curtain that Lesley now led him. "That'd be your bunk there," Lesley pointed to one of the cots along the wall, "and that's the library," he looked meaningfully at Warren.

A series of shelves glowing with brightly colored paperbound editions nearly covered one wall. "All the latest titles," Lesley said. "We get first pick. The rest go to the troops."

The screen door slammed and someone came into the outer office. "All the comforts of home, huh?" Lesley asked before going out into the office. Warren followed him.

"Dan," Lesley announced, "this is Warren. I've told you about him. He's interested in getting into the office here."

The sergeant, a stocky, rough-hewn man with pock marks on his square face, held out his hand. "It's a good deal," he said. "You got any experience along this line?"

"None, Sergeant."

"He's just modest, Dan," Lesley cut in, "why he can type, he's been halfway around the world and he's—"

"As I said, Sergeant," Warren interrupted, "Bob's trying to do me a favor, but I've got no experience with this work and I want to go on line."

The sergeant turned gray-green eyes on him and smiled slightly. "Okay," he said, "Private Lesley here told me you were a little glory happy."

"That's not it. I just want the experience."

"I've had it," the sergeant said flatly. "If that's what

17

you want, go ahead. Just keep your helmet on and your ass down."

"Thanks for the advice, Sergeant." Warren held out his hand. "Also for considering me."

"No trouble at all."

Out of the quonset hut, with its cooling fan, Warren stepped into the wracking heat.

"Glory happy." The words stirred in him an angry memory. Lesley had used those words before.

——He had been home on leave, sitting in a bar waiting for Jean to get off work. It was spring and the air was sweet with the smell of trees and flowers. He disliked bars and had often wished that sidewalk cafés existed in America. Women were walking by in light frocks and wide skirts, and one could watch them or, less frivolously, study the faces of their men. But in the artificial darkness of the bar he could only sit and drink cognac and stare at stupid murals on the walls, or watch some suited businessman nearly fall off his stool attempting to pat the bargirl's rump.

Bob Lesley had entered beaming. Warren hadn't thought of him as pig-faced then, but merely as a pudgy and smiling boyhood friend much too pampered by his parents.

"I thought you were in CIC school."

Lesley slumped into the chair opposite the little table. "Naw, been home three weeks."

"Quite a deal. Didn't you get a two-week leave a short while ago?"

"Sure. You just gotta know how to work things, Warren."

"What's the story?"

"No story. Just that my security clearance didn't go through and now I'm on orders again."

"Where'd the extra leave come from? Come on, they gave you all the leave you had coming before you went to CIC school. I know that."

18

"It's sort of a personal vacation."

"What do you mean by that?"

"Just taking it."

"You mean you're AWOL?"

"Now don't go using nasty words, Warren. I'm just taking a rest. They gave me a raw deal."

"They'll give you a rawer one when they catch up with you. You'd better get your can back to your post."

"Got no post."

"Well, wherever they've put you on orders to . . ."

"I'll do that when I'm good and ready."

"That's what you think. This is serious."

"Getting killed is more serious."

"So they're shipping you out?"

"FECOM, Far Eastern Command. You know what that means. Sure death."

"Oh, the hell it does. A lot of guys come back. Don't be an ass."

"Don't give me no sales talk, Warren. What've you got to worry about? Sweet post stateside telling the troops the news of the day, giving 'em pep talks about Korea in those damned propaganda lectures of yours. Easy for you to sit there and tell me to go get killed."

"Easy, sonny. I'm on FECOM orders, too."

"That's a laugh."

"Read for yourself," Warren said, taking the mimeographed sheets from his pocket.

Lesley read the orders. "Well, I'm damned! But you can get off, Warren," he said accusingly, as he handed the papers back. "You guys on Division Faculty have it made. You can get off. Forti got off, so did Pearson."

"I don't want off. I asked to get on."

"You what?"

"I volunteered. I wanted to get on."

"You're a damned fool."

Warren watched Lesley growing more agitated. "No more so than you."

"I'm disgusted with you, Warren. I never expected you to get glory happy."

"No one's glory happy. I know why I want to go and it's not for glory."

"Don't feed me that stuff." Lesley's voice took on an unpleasant, high pitch. "You're glory happy. You've been talking so long to basic trainees about the chicken-shit traditions of the army that you've gone gung-ho."

"Even so, it would be better than what you're doing."

"The hell it is. I'm playing it wise. I figure this war may end soon, a few days may make all the difference. I'm just delaying a little."

"Delaying a little! You admit you've been AWOL for three weeks. Another week and you're a deserter. They can send you up for twenty years, maybe give you life. Desertion under overseas orders is desertion in the face of the enemy."

"So now I'm a coward."

"That's not what I said, and keep your voice down."

"You didn't have to say it. All right so I'm a coward. What of it? Better a live coward than a dead hero. If you knew what was good for you, you'd get off orders."

"And if you knew what was good for you, you'd report in."

"Boy, you've really gone army."

"Just using common sense. They checked up on you yet?"

"Nope."

"They will, you know."

"Sure, I know. I'm no damned moron."

"My mistake." Warren sipped his cognac. "Well, what *are* you gonna do?"

"Oh, I'll turn myself in when I'm good and ready."

"Meanwhile?"

"Meanwhile I'll live at home."

"That's the first place they'll come."

"I know. The folks'll cover for me."

"You mean they know?"

"Of course they know."

"And they don't care?"

"Whatever I do is all right with them. Dad says it's my decision and Mom's happy as a clam to have me home."

"You're all stupider than I thought."

"Goddam it, you glory happy son-of-a-bitch!" Lesley stood up, his face quivering. "You can't insult my parents."

Warren sipped at his cognac. "Sit down. Act rational for a change."

Lesley dropped back into his chair, his body shaking with nervous sobs. Warren was glad of the bar's darkness. The flabby man opposite him might be giggling for all anyone would know.

"What shall I do?" Lesley whimpered.

"Do as I've told you. Pick up your orders, pack and get going. They'll go much easier on you that way. I won't be leaving for a week or I'd go with you. You going to Lawton?"

"Yes."

"I'll probably see you there."

"But I don't want to get killed."

"Who does? Look, you know what they say about the fourteen men behind the lines for each at the front? You stand just one chance in fifteen of seeing real action. Let's face it, the odds are better than fifty-fifty; but if you sit here, they're bound to catch you and then you really get racked. Getting killed isn't inevitable. Use some common sense. Going back now you might even get off. They're lenient with AWOL's who return for overseas shipments. Happy to send more over."

"Who's happy?" Jean's voice was a bright interruption and he turned to see her standing beside him,

21

her smile a warm benediction upon them both. As she gathered the folds of her mint green skirt and took her place beside Warren, Lesley got to his feet.

"I do have to go," he said, looking at Warren.

Jean turned her gaze from Lesley as he crossed the room and asked, "Did I frighten him away?"

"No. Care for a drink?"

"Not now. Let's go outside. It's too good a day to waste indoors. Why's your friend unhappy? Girl troubles?"

"I've got those," Warren said, shaking his head. "His are parent troubles. They've kept him a baby. He doesn't have to do anything, just eat and sleep and they're happy." He downed the last of his drink. "Let's go."

As they entered the sunshine, she turned and held out her hand for him. He took it. "I like your outfit," he said, "the blouse makes you look very peasantish. So healthy and young."

She pulled away as far as their joined hands allowed, as if doing some dance step, and faced him. "You sound like an old man." She made a long face at him and laughed. He had to smile. "That's better," she said and returned to his side, swinging their joined hands in a wide arc as they walked.

"You're bubbly," he said, "spring's gotten to you."

"Spring? Don't be silly. It's you. I'm like that fellow's parents. Just being with you makes me happy."

"And yet . . ."

"Oh, so that's it? Well, long faces aren't fair," she said. "We agreed, remember?"

"But we can't forget . . ." He didn't go on.

"You're the one who said we could and I'm willing to try. Come on, now. The future is a long way off, remember?"

He was silent.

"Was it unfair to remind you the idea was yours?"

"You've read my thought."

22

"Well, I think it's a good idea. We've only a week before you leave. Let's not worry about the future and marriage or anything like that. Not now. Let's just enjoy every moment of this week together. I love you and it's a glorious spring day and I'm happy. Come on," she coaxed, "I can't be happy for long if you're not."

And later she said, "Besides, I've a good feeling about the future."——

Fears of the future had tormented Lesley back then and now he's happy, Warren thought as he walked through the heat to his squad tent.

At Fort Lawton Warren had seen his bluff, smiling face following behind his outstretched hand as he hailed him in the service club.

"So you made it?"

"They didn't even miss me," Lesley had smirked. "I think the CIC school on the orders had 'em buffaloed."

But Lesley had worked hard at making his future. At Lawton he had hounded the Classification and Assignment section for a post there and when he was shipped out—they had both been on the same shipment roster—he buttered up every officer on the ship, trying to convince somebody that he shouldn't be sent to the front. In Japan, at Camp Drake, he had done the same thing; when he couldn't get permission to go to C and A, he would sneak out. Now, finally, it had all paid off for him. He's got books, a cot, a fan in this hot weather, and a pistol he'll never have to use.

Men sagged, shifting under the weight of stagnant heat as they waited their turn at the desk of the interviewer. The pounded earth under their feet was unyielding, offering no relief to the replacements waiting for another part of the too-familiar "processing." This time it was the Classification and Assignment routine.

Easing up to the desk, each man fell silent and gazed

ahead at the officer whose decision meant comfort or combat; they scanned the young lieutenant's broad, tanned face for some sign of hope. His blue and silver Combat Infantryman's Badge glistened in the sun, a bright spot above the left breast pocket on his dull green fatigues. His laconic repetition of the questions underscored the disheartening impression that the whole procedure was a mere formality. The replacement could not be sure, however, what the officer wrote on the 201 card. No matter what answer was given him, the officer simply made a notation, handed the card to the sergeant sitting beside him and called out the next name. He never seemed to look up from the cards before him. He didn't really need to, for the 201 file virtually was the individual soldier, containing his history, background, accomplishments, test scores; it was on this that the army based its decisions.

"Thompson," the officer called, glancing over the yellow surface of the card.

"Here, sir."

Pencil poised, the officer directed his words to the card. "You're down as a rifleman. Any preference as to position?"

"I'd like to drive a truck, sir."

The officer turned the card over, sighed. "Been to driver's school?"

"No, sir, but I can drive a truck."

The officer scribbled something on the card, shoved it at his sergeant assistant and picked up the next one.

"Trumph," he called, taking his eyes off the card long enough to glance at his watch.

"Here, sir."

"You're down as a rifleman. Any preference as to position?"

"I'd like to be an M.P., sir," the young man said, "or," he hastily added, "if you've got anything in quartermaster, that'd do just fine, sir."

24

The lieutenant scanned the face of the card, made his notation and gave the card to the sergeant, who filed it away.

It was Warren's turn. The officer lifted his eyes from the card when Warren answered: "Rifleman, sir."

Warren expected this reaction. He also knew what came next, as the officer looked back at the card. "It says here you have two years of college, Warren, and that you can type." He looked up again. "We need a man at the repple-depple as clerk-typist."

"No thank you, sir. I'm a rifleman."

The lieutenant looked back at the card. "Your area one test scores are pretty damned good, too good for a rifleman's job," and again he looked at Warren. "We could use you in G-2. I've a request for a man. They're short-handed."

"Sir, if it's all the same to you, I just want a good rifle outfit on line."

The lieutenant looked at his sergeant and smiled quizzically. The sergeant shrugged and lifted his hands, palms upwards. Then the lieutenant shook his head. "You know what you want, I suppose." He made his notation on the card and handed it to the sergeant. "We'll see what we can do about the 'good outfit,'" he smiled. Picking up the next card, he called, "White."

Warren moved off to one side, scrounging in his fatigue pocket for his cigarettes, waiting to hear how White made out.

White's bearing marked him off from everyone else in the shaggy line-up. While the others seemed beaten by the heat, their shoulders slouched, their bodies flabby, White maintained squared shoulders and a rigid spine. Although shorter than most of the men around him, he possessed a solid muscularity which even the baggy fatigue clothes could not hide. His full oval face seemed from the distance at which Warren stood to be soft, but Warren

25

knew better. Like the rest of the man, the face was set, tensed for violent activity.

Warren had first met White at Camp Drake, then again at Inchon and now they found themselves assigned to the same tent at the replacement center at Chunchon. They had made small talk and Warren had been struck by White's English. It was precise, formal, strengthened by a Slavic accent. Watching, Warren saw him snap a brisk salute as he came to attention in front of the lieutenant. The others, Warren himself, had merely shuffled to the desk in their turn.

"At ease," the lieutenant said self-consciously.

Warren smiled as he saw White shift into an "at ease" as rigid as any "parade rest."

"Do you have any preference as to position?"

"Rifleman, sir."

Looking up sharply, the officer glanced over at Warren. "What's going on here?"

"I don't know, sir," White clipped the words out swiftly.

The lieutenant turned the card over and read it carefully. "You've quite a record, Private . . ." He paused to look at the name again. "White. Do you speak all these languages?" His index finger tapped a spot on the card.

"Yes, sir."

"Russian, too?"

"Yes, sir."

The men behind White were quieting down, bunching up to hear the dialogue at the desk.

"You commanded a company once?"

"Yes, sir."

"And you want to be a rifleman?"

"Yes, sir."

"What if I were to assign you to G-2, intelligence, White?"

"You can't, sir. I am not a citizen and could not obtain a security clearance."

26

The officer looked at the card again and nodded his head. "You can type." He stared at White. "I could put you in as a typist here."

"You would do me a disservice, sir." White still looked straight ahead, as if at attention. "It is urgent that I see combat."

The lieutenant gazed at him thoughtfully for a moment. "Have it your way. God knows, few men on line want to be there."

"Thank you, sir." White snapped to attention, saluted, and marched from the table. The officer looked after him and then toward his sergeant before making his notation on White's card. Raising his pen, he studied the card a moment longer, then handed it to his assistant. After glancing at his watch, he took up the next card and called, "Winklish."

Warren fell in beside White as the latter left the table. White's solid, compressed build contrasted with Warren's own lean, almost skinny, frame.

"The only two men in the army who want to go to the front," Warren chuckled, "and we have to fight to get there."

"That's so," White said.

"Do you think we'll make it?"

"I think so. If not, we could always go to the I.G. and complain."

"We'd end up in the infirmary," Warren laughed.

"Why?" White asked.

"Complaining to the I.G. about not being sent into combat," Warren explained. "He'd send us down for psychiatric treatment."

"Do you think so?"

"I wouldn't put it past them, but I was only joking."

"Oh," White said, relieved. Then he chuckled drily, almost as an afterthought. "Yes, that would be funny."

27

Warren got the impression that White was not really amused at all.

"Got a particular reason for wanting the line?" Warren asked.

"Yes."

"Mind if I ask what it is?"

"Yes." Unexpected, the answer shoved Warren into silence. "Perhaps," White went on, "we will be together on line. It is a long story."

They reached their squad tent and Warren flopped on his cot near the door. It made no difference that the tent sides had been rolled up and secured by small cords. The tent covered a pocket of rank, humid air, but it was the only refuge from the hammering sun outside. Across the hard hot earth, in other tents, Warren saw men moving about, playing cards or lying on their cots. Laughter flowed from one tent in a sudden cascade. At one end of the camp were slightly more permanent structures than their own: a row of quonset huts and one or two wooden buildings. Around the camp ran a high, barbed wire fence. They were, in effect, prisoners.

Turning on his side, Warren studied White who was standing by his bunk near the center tent pole. Warren watched as White removed his fatigue jacket and his stubby arms moved quickly like pistons over the coarse fabric, folding, turning, patting it into a small square, then putting it on top of his fatigue cap which rested on his duffle bag. With the same swift precision White removed his tee-shirt, exposing a trunk like that of a tree with the bark stripped off its three sides, the cambium layer of flesh emphasized in its paleness by the dark brown bark of hair. The tee-shirt, put through the same energetic maneuvers, was shaped to the same size as the jacket upon which it was then placed. Stretching out on his cot, White put his hands under his head and stared at the green, heat-soaked canvas above him.

28

Turning over, Warren gazed out at the parched earth. White's whole being conveyed a sense of strength to him, a strength that bespoke violence lived through.

On noon of the next day a convoy of trucks rolled into the area. The replacements had been waiting in the constant heat since nine o'clock that morning when a sergeant had called them into formation only to leave them standing. Now the same sergeant, a thin fellow with a querulous voice, climbed upon a small wooden platform in front of the troops and stumbled through the list of names as he called the roll of those ordered to one of the three regiments. As Warren understood it, this was merely a shipment to another replacement compound where there would be more waiting, another processing routine before they would hit a rifle company.

Warren was pleased to find himself and White clambering onto the same truck. As he seated himself on the truck, Warren saw a jeep swing alongside. Screeching to a halt, its dust cloud billowed over the truck as Lesley swung himself out of it, and with his .45 slapping his generous behind, strode up.

"Saw you getting on here as I came in the gate," Lesley said officiously. "Just want to wish you the best of luck. If you change your mind, phone back down to me and I'll see what I can do." His face broke into the smile of one who waits for a laugh after telling a dirty joke.

"The phone works both ways. Come up and see me sometime. I'll tell you when it's safe."

Lesley laughed. "I've got to get the beer over to the hut or it'll get hot. So long now."

"Take care of the beer." Warren watched Lesley swagger back to his jeep and mount it like a dashing hero. Lesley waved off in a burst of dust.

The convoy, gears grinding, pulled out of the compound, and Warren looked at the nearby village. The shops bordering the road were made of wood and roofed with dull red tiles. Flattened tin cans and other salvageable refuse had been used for patching. In one of his lectures back in the States he had spoken of the five-thousand-year history of this country. On the surface, this ramshackle village gave no hint of what that five thousand years had been straining to produce. Surely not these awkward shacks.

"Lookit the joy girls," somebody said and Warren's head turned with the rest to look at three girls wearing Western style skirts who were waving at the trucks and shouting "Halloo GI" to the occupants. Their mouths, a garish red, gaped with laughter at the passing troops. They were leaning against a small shop front and another girl, as though pushed out by unseen hands, joined them and stood shyly beside the other three and waved without enthusiasm.

In front of the truck Warren saw a woman scurry, balancing on her head a great bundle. Her black skirt caught the full blast of dust from the truck's wheels and she turned to shake one feeble fist.

Another woman, carrying a large urn on her head, stood off to the side of the road by an open store front. Her haggard face was without expression as she waited submissively for the vehicles to pass. Her white blouse hung open and Warren saw that her dry breasts sagged lifelessly. On the table near where she stood, strange tuberous vegetables lay exposed to the sun, and behind her, wrinkled as her breasts, hung great slabs of dried fish. The repugnant smell that saturated Korea was strongest in the towns, Warren thought, just as the misery of this country was most visible there.

At one corner of the village, near one of the more stable-looking structures, stood a thin old man, his tall black linen hat announcing his advanced station in the community. With his flowing robe, his stringy beard and time-

30

etched face, the patriarch puffed on his long-stemmed pipe as he watched the trucks roll by. There was dignity in the silent figure and it was not difficult for Warren to imagine such a man standing in the same wise silence when in another age, the strange troops of Genghis Khan had marched through this village.

Through an open window, Warren caught sight of a young man sitting on a mat, talking, gesturing, his arms moving smoothly toward someone out of sight. The upper part of his bronze body was naked. A woman's hand stretched gracefully to touch his face.

"Look at them gooks run," somebody said and Warren realized that Duke was aboard the truck. Duke had first made his presence known to Warren on the tedious train trip from Pusan to the repple-depple.

All in all, the train trip had been an unpleasant experience. The narrow, wooden seats with perpendicular backs had been instruments of torture, making impossible any relaxed sitting position or any attempt at sleep. The train seemed to move forward by inches; during the night it had made innumerable long and unexplained stops. Some lucky individuals had staked a claim on the only open area on the train floor, a space near the urine-soaked little room with a hole in the floor that was a latrine. There they stretched out, with heads upon their duffle bags, to sleep. Warren had not been as fortunate.

———Aside from the cloying heat and the uncomfortable bench, Warren had also to contend with Duke, who sat across the narrow aisle from him. Duke stripped himself to the waist and sat on his bench flexing his muscles for his admiring companions.

"Man, Duke, you got *the* body beautiful."

"Hell, man, you ain't seen nothin'," Duke replied. "Look at this." Assuming a new pose, gripping his left wrist with his right hand, he filled his chest with air and flexed his biceps.

31

"Oh, baby, you is some cat," another chimed in.

"Honey, the gals must go for you, yum, yum, must lap you up."

"The Duke, that's what they call me. Nobody fools with me. I'd like to see the bastard I can't lick." He looked around the car arrogantly.

"Oh, now, Duke, that's just so."

"You bet your damned life it's so." And so the dialogue went.

Warren judged that the Duke was about twenty. With his blond hair and well-developed torso, he might have been good-looking, but his face was marred by a lip curled in constant contempt.

Later in the evening, one of the lucky individuals sleeping in the open area went to the latrine. This was what Duke had been waiting for. He immediately jumped up, dragged his duffle bag to where the fellow had been and put the other's duffle bag on his own seat. Lying down he feigned sleep.

The latrine door opened; a soft-faced young man came out. A quiet fellow, he just stood above the Duke looking down at him before he nudged him with his toe. "Hey, guy, that's my place you're in."

"Get your goddam toe out of my rib," the Duke snarled. "Let a man get his sleep."

"I said you've taken my place."

"Beat it, Buster, you'll find your bag on that seat over there."

"But you're in my place."

"Look, sonny, unless you want a quick bloody lip, you'll just get your can over to that seat."

Duke had chosen his man well, for the fellow gave up and went to the seat indicated to spend an uncomfortable night.——

Now the Duke was on the truck as it made its way along the dusty road, but his worshipful companions were nowhere to be seen. Undaunted, he took off his shirt and flexed his muscles a few times. Tiring of this, he dropped to the floor of the truck and began to do push-ups, executing them with precision, his back and shoulder muscles rippling. When he tired, he changed position and began to touch his toes with the tips of his fingers.

Warren exchanged glances with White who had also been watching the exhibition, his broad nose flaring, his face registering his disgust.

Then, from the forward distance they heard the first muffled sounds of artillery.

The regimental replacement area was in a small valley between two low ridges; stretched across the valley were rows of pup tents to which the incoming replacements were assigned. A rugged-looking sergeant with a scar on his cheek gave the new arrivals their briefing.

"You'll get two hot meals a day brought in by truck from the regimental headquarters kitchen," the sergeant shouted. "For the third meal you'll be issued C-rations. The latrine you'll find in the large tent at the far end of the area." He waved an arm at the large tent. "No pissin' around the pup tents or you've had it. Drop your mail at the large tent at this end of the area—that's the orderly room. The only processin' you'll do here is to have one interview with the C and A officer who'll decide what job you'll have. Anybody wantin' to go on sick call come to the orderly room. Homesickness doesn't classify. There'll be reveille and roll call each morning. Be there! Some of you'll pull guard duty here and you'd better remember this isn't stateside."

He began to walk up and down in front of the men. "You're using loaded weapons and the sound you hear may be the enemy. You're only five miles from the front. The lines are so thin up there a troop of Boy Scouts could march through. No campfires or flashlights allowed after dark. You can smoke after dark, but only inside your tents. A replacement unit was attacked not too long ago by guerillas and pretty badly hacked up, so you'll understand the precautions. That's all, men." He started to turn away. Then, abruptly, he turned back and added, "Oh, yes, tomorrow the colonel will give you a talk on the situation. He's a damned good man—a gentleman and a soldier. That's no horseshit. You're going to be proud to serve under him. Dismissed!"

In their pup tent Warren and White stretched out on their blankets.

"Cigarette?" White asked.

Warren accepted the cigarette and White lit it for him. They lay back and listened to the steady slam of the artillery fire. After an interval White spoke. "That's a good sound."

"Artillery fire?"

"Yes. A good sound. I can remember times when I prayed for artillery fire."

Warren said nothing hoping White might go on.

"Well, not really prayed," White continued. "I am an atheist. But I remember saying, 'God, if we could only have some artillery cover. Please, God, some artillery cover.' Funny thing for an atheist to say. If I had gotten it, I might not be an atheist," he chuckled drily.

"I hope the sergeant is correct," White said after a pause, "about the colonel. Americans have few good soldiers. Two things won the last war for you: your production in places like Detroit and the fact that your soldiers can use their brains in a tight spot—the privates, I mean. The Germans are better soldiers than the Americans, so are the Russians, but they are only good when they have good officers. If somebody is not there to tell them what to do, they are lost." White's thick lips sucked deeply at his cigarette. "In my office I made two hundred dollars betting that the Chinese would intervene in this

34

war. Everyone thought MacArthur knew what he was doing, but I could see from my office what was going to happen." White shoved the stub of his cigarette into the dust, grinding it down with his thumb.

"Your office?" Warren asked.

"I am a chemist. No, not really a chemist, but I have become one. I am really a soldier. I have been a soldier all of my life."

"Is that why you're here?"

"Partly. I was drafted. I am twenty-seven years old and I could have gotten out of it, but I let them draft me. When World War Three begins, everyone will be in. I want to be an officer."

"Do you think World War Three is coming?"

"Coming? It is here! This could be the beginning. We should start it before the Russians do. We are giving them too much time to catch up with us. It is stupid to wait until they are ready. Then they can beat us." The precise, formal way White had of speaking underscored his vigorous delivery.

"Do you really believe they want war?"

White plunged one fist into the palm of his other hand with a loud smack. "Of course they want war. I know them. The unit I commanded was a part of the Russian army. Do they want war? Huh!"

"Isn't it conceivable that they will have a lot of little wars, just like this one?"

"Oh, yes, they are clever. Never forget that they are clever. But little wars can only accomplish so much. They give them time to prepare. Then comes the big one." White sat erect in a swift movement. "Then we will kill Russians." He paused thoughtfully. "That will be almost as much fun as killing Germans." He glanced at Warren. "Let us not talk any more about it." Opening his fatigue jacket pocket, he took out a black leather wallet and flipped through a series of celluloid-encased photos. He

35

stopped at one and then thrust it at Warren. "Pretty, eh?"

"Very," Warren scanned the smooth, delicate features of a black-haired girl.

"She wants to marry me."

"Oh."

"But I cannot marry her." White retracted the wallet and looked at the photo again. "She is a devout Catholic," he said scornfully. "Besides, I cannot marry anyone. A soldier should not marry. He thinks of his wife when he should be thinking of the enemy."

Just after dusk some of the Negro troops began to chant —probably one of the obscene "monkey chants" he had heard before, Warren thought. They had begun slowly, accompanying their voices by beating their hands upon wooden boxes or clapping them together. The words were lost in the night, but the rhythm, the ever-increasing tempo of the beat of the flat palm on the wooden box, the clap of flesh against flesh, sounded like a primitive appeal to a pagan god.

Warren lay in the tent and listened. Beside him he sensed White's taut body. He was certain White was awake, though the other lay silently, his arms folded under his head. He spoke only when he wished, then in short bursts that brooked no opposition. To Warren he seemed to be made of coiled steel held tight by an inner tension. For the present, Warren was glad of the silence. Stretched out next to the earth he could enjoy the sound of the husky voices in the dark and feel the throb of that mounting rhythm as it vibrated its way into his consciousness. His own pulse beat seemed attuned to those undulating sounds.

"Damned fools," White snapped in the darkness.

"What?"

"The enemy could be around here. They are asking for it."

36

"The sergeant only said no fires. He didn't say anything about singing."

"He did say that the enemy could get through to here! And those damned fools sing!"

"They're just letting off steam."

"Of course they are," White said impatiently. "But they could be endangering everyone."

The chant seemed endless, its tempo increasing until it was wildness itself. The two men listened. Warren noticed White growing more tense. A few minutes later he pounced. Before Warren had fully assimilated the sound of the shot, White was out of their tent, his rifle in his hand. Then Warren grabbed his own rifle and rushed out of the tent, his heart-beat sounding in his ears. Others in the immediate area were crowding out too. The chant had ended abruptly, but there was laughter from that direction. Then the chant began again, this time with more shouting and laughing mixed with the words.

"Who fired that round?" White demanded.

"I dunno," came a reply. "Somebody over there."

White was already charging toward the group of singers. He thrust himself into their center. "Who fired that shot?" The singing stopped. He stood there, his short powerful figure a dark menace demanding an answer. No one said a word. "I want to know," White said from between clenched teeth, "which of you fired that shot."

"Nobody in this group fired any ol' shot," one deep voice said. Warren could see the terrified faces soften, the white eyes laughing.

"That's right. Sure you ain't just 'maginin' things there, boy?"

White pushed his weapon into the second speaker's chest. "I'll kill you right now unless I know who fired that shot."

Terror returned to the eyes. Faces once again stiffened with fright.

"It was only a blank, guy." The Duke swaggered out of the fringe of the crowd.

White descended on the Duke who stood impudently in front of the audience, his blond hair waved carefully back, an ambiguous smile staining his lips.

"Only a blank! This is a combat zone, punk! You use a weapon to kill, not to play with!"

"Look, guy, don't get excited now . . . Just—"

"Listen. Fire another round and you will pay dearly."

Furious still, White strode off; Warren fell in alongside of him.

"Punk kids," White scowled, "playing with guns." As he spoke another shot came from behind him. White swung around and before Warren could catch up with him, he had wrestled the M-1 away from the Duke and thrown the blond to the ground. The latter reached for his bayonet. In a swift movement White was holding that same bayonet at the boy's throat. "I'll kill you! I'll kill you now!"

Clapping his hand on White's shoulder Warren cautioned, "Take it easy, White."

White wrenched his shoulder free. "I'll teach you a lesson you will never forget."

"Lay off, White. He's learned it."

"He had better." Breathing hard, White continued to sit on the Duke's chest, pressing the bayonet's point on the soft throat. "You do not know how close you have come to dying tonight. You are not in a kid's game. You had better become a man, fast!"

White stood up and looked down at the Duke. Then he spat into the boy's face. Turning, he hurled the bayonet and it impaled itself in one of the wooden boxes that had been serving as a drum. "That goes for all of you," he said. "You should all be in bed, anyway." With that he turned his back on them and strode off.

"I'll bet that Duke is a German," he said bitterly as

38

they stretched out in their sleeping bags. "I should have killed him."

Assembled in a natural pocket on the hillside, the troops sat as though in a Greek theater while the colonel in starched fatigues pointed at a war map and explained the situation. "Papa-san is the highest ridge in our sector," he said in a low voice that did not lack firmness. "Sniper's Ridge is to the right and Jane Russell to the left." As he spoke, he tapped his pipestem on a series of brown lines which marked the location of the hills. "All three are held by the enemy, but Papa-san, the largest and highest, is our objective." Tall and lean, with a tanned friendly face, he had upon arrival lit his pipe and given the men permission to smoke. Now his pipestem alternated between his mouth and the acetate-covered map which rested on an easel beside him.

"There is a rumor," the colonel continued, "that we shall pull into reserve soon." A smile lit his eyes. "Only a rumor, though, so don't go saying the colonel told you that." He rubbed his gray temple with the palm of his hand and grinned. His manner seemed to take the whole group into his confidence. "Any questions?" he asked.

White shot up, his arms rigid at his side. "Sir?"

"Yes?" the colonel nodded.

"Would you mind telling us what significant action has occurred in our sector recently?"

"A good question, I should have included something about that in my talk. Thank you." He nodded. "You may sit down."

White resumed his seat beside Warren and the colonel proceeded. "As I have said, we are pulling mostly recon and ambush patrols, with an occasional combat patrol. If I tell you about the last three major actions we have taken, you will see what sort of thing we are up against. Earlier this month we held a turkey shoot." He turned to the map in a business-like manner. "Our tanks penetrated this valley, up to this point here and effectively shelled the rear side of this ridge 492." His pipestem moved along the route to the ridge. "As you can see the ridge is an extension of Papa-san. The enemy was deeply entrenched and had a heavy mortar contingent there. Utilizing forward observers on Papa-san, those mortars had been doing considerable damage both to our lines and to any patrols which we sent up this road. Our tanks rolled up that road in broad daylight, took the enemy by surprise and hammered that rear slope with about two hundred rounds of ninety millimeter High Explosive and White Phosphorus shells. Then the tanks withdrew. Unfortunately, we lost one man, a turret machine-gunner, but the operation was otherwise successful.

"Two nights later," he continued, "we sent Baker company out to take that same ridge. Elements of Baker company reached the top of the ridge, but were pushed back and the mission was not successful. Last Thursday night a reinforced combat patrol was sent out to the right flank of Papa-san with instructions to make contact there. They succeeded in reaching this point here," he tapped a spot on the map, "when contact was made. The position is heavily manned and our patrol had instructions to pull back upon contact." The colonel looked at White. "Does that answer your question?"

Standing up, White answered, stiffly, "Yes, sir," and then sat down again.

Since there were no more questions, the stocky sergeant with the scar on his cheek who had first met the replacements stood up and came forward. "Te-en, hut," he snapped.

The men sprang to attention and the sergeant about-faced smartly, throwing the colonel a salute. The colonel scanned the faces in front of him before his gray eyes

40

turned to the sergeant. He saluted and moved off toward his jeep with long easy strides.

"At ease, men," the sergeant said. "You can sit down." They sat obediently. The sergeant waited until the jeep had pulled away.

"I was glad somebody asked a question," the sergeant rubbed his scar. "The colonel likes to have the troops ask questions. Shows they're alert. Just so you'll know I wasn't slingin' you any horseshit the other day, I'm tellin' you that the colonel was out on that tank shoot he talked about." The sergeant threw a belligerent look at the men in front of him. "He was in the lead tank manning the machine gun. We hear he got his ass chewed by division for riskin' his life. But that didn't stop him. That Baker company attack he told you about was no joy ride either. They got in a tight spot. So what happens?" He paused as if to give a greater effect to his answer. "The colonel goes out and pulls 'em back in, that's what. The Thursday night patrol got itself pinned down and the colonel starts right out to it. He lost radio contact with that patrol and so he gets a radio man and heads out there. He brought 'em back too! Carried one guy dead in his own arms right back to our lines. Blood all over him and crying he was. I tell you he's the best goddam officer you could get." He paused. "You better know it!" he added with a bite. "All right, now get your cans out of here." Feet shuffled and men began to talk. "Wait a minute, I almost forgot." The sergeant rubbed his thick hand across his scarred cheek again and remarked casually, "Some mail came in and we'll be holdin' a formation just after noon chow. Okay."

White returned from mail call with a letter. Warren had none, had not expected one, for he and Jean had made an agreement not to write.

"It is from Carol," White announced.

"The one in the picture?"

"No, no, another one. I would not have given her my address, only she cried."

White scanned the letter muttering, "I thought so, I thought so. You see, the return address is Hollywood. She has gone to Hollywood to get in the movies. She is a starlet now. Ha!" He hacked out the word. "Starlet, harlot. In Hollywood they are the same." He continued to peruse the letter, his heavy cheeks hardening as he clenched his teeth. "She says she loves me," he announced, "which she has said before. I never said it to her, though. I am no hypocrite. I lived with her for six months and yet I never told her I loved her. Not once." He smiled slyly at Warren, "And that is difficult."

Having finished the letter he tossed it at Warren. "You may read it if you wish. She asks me to marry her."

"No thanks."

"It is just a love letter," White said. "She could never talk of anything that mattered." He scooped up the pages of the letter, placed them one on top of the other and deliberately tore them up with the same definiteness as he did everything. He stacked the little pile of paper in the dust and touched a match to the stack, igniting it on all four sides. "I have a picture of her," he announced, thrusting two fingers into his fatigue jacket pocket and extracting his wallet. Flipping the celluloid pockets, he stopped when he came to the picture he sought and handed the wallet to Warren.

The blond smiling face in the photo was closer to Warren's idea of White's type of woman than the dark, thoughtful girl had been. The face was pretty, the eyes large and untroubled, probably blue.

White's stubby finger tapped the picture below. "That's her, too."

It was a snapshot of the same girl reclining beside a pool. Her mouth was open in unrestrained laughter and her hair flowed down over a tanned body clad only in a Bikini swim suit. She was half-sitting, leaning back on her hands, her legs were spread slightly apart and her whole body was fresh, intimate.

"I took it," White said.

"Pretty nice," Warren commented, handing the wallet back.

White took another look at the snapshot. "To live with, she was fun," White said, "but she wanted me to love her too. Women are never content unless they defeat you."

Sticking his thumb under the celluloid, he pulled the snapshot out. The dark-haired girl's photo was likewise removed. Lighting a match he ignited the snapshots, holding them in his hand until the upward curl of flames forced him to drop them. "Oh, the envelope," he said, having discovered it lying beside him. He picked it up and looked at the return address. "Hollywood," he spiced the word with disgust. "She will become a whore." He touched the corner of the envelope to the burning pictures and watched the flames creep up its sides, then dropped it onto the miniature pyre.

"That ends that," he said.

The next morning a sharp looking non-com came down from division to give the replacements a refresher lecture on escape and evasion. "Whatever you guys do when you get caught, and escape, don't hole up with any women." The instructor's tone was aggressive and high pitched. "Women get possessive, they fall in love with ya or they want to mother ya and then when you try to get back to your own lines, they don't want ya to leave. You can bet your life they'll even turn you over to the enemy before they'll let ya desert 'em. That's women's logic. So whatever ya do . . ."

The classification and assignment processing routine was gone through again that afternoon. The regimental personnel officer, a short, ruddy-complexioned warrant officer, advised White and Warren to accept assignment in a counterfire unit. The W.O. did not seem willing to assign them summarily, but wanted them to volunteer. They declined, yet were left uncertain of the officer's final decision.

"He can send us where he wants," Warren said, "I don't know why he bothered asking." Overhead, a brown Piper Cub made drowsy hornet sounds. "What's counterfire, anyway?"

"A unit that picks up the sounds of enemy weapons and calls artillery fire on them," White replied.

"The first I've heard of it."

"The Germans perfected the sound-locating equipment toward the end of the last war."

"I don't want to get this far and not make the line."

"I had better get into combat," White threatened.

The artillery, erupting in the distance, punctuated his words with emphatic, dull thuds.

Despite the humid days, the nights were cold. Lying awake on the ground, Warren felt the throb of the artillery, as if giants in some distant workshop were pounding at the earth with great sledges. He thought that he could hear, far off, the sound of machine gun fire, but he wasn't sure. Overhead the grinding whir of a helicopter was softened by the fog which accompanied the descent of the night over the rice paddies and the hills.

White was breathing with a solid evenness beside him, and Warren wondered what reason the sleeping man could have for so violently desiring the line. It was assuredly not the same as his own, which he felt would not bear too close scrutiny. So many loose ends in the fabric of his life were tied in with this desire. The vision on the French train ride was one; indeed, the greatest one. War had broken out soon after that experience. In Basic Training he had the vivid sensation of beginning to walk into that dream, but, abruptly, his course had swerved.

——Late one night while he was sitting in the latrine,

44

Sergeant Thorne came in. Red faced and puffing, he leaned unsteadily against the wall, propping himself with one red hand while he urinated into the porcelain trough.

"Too much beer," he wheezed. "Too damned much beer." He turned his spectacled gaze on Warren, "What in hell you doin' down here this late, and with all your clothes on?"

"Writing."

"Writin' what?"

"A poem."

"A poem? Read it to me." He fumbled at his buttons. Warren read the poem while the sergeant, staring at him through steamed-up glasses, eased his bulk against a wash basin.

"Beautiful," the sergeant said when the poem had been read. "Lotta pretty words in there; I don't understan' it, but it sure sounds beautiful. You got talent, know that?" He walked unsteadily over to the row of toilets and sat down on the seat next to Warren. "You got real talent." He planted one heavy hand on Warren's knee for a moment and then went on. "I got a sister what's got talent, she writes poems for our little home-town paper back in Alabama. She's a cripple, but she's got real talent, too." He belched heavily and expelled a large wind of beer and tobacco near Warren's face.

"You shouldn't be in this goddam company. All these guys are goin' to Korea. That's all right 'cause most of them ain't got no talent. Now you, you shouldn't go to Korea. You should volunteer for Leadership School!" He slapped his hand down on Warren's knee in a firm grip. "Yeah. You volunteer for Leadership School. What's your name?"

He did not consider the conversation anything more than an incident. Convinced that Sergeant Thorne would not remember it the next day, Warren was startled when the sergeant's red face approached and commanded, "Sign this!" One thick hand thrust an application for Leadership School in front of Warren. Warren protested, but the red face only firmed up. "You sign this goddam thing, Private! I know what I'm doing."

So Warren was among the ten "volunteers" for Leadership School and upon graduation he was assigned to Division Faculty. Lesley was right in calling it a "soft post." Warren could have remained there until his discharge, that was certain; other men, put on orders, had been taken off because they were "valuable to the training mission." In fact, when he decided to volunteer for Korea, even the formidable Lieutenant Ordway, his group chief, was shocked.

"Personal problems, maybe?" the lieutenant asked in his condescending manner.

"No, sir."

"Come, come, you can talk to me. Girl jilt you?"

"No, sir."

"Somebody here on faculty? Some situation at home?" Lieutenant Ordway rubbed his square chin for a moment. "You need a three-day pass to think this over. Here. Get out and come back sane. I'll get somebody to handle your classes."

On that pass Warren had met Jean, but even that encounter did not change his mind. Finding him still adamant, Lieutenant Ordway gave him another three-day pass, but not before calling him into the office for a strange consultation.

Lieutenant Ordway was a large-boned man in his late thirties with a face like Franklin Roosevelt's. Never absent from his left breast were his four rows of ribbons. Once he had commanded Warren to tell him what each ribbon signified and Warren had missed one. Ordway promptly restricted him to the post for the weekend to "learn thoroughly the medals and decorations of the United States Army." The enlisted men were accustomed to such orders from the lieutenant, for Ordway had never acclimated himself to the relaxed atmosphere of Division Faculty. He heartily detested the idea of enlisted men going to the coffee shop with officers, as was the faculty custom, and he muttered all along the way if he accompanied such a mixed group. That the major condoned and even took part in the practice caused Ordway to voice even louder resentment. "The major's a reservist," he affirmed one day, "that's the whole damned trouble with this outfit."

One afternoon, Lieutenant Ordway, Lieutenant Encimer—a new and shy addition to the group—and three enlisted men started on foot for the coffee shop. "What's your date of rank, Lieutenant?" Ordway asked. When the lieutenant told him, Ordway announced, "You're on my left, then," and stopped to allow Lieutenant Encimer to cross over. "Sergeant, you're on the lieutenant's left. You privates can stay where you are." Then, the formation having been organized according to proper military protocol, the group continued to the coffee shop.

Lieutenant Ordway lost no opportunity to blast the "new army" and to berate the officers and men who allowed what he considered laxity in discipline. "Once," he said to Warren who stood rigidly at attention for the dressing down, "they had the old army," he dragged the sentence like a slow burning fuse. "Then," he continued, his voice sarcastic, "they got the new army. Then," he exploded, "then they drafted you!" His large jowls turned purple in rage as he thundered: "I don't know what's happening! In the old army they said: 'Officers and their ladies, enlisted men and their women.' Today they don't make such distinctions. But it's only those distinctions which count! Do you understand? You failed to append the word 'sir' to a statement you delivered to a first lieutenant! What have you got to say for yourself? Nothing! You can't say anything! There is no defense for such an inexcusable oversight! Oh, it was probably deliberate. I

47

know this 'new army.' Well you listen to me, Private Warren! Outside that window there's a pipeline running directly to Korea, and if you blunder once again like this, I'm going to shoot you down that pipeline so fast you'll wish you'd never left your mother's womb! Dismissed!"

Thus, Warren was surprised to meet a different Ordway on the day that he was called into the office after returning from the three-day pass.

Closing the door of the office, Ordway moved to his desk. "Sit down, Warren," he said casually, without the usual emphatic "Private." "I'd like to have a chat with you." His eyes scanned Warren's face as he seated himself behind his desk. "Tell me, first, how can a private like Forti get married?"

"What do you mean, sir?" Private Forti was being married in another month.

"I mean that I couldn't get married now if I wanted to. I'll have to make captain first. How can anyone dare to get married on a private's pay?"

"Simple, sir. It costs two dollars for the license and a few more for the ceremony. He just gets married. Then he's got his allotment—"

"Damned fools, that's what they are! Do you know that for the past three years I've never held a post that called for less than the rank of captain and yet I've never made captain?" He peered intently across the desk at Warren. "My whole family is military. Our tradition goes back to the French and Indian War. My father was a colonel, and I can't make captain."

"Maybe you're trying too hard . . ." Warren suggested.

"Private," Ordway snapped, "you will speak when I ask you to. I called you in to talk to you, not to have you," he underlined his words with sarcastic vigor, "tell me what's wrong."

"Yes, sir." The barriers, or more aptly the bars, were up again.

48

"Now tell me," he lapsed into the tone he had used before his outburst, "what would a man like me do on the outside? I mean, where could I put my talents to best use?" He did not wait for Warren to answer him. "Insurance, banking, those are respectable. I can't be a doctor. I'm a little too old to be studying law." He picked up a pencil from the desk and began toying with it. "I'm thinking of getting out of the army, Warren."

"Yes, sir." The man was trying, but he was incapable, or afraid, of being really confidential.

"Yes. I can't take this 'new army' any longer. I see officers, officers, mind you, pushing baby carriages or lugging packages for their wives in the PX. It's ridiculous!" He tossed the pencil down.

"Yes, sir." Warren expected him to leap from his chair in indignation, but hoped agreement would pacify him.

"Now I'd go back to college if I got out; I've one more year to go to get my B.A." He shoved a slip of paper across the desk. "I've listed them in the order of their social preference. I believe Yale or Harvard would be the best, don't you?"

Warren glanced at the darkly printed list. "Yes, sir." One could cope with a chewing out, he thought, but this formal informality was puzzling.

"Harvard first, naturally. Then Yale." The lieutenant stretched his arm across the desk and his soft fingers drew the paper back in front of him. "Princeton, perhaps a poor third," he mused looking at the piece of paper. "Did I see you at the opera last week?"

"You may have, sir."

"Hmm," Ordway pursed his wide lips, "and would you mind telling me what enlisted men were doing at the opera?"

"Enjoying it, sir." He was absolutely serious, Warren decided.

"Enjoying it. Tell me, Warren. All the enlisted men

49

in this building have some college education. Two of them are Yale men. Why aren't they interested in becoming officers?"

"The smart ones want to serve the shortest possible time and get out."

"So I see. I was a first sergeant in the last, The Great War, you know. I tried the outside and decided to come back. I made this bar," he rubbed the silver bar on his shoulder with one loving finger, "in Korea. There should be two there, maybe even a major's leaf by now. Look at the major. Not even a career man, a . . . a . . ." he sought for a word, then hissed, "a reservist." Stopping, he picked up the pencil again and began to scratch at a pad in front of him. "Tell me," he said pensively, "what do you think of men whose wives are school teachers?"

"Nothing wrong with that, sir."

"No children, of course," the lieutenant said determinedly. "I won't be reduced to caring for some squalling little runt who defecates every hour on the hour." His pencil poised, he reflected, "Maybe a son, though. One son would be fine, carry on the line." He watched the point of his pencil as it filled in a square that he had marked off on his pad. "You still intent on going to Korea?"

"Yes, sir."

"Why?"

"I feel it is the right thing, sir."

"Nasty, very nasty there. You could make rank there, though. Quicker than here where rank's frozen. Is that why you're going?"

"No, sir. I just think it's the right thing for me to do."

"Field army's not like garrison life." The lieutenant was still marking the square on the paper with short, black strokes.

"So I understand, sir."

Abruptly, the lieutenant stood up. "You haven't changed your mind?"

50

"No, sir."

"Been to C and A yet?"

"Not yet, sir."

"Why don't you take another three-day pass and think it over some more?" He stalked over to his desk and opened the drawer. "Here," he said, throwing the pass down on the desk. "If this doesn't do it, you can have another one when you come in again."

"Thank you, sir."

"Now get out of my sight. I'm sure you're demented."

"Yes, sir." Warren did not fail to salute before he left the office.

How could a person like Lieutenant Ordway ever understand his decision and the reasons behind it? Could anyone? Jean might . . . Bernhardt surely . . . his decision was triggered by Bernhardt's letter.

He and Bernhardt had met only three times in Basic Training: once for an afternoon as they assisted one another in rifle practice, another time when the company was out on bivouac. In different platoons, they were seldom thrown together. Their longest talk had come when they pulled guard duty together. Between shifts of marching around an empty shack they lay on their bunks, a chessboard on the floor between them. Quiet, mature for his age, Bernhardt shipped out with the ninety per cent of the company who went directly to Korea. Bernhardt had found his address somehow and three months later had written Warren a letter telling mainly of the men they had both known, some dead or missing. Most important, Bernhardt had written a passage that hounded Warren's thoughts. "In the big fear all men turn to God. Funny you have to come here to find Him."

Could the restlessness that gnawed at him be such a search? He had turned from the thought in disgust, thinking of churches as filled with psalm-braying jackasses; but he could not deny that he had sought for something

51

throughout the cities and villages of France. In cathedrals, along dung-strewn country roads, to the accompaniment of chanting monks in the abbey, he had searched, but he had not found. Then, toward the end, the vision on the train had occurred. Bernhardt's letter had arrived when he had begun to doubt the meaning of the vision. The letter stung his conscience like a reproach. He replied to it, asking Bernhardt to write to him again, but his own letter came back sloppily stamped, "Returned Undeliverable." A check mark appeared in a little box next to "Killed in Action."

Within him had been growing the fear that he was a coward, that somehow he was turning his back on destiny. At last he chose to volunteer for Korea.———

The pulse beat of the artillery trembled through the earth as Warren shifted his position that he might sleep.

"The land of the morning calm," somebody said as they clambered aboard the trucks that morning. "I'll be damned if it is."

"It kept up all last night, too," somebody else said.

"Wonder if it's the 'softening up' before an attack?"

White leaned toward Warren to speak. "It probably is. Too much of it to be just harassing fire." He rubbed his palms together jovially. "I think we shall see action very soon. Maybe even tonight." He grinned at Warren as if they were accomplices in some practical joke.

When the orders were read, Warren found himself anxious to hear that he had been assigned to some "safe" post.

"We made it," White exulted when the sergeant announced their assignment to the first battalion, Baker company.

Warren did not share White's enthusiasm, a clinging uncertainty gripping him. While they cleaned up their tent, putting their gear in order for the move, White hummed cheerily. A dizziness on the edge of nausea overtook Warren. He restrained himself as best he could, but finally he could no longer and he sat in the dust and put his head between his knees, trying to steady the revolving world.

"What's up?" White asked. "Heat getting you?"

"I think so," Warren responded. "Got some water?"

White poured him a canteen cup of water and watched him while he drank from it. "That happens," White said. "You had better keep a batch of salt pills handy. I always do. Here, take these." He extended two white pills which Warren obediently swallowed with the water. "Get some from the medic before we leave. The ride will be hot."

By the time the trucks had arrived, Warren had steadied himself.

The driver came around to secure the tail gate. "Somebody get behind that machine gun for this trip." He pointed at the fifty caliber machine gun mounted on a ring above the driver's cab. "Regulations."

A young man leaped for the gun.

"Oh, God," Warren moaned, recognizing the Duke.

"It's loaded," the driver said, "so be careful."

"We can pray that he will not be in our company," White said.

"For an atheist you rely a lot on prayer."

"I am a poor atheist," White chuckled, "or maybe a good one, eh?" In his overflowing good humor, he punched an elbow into Warren's ribs.

The Duke began to remove the canvas covering from the machine gun, but a shout stopped him. The driver, entering the cab of the vehicle, turned bellowing, "Leave the damned cover on unless you need the weapon! You want to clog the damned thing with dust?"

"Okay, buddy." The Duke pulled the cover back down again.

"Unhappy," White winked at Warren and pointed in the direction of the Duke, "he cannot play hero."

The convoy pulled out of the camp area and onto the main route. The trucks ahead of them were whipping up a great cloud of dust through which they had to drive, and in an effort to keep the dust from hitting their eyes most of the men turned their heads to the rear of the vehicle or looked out over the side; some unbuttoned their fatigue jackets and pulled them up over their heads; White tied a handkerchief over the muzzle of his M-1. The Duke, in his gunner's position, caught the full brunt of the dust. He put on a pair of dark glasses and peered theatrically to the front and the two sides of the road, ostensibly looking for the enemy.

The hills upon which Warren gazed were almost bare of foliage. The rice paddies between were, for the most part, dried up and deserted, though in one green valley, not unlike the one where they had been staying, there was a village of straw-domed mud huts, while the hills on either side had been terraced into paddies. Not able to tell whether the village was still occupied, he wondered what sort of life was lived there, or had been . . . Attracted by a sound overhead, he saw a brown helicopter whirring in the direction they were headed. Its bare skeletal structure surmounted by a glass bubble gave it the look of an overgrown grasshopper. Along each side near the ski-like landing runners extended a coffin-shaped container.

"Wish we had had those in the last war," White nodded at the whirlybird.

"Yeah?"

"Cut casualties about ninety per cent. Get the wounded to major surgery in five minutes."

They watched the ugly little machine as it disappeared over the hills in the direction of the artillery firing.

Warren's face felt dry with dust, silt clogged his nostrils. Over all the men he could see the same powdery film.

They passed the artillery unit, where the 155's could be seen leaping with each slam. In the sand-bagged pits, shirtless men rammed shells into the breeches and jumped away from the recoiling weapons as they spat the charge into the air. Other men came out of an underground bunker, visible only because of its sandbagged roof, and walked over to one of the belching pieces. The crew there fired the round and, picking up their shirts and canteens, left the weapon to the relief.

Further up the road the caravan passed a reserve battalion. Some men stood where the entrance to the battalion area joined the road and shouted at the passing trucks.

"Say, are you my replacement?" one man yelled.

"You guys gonna end the war?"

"Hey, guy, I can go *home* now."

"Got any women aboard?"

The trucks rolled by, few of the replacements replying to the jeers thrown at them.

"Look at Hollywood with the John Wayne gun," somebody shouted, pointing at the Duke.

"Bastard!" The Duke thrust his middle finger in the air.

The regimental C.P. was cut out of a hillside. As they passed it, the men could see that most of the bunkers had only a minimum area exposed to view—and that covered by sandbags. Vehicles were surrounded by sandbags; the open area was dotted with mounds of sandbags, but stairs cut down into the earth revealed their function as underground dwellings. The trucks stopped. Their driver got out and climbed the railing.

"All right, you guys: from here on out, on your toes!" he shouted hoarsely. "Parts of this road are under enemy observation. When we come to those parts, we'll be going like hell. Don't be horsing around or you'll fall off. Don't panic if a round comes in. Unless we're hit, we're going right on. It won't take more than twenty minutes to get where we're going." All of the drivers were giving their passengers the same warning talk. Then, a signal was

55

passed down the line; the drivers started their trucks and, at timed intervals, pulled out.

The trucks picked up speed as they whined their way along the twisting route. They were in the hills now, the road following a small mountain stream which, despite its greenish color, seemed inviting to Warren.

The Duke's hands moved nervously over the still-covered weapon.

"You'd make a good target there, Duke," one of the men said. Whether the Duke heard or not, he made no reply.

There was no more talk until someone pointed to a bare hill that showed between two ridges. "That's Papa-san, I'll bet."

Warren and White looked at the hill. "See that smoke?" White said, pointing. "They're hitting the rear slope of the hill."

Overhead, two jets screamed by in a swift strike at the hill.

"Look at those babies go!"

The sound of machine gun fire, short ripping sounds, reached their ears as the planes swerved upward from the slope.

"Strafing."

"The hell they are! Look at that slope! Napalm."

Gushers of black smoke were rising from the hillside as the flames sloshed over the face of the slope. The planes made another run, this time at the rear slope of the hill. The crackle of machine guns was heard long after the aircraft were swooping upwards and the dense, black smoke bulged over the edge of the hill like an ugly monster roused in anger.

"That'll fix the bastards."

"Anyone want fried Gook for supper?"

Without encountering fire, the trucks slammed to a halt

56

at first battalion headquarters and the men were rushed into jeeps.

"Baker company men over here," a driver called and Warren and White went toward him, while the other jeep drivers collected their men. An officer walked around with a sheaf of orders and checked each jeep-load to see that all the men were accounted for. Warren and White had settled themselves in the back seat of the jeep when Duke jumped into the front seat, pulling his pack in after him.

"Hi, guys," he said in a friendly tone, turning with out-stretched hand. "I'm the Duke." Then he recognized White and his hand froze in mid-air.

"What's your real name?" White asked, ignoring the hand.

"Hank, Hank Schmidt."

"Well, Herr Schmidt," White said slowly, "this army has no rank of Duke that I know of."

"It's just a nickname, guy."

"I see. Well, do not let it go to your head."

Warren grasped the still extended hand. "My name's Warren."

The Duke settled into his seat. The officer came by. "Baker company jeep?"

"Yes, sir," the driver answered.

"Schmidt, Warren, White, that correct?"

"Yes, sir," White replied.

The officer checked the names on his list. "Good luck, gentlemen," he said and moved on to the next jeep.

"We've got a number one outfit," the driver said as the jeep moved along the narrow mountain road. "We've had hell lately. You're the smallest batch of replacements we've gotten in a month. Need more. Hell, man, we've really been getting it. More casualties than any other company on line. Got another big deal comin' up tonight. You're just in time."

"I told you," White nudged Warren.

"You mean we're going, we're going *out* tonight?" the Duke asked.

"You're not gonna play tiddly-winks."

"Just let me at those bastards," the Duke said. "You'll really see something."

"Oh, no," the driver slapped his forehead. "Not another hero. Listen, bud, for your own good I tell you this. Don't be a hero. Somebody might shoot you." The driver lifted one hand from the wheel and turned halfway in his seat. "I'm Roger Zikowlsky—coward." He held out his hand, smiling. Warren and White shook hands with him and introduced themselves.

"You guys'll probably go to first platoon," Zikowlsky said. "They're short. We're all short. If you do get first platoon, you'll have Sergeant Prevot for a platoon leader. He's a good man."

"A sergeant for a platoon leader?" White asked.

"We've only got two officers in the company. They're begging people to take battlefield commissions. Prevot could be a lieutenant tomorrow, but he won't do it. We've got a first louie for a company commander and a warrant officer. That's all our officers."

The jeep passed a metal shack with a straw roof, surrounded by other more substantial sandbagged dwellings. "That's where our KSC's live. They're Korean men who couldn't pay their taxes so they work it off in labor battalions. We use them for heavy work like carrying ammo and sandbags up to the line. Undependable as all hell; run like rabbits when a shot is fired, but they come in handy for the manual labor. Keep an eye on them; they'll steal you blind."

"Doesn't anybody worry about spies?" White asked.

"Oh, sure. Probably a spy or two in that group there, but how do you know? Hell, some colonel had a twelve-year-old houseboy who turned out to be a top Commie spy. You never can tell. That's our company there." He

58

pointed to the ridgeline above them, but aside from one or two rugged splotches of sandbags, Warren could make out little. "Joe Chink's on the other side of the hill. We'll probably go out to see him tonight. The boys have already been briefed, you'll probably get a special session, if that. Everybody's damned shorthanded."

The jeep made a left turn at a fork in the road and stopped at a bridge where a road guard took one look and waved them on. Then the vehicle began to whine up a narrow road which doubled back above the road it had left. "Keep your head down from here on in," Zikowlsky cautioned. "Joe Chink can see this part of the road and he snipes at us occasionally." The men crouched obediently while the driver pressed down on the accelerator. After a few minutes he said, "It's okay now."

The road was bumpy. "Joe Chink lobs mortar rounds in here all the time," Zikowlsky commented. "That's how our captain got it. Coming back from a Battalion Commander's meeting, right about where we are now, Joe threw about eight rounds onto this road. One hit right near the rear end of his jeep, throwing it over. He was picking himself up when another one got him, landed nearly on top of him. A good guy, too. Brand new lieutenant with him. The lieutenant didn't even get to see the line. Really cut up. Guess he's home now—if he lived." After a pause he added, "Battalion mortars are over in that draw, other side of that ridge there."

Zikowlsky continued his commentary until he braked the jeep to a stop in front of a bunker near the top of the hill. "Be right back," he said swinging himself out of the jeep and entering the C.P. He returned, following behind a thin, tired-looking sergeant.

"I'm Sergeant Prevot," he said, extending a hand. "You men will be in my platoon." His brown eyes surveyed the three replacements almost sadly.

59

The three shook his hand in turn and introduced themselves.

"Had chow? Well, we'll take care of that. First, let's get you to your bunker. Follow me and keep your heads down."

Prevot led them through a trench beside the Command Post bunker. "It's always safer to use the commo trench," he said, "though you can take the road if you want. Some people take the road 'cause it's quicker and more comfortable, not all this bending over. Could get picked off by a sniper or an incoming round, though." Crouched, keeping their heads below the level of the trench, they came to a position sandbagged and camouflaged with earth. "Unbend and we'll give you a look at the enemy." The men straightened up and Sergeant Prevot pointed one knobby finger out of the narrow slit in the front of the fortification. "That," he said pointing to the great brown hill directly in front of them, "is Papa-san."

The mountain, at this distance, impressed Warren with its naked strength. A stream approached the massive rise and then, abruptly, split in two: its separated waters encircled the mountain like the white arms of a tiny bride trying to embrace her burly, gigantic groom. "How come they've stopped shelling it?" Warren asked.

"Joe Chink's gone underground," Prevot answered. "No sense wasting shells. We'll have another air strike before nightfall. The mosquito plane is up looking things over."

A man entered their position from the other direction. "Damned sound power went out," he muttered. Sweat trickled through the dust on his round face. "Had to find the cut. Bad splicing job." He picked up the phone and whistled into it. Warren heard a voice come through the earpiece. "Rutledge here," the dusty man said. "Just fixed the line. Work okay now? Good. Out." He hooked the phone up and turned to them. "New replacements, eh?"

He thrust out a paw. "Rutledge. We need you. Isn't that right, Sarge?"

"Could use another twenty," Sergeant Prevot replied, his Adam's apple bobbing.

"They going out tonight?"

"Yes." Sergeant Prevot started along the trench from the direction from which Rutledge had emerged. "Let's move along."

"Good luck tonight," Rutledge called as they left.

"We'll all need it," Prevot smiled wryly.

The men crouched down and once more worked their way through the trench along the ridge. They passed other men in other positions like Rutledge's, but did not stop again until the trench opened out onto the road. "That whole stretch of road behind us," Prevot pointed, "was under direct enemy observation. No sense tempting Joe Chink."

Continuing along the road, they passed great stacks of sandbags with doors in them. Before one of these a burly fellow was sitting on the ground explaining a fifty-caliber machine gun to the ROK soldier in front of him. His arms were in constant motion as he shoved one part of the weapon into another, gesticulated elaborately with a bolt and the opening into which it fitted.

"How's it coming?" Prevot asked.

"Either he's gotta learn English or I've gotta learn Korean," the instructor paused. "But he's a good boy. He's getting it." The Korean soldier stood up and grinned expansively.

"Keep at it, Lim, you good ROK." Prevot patted the Korean on the shoulder. "Tonight you use that." He pointed to the machine gun.

Lim's grin broadened and he sat down. "Number one, Sergeant," he said pointing to the weapon. "Number one."

"You bet, Lim, number one gun. You number one soldier." Prevot led the replacements past other bunkers before they entered the dark coolness of one of the cave-like dwellings. "This is it," Prevot said, "but keep your M-1 with you at all times. Those three bunks are yours. Take your pick. Two hot meals a day here, if Joe Chink permits. We've already had ours for today. I'll see if the cook has anything. If not, I'll trot you up some more C-rations. You'll find some under that cot, I think, but the selection is limited." He went out. A moment later he returned. "Anybody need water?"

All three had emptied their canteens on the dusty ride from the replacement area. "Somebody bring them and I'll show you where the Lister bag is." Warren collected the canteens and followed Prevot from the bunker.

"After I get you guys fed, we'll go down to the C.P. and I'll brief you." He shook his head. "Hate to send new replacements out before they know the men they're with, but there's nothing I can do. That's the kitchen area, there," he pointed. "You can tell the others." Warren saw a row of garbage cans, the usual three with heater equipment for mess kit cleaning. A large bunker, close in to the rear slope of the ridge, was the kitchen.

"Just sent the leftovers down to the KSC's," the cook informed them. "Really don't got a damned thing left. Maybe a little bread to go with the C-rations. If you'd only got in here twenty minutes ago . . ."

Taking a loaf of bread and a couple of boxes of C-rations, Prevot and Warren stepped outside again. "There's the Lister bag." Prevot waited while Warren filled the canteens from the bulbous green sack suspended from a tripod. Then the two men returned the way they had come. Prevot turned to Warren when they reached the bunker door. "You know the way to the C.P. When you guys finish eating, come on down. I'll explain what's up." He turned away and then remembered something. "Oh, yeah, latrine's down there." Warren looked to the small box about fifty feet down the rear slope of the hill. "Don't stay on it too long. It's not made for meditatin'. See you in a half hour."

After a meal of C-rations heated one can at a time on a small Coleman stove, Warren and White, trailed by the silent Duke, returned through the trench where men were now test-firing their weapons, to the company C.P. Even as Sergeant Prevot pointed his bony finger at the map he had spread out before them, the rifles along the line were sniping at the impassive brawn of Papa-san.

"Those are the check points, then?" asked White, placing his own stubby finger upon the several locations.

"Right," said Prevot.

"This area to the left of this ridge," White pointed again at the map, "is it zeroed in for a mortar barrage?"

"Yes. This whole area is boxed. Don't worry about that. We'll have every mortar in the battalion at our disposal. Division artillery, too. The artillery F.O. is going out with us. This is a big deal."

White's seeming satisfaction with Prevot's answers gave Warren confidence. Earlier, while eating his C-ration corned beef, he had tried to escape thoughts of the impending action. More than once during the day he had wished that the moment illuminated so long ago on the train could be accomplished without all these preparatory gestures and words.

"I've got a rather crude sand-map of the terrain outside," Prevot said. "It'll give you another view of the situation." He pulled back the bunker flap and they stepped out to his sand-map near the side of the C.P. There, looking down at what might have been a child's sandbox of hills, castles, and valleys, Prevot pointed out the route they would follow into enemy territory. "We cross the barbed wire at precisely twenty-two hundred hours tonight. That's this point here. We know this stretch well, so we'll make time up to this point here." He made an indentation with his finger at a spot on one of the ridges of sand. "As you can see,

63

that's a southern finger of this ridge here that cuts into Papa-san. Anyway, that's our first check point. We'll wait there until we get a runner from the second platoon telling us that they've gotten to here." Again he made an indentation with his finger, at a point to the front of the same slope. "They'll lay down a base of fire for us when needed. Second radio check comes here," he pushed a twig into a sandy ridge, about halfway up the slope. "We'll try to make it to here without being discovered. That'll be tough. A recon patrol got hit there not long ago. Anyway, when we reach that point, the third platoon should have moved ahead and be here. Then we'll call in the mortars on the top of the ridge. As they lift, the third platoon will be moving up from the front while we go up the side. We want a prisoner. We don't have the slightest idea what outfit holds this area. We'll pull back when we get orders to do so. Got artillery and mortar to cover our withdrawal. The second platoon will also cover, then pull out last. And get this straight: no wounded or dead left behind." His Adam's apple wobbled violently. "If anybody's missing when we get back, we go right out and bring him in. Get your armored vests at that bunker over there, together with whatever ammo and grenades you need. Don't, for God's sake, weigh yourself down so you can't move. Test-fire your weapons and get some sack time. You're going to need it."

Warren followed White's advice on the number of grenades and M-1 rounds to take with him. "Tonight I will show you how to fix the grenade for rapid use," White promised. Warren nodded, but he was sure that if White knew what fears now gripped him, he would be despised as much as Duke was.

Warren and White worked on their rifles while Duke merely sat on his bunk watching morosely. Finished, they put on their armored vests to go to the forward trench and test-fire their M-1's. Before leaving, White took his first notice of Duke since their arrival. Tossing his cleaning

64

equipment on the bed near the boy, he said, "Here, kid, put this to good use. Tonight you may get to kill somebody." He chuckled. "Maybe vice-versa." The boy mumbled something. Warren wanted to soften White's statement, but didn't know how. He hesitated, then followed White from the bunker.

"Aren't you being a little hard on him?" he asked as they entered the commo trench leading to the forward position.

"He is a German. It is impossible to be hard on a German. Besides he is too cocky. To be a little humble tonight may save his life."

After firing a couple of clips each from their weapons, White pointed out the features of the terrain that Prevot had shown on his map. "It is a well-planned attack," he said knowledgeably. "We should have some real fun. Only there is not much cover out there. Everything is burned off. We will have to make use of every hump of ground."

Later, flopped on their cots, Warren saw that Duke had not finished cleaning his weapon. The boy sat listlessly on the edge of his bunk and wiped the rifle bolt again and again with the same cloth.

Warren wanted to speak, to talk to him, but the words wouldn't come. Finally, his desire smothered in wordless turmoil, he turned his face to the wall and tried to sleep. If the boy was frightened, what about himself? Everything since their arrival was like an underdeveloped photograph, full of meaningless gray blurs. All of this travel back and forth through trenches hacked in the hard earth, the dry instructions concerning future movements, instructions listened to as if they did not concern him, all of the events and men were disconnected from the reality of the vision. Something was lacking. He had asked for this and now his inner being seemed ready to shatter at the prospect of combat. Why had he come—leaving Jean and the safety of a stateside post to lie on this bunk and stare at sand running out of a small hole in the wall.

Sergeant Prevot awakened him and White. "It's all off. Regiment just called. Nothing doing tonight. Intelligence says the enemy is wise to it." Then he turned to the empty bunk, "Where's the other guy?"

"Dunno," Warren said sleepily. "He was cleaning his weapon when I hit the sack."

"Could be on the latrine," White stated.

Pulling the flap back, Sergeant Prevot stepped outside. Warren peered through the doorway into the darkness. "What time is it?" he asked White.

White looked at his watch. "Twenty hundred," he replied.

"The kid's not on the latrine," Sergeant Prevot said when he returned. "Where in hell could he have gone?"

"The trench, maybe."

"Well, we better find him. C'mon."

They searched the trenches without success. Prevot called the C.P. bunker and one or two of the other positions. Duke had not been seen.

"Could he have buggered out?" Prevot asked. Then he went to the C.P. phone and called the road guard down the hill. "A blond kid . . . No? . . . Okay."

After another half hour of fruitless search, Prevot said, "Hate to say it . . . only one thing left . . . he must be hiding out somewhere. There's a bunker next to yours. I didn't think of that. It's empty except for some ammo. He may be there." They headed back to their bunker, taking the road this time. "It's safer at night," Prevot explained, "and I don't want to take an hour getting challenged by every man in that damned trench."

A pale moonlight covered the denuded hills with an eerie glow, casting into relief the projecting timbers of bunkers, the smashed trunks of trees, the earth's surface where projectiles had caused it to erupt. To Warren, the

66

jangling aspect of the world about them was in sharp contrast with the polished stillness of the night. There was not a sound save their own swift movement up the road.

On the left of the bunker in which Warren and White had slept was the one they sought. As they approached it, Prevot was saying, "If he's not here, I don't know where in hell he is."

"Keep away, bastard, or I'll kill you." The cry, unnaturally pitched, was followed by the crack of a rifle. Even as Prevot threw himself on the ground, White pushed Warren back behind their own bunker, out of the line of fire. "Off the ground, you sonofabitch, get back with those others. I've got a gun aimed right at your head. I'll kill you if you don't get away." Prevot scrambled to where Warren and White stood.

"Come on, kid," Prevot called, breathing heavily. "Cut the foolishness."

"I'll kill you if you show your face," Duke screamed.

"White, get down to the C.P. and tell Lieutenant Fregni what's going on. I'll try to talk him out of there."

"Hey, kid, that's not the way to act."

"I'll kill the guy who comes near me."

"Look," Prevot paused and turned to Warren, whispering, "What's his name?"

"He calls himself Duke."

"Look, Duke, the mission for tonight has been called off . . ."

"Lying bastard, who in hell are you kidding? I'll kill ya for lying! Nobody's gonna kill me. You can't send me out, ya lying bastard! Who are you? You're just a lying bastard sergeant! You're not God! I'll kill ya!"

"I mean it, kid, it's been called off. Now come on out of there. You'll only get in trouble . . ."

"I'll give you trouble, lying bastard of a sergeant, I'll kill you if you come near. I'll kill anybody shows his head 'round that bunker. I've got my sights on the spot. Ha! The

67

Duke isn't going to get sent out on any goddam patrol and get killed. Not by any friggin' sergeant. I'll kill ya first."

"Duke!" Prevot called. "I'm not lying! There's no patrol tonight. You'll only get yourself court-martialed if you don't come out of there."

"Lying sonofabitch! Sergeant bastard! If anybody tries to come near me, I'll kill him! The Duke's not going out there."

White returned with Lieutenant Fregni. Prevot warned them away from the bunker edge with his hand. "He's gone psycho, Lieutenant. Threatens to kill anybody who steps out there. Listen. Hey Duke," he called, "everything's okay. You can come out and go to bed. Nobody's going out tonight."

"Lying bastard sergeant," Duke screamed. "Step out from behind there. Let me see ya. I'll kill ya for lying to me. I'm the Duke."

"See what I mean, sir?"

"Can we sneak up on him?" the lieutenant asked.

"We could get up on the roof of his bunker, if that would help," Prevot replied. "Somebody could take the trench around to the other side of the bunker and sidle up along that wall. But he's covering the entrance and I don't know which side he's on or whether he's standing or lying down. If he's at the back of the bunker, we can't get in without making targets of ourselves."

"I see," said the lieutenant.

"Sir," White cut in, "with your permission, sir, I will get him out."

"How?"

"I have handled this sort of case before, sir. I can get him out."

"You're sure?" Lieutenant Fregni frowned. "I don't want anybody to get hurt if it can be avoided."

"I assure you that nobody will be hurt, sir. Just give me permission to get him out and I will do it."

68

The lieutenant looked doubtful. "I wish we had some tear gas," he said ruefully.

"Even then he might come out firing," White said. "I know how to handle this, sir."

"All right," the lieutenant reluctantly nodded. "See what you can do."

"Thank you, sir. Now, regardless of what you hear, don't interfere. Whatever you do, don't say anything to him or to me."

Then White stepped out from behind the bunker and into the range of fire. A shot rang out.

"Come, come," said White with soft laughter. "You are a better marksman than that, aren't you?"

"Get back, bastard, get back you lying sonofabitch or I'll blow your goddam head off."

"How can you blow my head off," White said, deliberately stepping toward the bunker door, "when you are so nervous that you cannot even hit me?" Still moving forward, White removed his steel helmet. "Here," he said, "is my head. I would prefer that you hit me between the eyes. Say, oh, about here." The men pressed against the bunker wall could imagine the stubby finger tapping the exact spot on the broad forehead.

"Stop! Stop! Don't come nearer!" the Duke shrilled. "You're not going to send me out on any goddam attack. I'll kill all the lying bastards who come near me."

"How can you kill any of us when you refuse to help kill the enemy?" White's sure voice sounded nearer the bunker. "If you cannot kill the enemy whom you hate, how can you kill your own buddies, eh?" The second question rang back, echoing from the dark hollow of the bunker now.

"I'll pull the pin on this grenade if you come closer." Desperation swarmed over the words.

Warren felt his body tense even closer to the wall against

69

which he, Prevot, and Lieutenant Fregni were pressing their backs.

"Pull it," White's steel hard voice replied. "Then we both go. You and I together. Our blood all over this bunker. I thought you did not want to die. But if you do, then pull the pin."

The three waiting men pressed against the side of the bunker wall heard the words smothered in a long scream, then the confusion and clatter of kicked metal and grunting men. Lieutenant Fregni's anxious face was sweat-covered when he stepped away from the wall. Prevot turned and touched the lieutenant's arm. "Wait, sir!" His dry lips, stretched thin, made the words a command. The lieutenant moved back.

"Take cover!" White's demand was an instant clear in the night.

The three men dropped prone. Bodies stiffened as the concussion from a grenade burst rolled up the slope of the hill and bits of shrapnel sang about them. A falling fragment of metal struck Warren's helmet. As the sound of scattered earth faded, they could hear again the thrust and push of bodies and objects from the dark chamber. Getting up, Lieutenant Fregni brushed his face against his sleeve. "You two okay?" he asked breathlessly, his damp face now streaked with dust.

"Yes, sir," Prevot replied.

"Yes, sir," Warren said.

"It's quiet," the lieutenant spoke and the others listened.

"Okay," the voice gasped, "he's yours."

When the three men entered the bunker, they found White sitting on Duke's back, pinning the boy's arms behind him.

"Lying bastards. Lying sergeant bastards. The Duke'll fix you all." Duke began to sob. Between curses his voice cracked and he cried like a child.

70

"Commo wire!" White commanded. "He should be tied up."

Prevot switched his flashlight around the bunker.

"Could straitjacket him in his fatigue blouse," White labored, "not as good as commo wire."

"Here's some," Prevot said, taking his wire cutters from his belt and snipping off a length of the wire.

"You tie him," White directed, "while I hold him."

"Private," Lieutenant Fregni turned to Warren. "Go down to the C.P. Tell the warrant officer we'll need a jeep to get this man to regiment. Have the jeep wait at the C.P. and we'll trot him down the hill."

Warren did as told. The warrant officer, a short, balding man in his forties, wanted more information. Warren gave him a brief summary. "The poor little kid," the warrant officer said, taking off his steel-rimmed, issue glasses and wiping them on his handkerchief.

When the trussed prisoner had been hustled down the hill to Zikowlsky's jeep, the lieutenant said, "Take these two men with you. I don't know what regiment will do with him, but battalion can't handle him tonight."

Warren and White climbed in the rear seat of the jeep, on either side of the weeping Duke. Prevot got in the front seat and Zikowlsky turned on his blackout lights. As the jeep moved away, Warren heard the warrant officer mutter, "The poor damned kid."

"Halt," shouted the roadguard at the little bridge.

The jeep halted.

"Who goes there?"

"Baker company jeep with five men."

"Lace," the sign was thrown out as a challenge.

"Brassière."

"Pass, Zikowlsky old buddy."

"Thank you, O Imperial Keeper of the Royal Bridge."

Searchlights now pierced the sky above them; there was not a sound in the peaceful night except that of the jeep's motor. "Somebody needs a little moonlight," Zikowlsky said. "How'd you like to have that at home, Sarge? Take the girl out and have somebody switch on the artificial moonlight. Bounce it off the clouds just for you."

"It would be nice," Sergeant Prevot sighed. "Get married to some little gal who could keep the bunker tidied up and heat the C-rations for me." Gazing up at the quiet sky, he mused, "I know just the gal, too. Met her in Hong Kong when the tub I worked on docked there. White Russian, a real beauty . . . saddest eyes you ever did see . . . said she had been a princess or should have been. I believe it . . . lots of ex-Russian royalty around Hong Kong. She worked in an exporter's. We had a fine time, but I couldn't touch her. She was very religious. Maybe I'll go back and marry her someday. I don't know, though. You see these eighteen- and nineteen-year-old kids getting married and you wonder. Perhaps that's the marrying age. Then again, maybe they just don't know what they're getting into. Myself, I find the older I get, the harder it is for me to think of getting married; you get to feeling how much responsibility is attached to it. Something the kids never think of . . ." He leaned back in the seat and stared at the sky. "It would be nice, though." He paused. "Then again, she's the only gal that might marry me, I guess, and I can't be sure of her. I'm too ugly for these American beauties." Turning around, he asked, "How's Duke?"

"I think he's asleep," Warren said with a glance at the Duke, whose head had dropped forward to his chest.

"He may have passed out," White warned, "but keep an eye on him, anyway. It might be a trick."

"I don't know what in hell regiment is going to do with him this time of night," Prevot sighed.

"What will happen to him, Sarge?" Zikowlsky asked.

"Oh, I dunno. Never had this happen before. Probably send him to the rear for psychiatric observation." He

72

turned to the back seat again. "We'll all have to write this up, I'll bet, probably in triplicate."

"Think they'll court-martial him?" Zikowlsky persisted.

"Maybe. Kinda doubt it. He just cracked up. One of those things." He looked around at White. "You sure got nerve."

"I've handled this kind before," White said flatly. "If they cannot get up the nerve to go out, where are they going to get the nerve to kill somebody in cold blood?"

"Fear. He was crazy with fear."

"A coward is a coward," White said, "whatever he is faced with."

"You say you've handled kids like this before." Prevot peered through the pale night at White. "Where?"

"In the last war. We usually shot them on the spot."

"You mean you executed men for something like that?"

"Sergeant," White said, "after a battle I have had as many as six men executed for cowardice. They could no longer be trusted in battle; they might destroy a whole unit by not fulfilling their duty so they were shot."

"Even kids like this?" Prevot nodded at the Duke.

"Sergeant," White said, "in war there can be only men. I was a company commander at seventeen."

"No kidding. What army?" Prevot's voice bore a note of incredulity.

"The Polish army. I had been raised in military schools and when the war broke out I was still young, fourteen. Two years later I was a member of a unit attached to the Russian army."

"How'd you get to the States?" Zikowlsky asked.

"I assassinated a Russian officer in Warsaw and was smuggled out of the country by the underground."

"Underground? There's an underground in Poland?"

"Yes. Someday you will hear of it."

"This assassination," Zikowlsky asked, "the underground plan that?"

73

"Oh, no. Not this one. One evening I saw a Russian officer pawing a waitress; he was drunk and she was not able to free herself from him. I went over and threw my drink in his face. In the struggle I took his pistol away from him and shot him through the eye. Then I had to leave the country."

"Halt!" A figure came into view pointing his M-1 directly into the windshield of the jeep. "Who goes there?"

"Friend," Zikowlsky replied. "Baker company jeep and five men."

"Lace."

"Brassière."

"The gooks couldn't mispronounce it that way. Pass, friend."

"Wish I could get a pass right out of this Mysterious East," Zikowlsky said as he geared up the jeep.

"What's the matter?" Prevot asked. "Don't you like the exotic orient?"

"Sarge, I've got a mother back home. She's a little Polish woman and she beats me over the head with a ball-bat when I'm naughty, but by God I'd like to be home. Which reminds me," he said, turning his head slightly towards White, "How come a name like White?"

"Security reasons," White replied. "Besides, it is easier to spell."

At regimental headquarters they were halted by another sentry before they pulled into the area where the trucks had stopped that morning. Zikowlsky parked and Sergeant Prevot went off into the darkness. A few minutes later he returned with the Officer of the Day.

"God," the O.D. said. "It's not bad enough to have to worry about the men shooting up trees along the road out there, but you've gotta bring me problems. Well," he sighed, looking at Duke, who still sat as if asleep with his head on his chest. "Take him over to the bunker where the relief guards are sleeping. I'll post a man on him. We'll send him back to division in the morning. I've already talked to your company commander on the phone. You'll have some reports to write up tomorrow."

"I figured as much, sir," Prevot said.

"Well," the officer yawned, "wake him up and let's get him over there."

White shook Duke's shoulder and the boy roused himself, looking around with wide eyes. Then staring directly into White's muscular face for a moment, he broke into sobs.

"Come on," White ordered, gripping Duke's arm. "Get out."

The officer led the men with their prisoner to one of the underground bunkers, where four fully dressed men lay sleeping on stretchers suspended from the ceiling by commo wire. The lieutenant nudged one awake and told him to guard the prisoner. "Each of you take him for an hour. I know that cuts an hour of sack time off everybody, but that's the only thing we can do. He's got his hands trussed, but he's a little off so keep your eyes on him. In fact, you might put him on a bunk and let him sleep."

Warren and White, with the aid of the still-sleepy guard, lifted Duke up and onto one of the stretchers.

The next day the colonel came through. It was his custom to make a weekly trek of his entire regimental front, chatting with his men and checking their positions.

To salute an officer along the line marked him as a prime target for an enemy sniper or mortar observer. "The colonel's an exception, though," Prevot had told Warren. "He gets a salute and he returns it. I remember one day I saluted him and almost as soon as I did it a slug plowed past us. The colonel hit the dirt and so did I. We crawled to cover and he gets up, cool as can be, brushes himself off, snaps me a return salute and says, 'Second time today.' " Prevot shook his almond head and his eyes sparkled as he thought of it. "There's a man for you."

The tall, easy-moving figure, followed by Lieutenant Fregni, came out of the commo trench while Warren was policing up the area in front of his bunker. Warren hurried inside to notify White of the colonel's approach and they both came out to greet the officers. A few yards behind Lieutenant Fregni was a sweating corporal, who alternately tugged at the sling of his M-1 and mopped his brow with a khaki handkerchief.

"As you were," the colonel said as he returned their salutes.

Like all junior officers, Lieutenant Fregni was nervous during the inspection. Warren could almost touch the anxiety of the man whose dark eyes swept the area and then focused on them while the colonel spoke.

"I spoke with you the other day, didn't I?" the colonel asked White.

"Yes, sir," White replied.

"Anything else you'd like to ask me?"

"Yes, sir." Warren was not expecting the affirmative reply, but it was Lieutenant Fregni who was most shocked by it. The normal routine upset, his eyes flitted anxiously from White's face to the colonel's and back again. Then he blurted: "This is the man I told you about, sir."

"Indeed?" the colonel responded. "You're to be commended on your exploit of last night."

"Thank you, sir."

"But you had a question," the colonel reminded himself. "What is it?"

"Well, sir," White began, his legs slightly apart, his hands behind him, "it is my understanding that we need a prisoner."

"That is correct."

"Then, sir," White continued, "if you will give me per-

76

mission to penetrate the enemy's territory for two days, I will bring you a prisoner."

"You'd like to do this alone?" The colonel's intent gray eyes studied White's face.

"One volunteer would help, sir. I could then take a radio. But if one is not available, I can go alone, sir."

"What is your name, Private?"

"White, sir."

"And you feel, Private White, that you could succeed in bringing back a prisoner?"

"Sir, I am convinced of it."

"Convinced? On what grounds?"

"I have done it before, sir."

"I see." The colonel rubbed his tanned jaw with the palm of his thin hand. "Your spirit is to be commended, Private White. About your proposal," he paused, "that I must take under consideration." He glanced at the fidgeting Lieutenant Fregni and then turned his eyes upon White again. "I will let you know of my decision." Then he saluted and continued his inspection tour, followed by the lieutenant, nervous as a terrier, and the heavily breathing corporal.

"Quite a proposal," Warren commented. "Surprised everyone."

"I can get them a prisoner," White said grimly. "They could specify the rank." His set face softened a little when he smiled at Warren. "But, of course, then I might need three days."

"You've done it before?" Warren probed.

"I have spent as long as nine months behind the enemy lines doing sabotage and intelligence work. I see no reason why I cannot go out and get a prisoner. It is silly to send out a huge patrol to catch one man. This way if it does not work, they only lose one man."

"You."

"What of it? I have killed my share of other men. It is my profession. If another man should kill me, why," he shrugged, "that is simply one of the risks of the profession."

"Think you'll get a volunteer to go along?"

"I was thinking that you might want to go."

"All right, guys, enough loafing," Sergeant Prevot said as he pulled aside the canvas flap over the bunker opening. "Gonna assign you a duty post, Warren. Bring your water, cigarettes, candy bars, ammo, and weapon and I'll show you where you'll pull duty from now on in. White, just come along and see. You'll relieve each other on four-hour shifts."

He led them through the commo trench and up forward to one of the enclosed positions through which they had passed earlier.

"Your home away from home," Prevot announced. "The sound power phone there is connected with the C.P. and the other posts. You can hear if the other guys report anything in. One whistle, you get the other guys, two whistles and the C.P. will answer. Not much activity right now, but keep your eyes peeled for snipers, for diggers, F.O.'s, movement of any kind. Report 'em in. Take a shot at anything you like, but restrain yourself. Tonight you can fire all you want. Harassing and interdictory firing keeps 'em from moving around too much out there. But do it away from the hole, out in the trench. Your muzzle flash'll attract return fire. At about six o'clock the password will come down; make sure you know it. Challenge everybody and everything."

"No patrols tonight?" White asked.

"We have patrols every night," Prevot answered. "Mostly ambush patrols, where you go out and sit and wait all night just in case Joe Chink tries to come in. Probably get yours tomorrow night. You pull 'em right along with your regular duty, unless it's a combat or

78

recon patrol. Then we try to get some sack time in before-hand."

When Prevot and White had left, Warren scanned the line. As if gouged by some giant plow, the single furrow of the forward trench had been cut along the sharp ridges for as far as sight carried him. From his right it appeared over the crest of a distant ridge; cleaving carefully to the uneven demarcations of the earth it reached his own position and then sliced off to the left where it descended into a valley out of sight; then, reappearing once again, it sloped upward and over the distant triangular hills. At frequent intervals the furrow bulged with sandbagged positions like his own—so many potatoes plowed up and left behind.

His post, roofed with timbers, sandbags, and earth, looked fragile to him. Since his arrival yesterday, the enemy had done no shelling, but he wondered how much his crude shelter was built to take. Like a hernia in the trench, the position bowed back into the hill. In the bulge someone had built a wooden seat. On both sides of it, strung on commo wire, hung grenades. Whoever had used the position previously had supplied himself well; there were strings of illumination grenades, as well as the regular fragmentation kind. He tried to remember what he had learned in basic about illumination grenades, but all he came up with was the purpose: to briefly light up the area. Then he noticed a thermite grenade. Taking the canister off the wire he looked at it. He had no equipment he'd have to burn if the enemy overran his position. He shook his head and hung the grenade back on the wire, then stepped to the forward opening.

He looked out across a low valley to the place where the two streams joined before they flowed toward his own lines through the valley on the left. Rising out of the waters of the streams, moated by them, was Papa-san, his massive bulk dominating all, his bare rounded form set in sharp contrast to the jagged razorback ridges behind him. Where their sharp edges seemed restless as sea waves thrusting themselves upward in angry motion, Papa-san sat glacier-like, his smooth solidity, his very immobility defying all the turmoil about him. "Our objective," the colonel had said that day of the briefing, "is Papa-san." There the objective sat, brooding over all. Gouge, burn, blast, insult it as they would, could anyone really take Papa-san?

Between the ponderous hulk and himself, in the valley over which Papa-san reigned, men had hidden high explosives, booby traps, and mines. The raped valley was a pregnant womb awaiting abortion. On the forward slope in front of his own post stretched two rows of barbed wire. At the slope's base coils of concertina stretched out of eye range like a wild tangle of children's hoops, stopped simultaneously, weirdly poised as if awaiting the magic of the child's touch to start them all rolling again. Closer still, regular barricades of barbed wire hung on timber supports. Was it all vain labor? Who would clean up the mess when the war was over? Smiling at his quixotic thoughts, Warren turned back from the opening and lit a cigarette before sitting down. Tonight a group of men, tomorrow night he himself, would go out there somewhere and wait. If he were to go with White, he would be out there two days, not just listening in the dark at some point between here and Papa-san, but moving ever deeper into enemy land—behind Papa-san itself. Was this what he had expected? He hadn't realized that there would be so much time to think, so many lulls. Somehow he had forgotten what he must have been told, that combat was an intermittent activity. Now he knew that the moment illuminated by the vision on the train would have to be approached. It could take place tomorrow night, or it might occur months from now. There was just too much time. Time to become afraid. White's suggestion flattered, but he did not like the

80

identity. He did not spill over with hatred for the enemy. He hadn't even seen him yet . . .

Pressing his cigarette out in the earth, Warren walked to the slit and scanned the jagged hills. He saw no life, but still stood there for a time peering at the unlovely hills, his gaze continually returning to Papa-san. He had come here in order to test himself. While most of his beliefs were still unsettled, he knew that he did not believe in killing. Yet, he was here. He had come because he could not live out his life feeling that he had been a coward.

There were ten men on the patrol which Sergeant Prevot led out that next night. The beaming ROK was carrying a thirty-caliber machine gun; another man lugged the tripod and a box of ammunition. Warren and White each carried, in addition to their own weapons and ammo, a box of ammo for the ROK's machine gun. Others carried extra clips for the Browning Automatic Rifle, which was in the hands of a little Mexican named Martinez. Prevot had briefed the two new men that afternoon. "We just sit quiet and wait," Prevot had said. "Be sure the man nearest you is awake. If Joe doesn't show up, we'll all be back here at 0600 hours. Otherwise, we hold a reception. Then we pull out under our mortar and artillery cover, but nobody pulls out until I say so. Remember what I said about going out to get anybody left behind? That still holds. We bring back all dead and wounded."

At 2130 hours they had passed through the barbed wire at the point of departure. Then began the journey through their own mine fields. Mines. Ours were kinder than theirs, some said. They set bouncing betties to jump and explode at testicle level while we more mercifully had them go off at the head. Mines. Big ones and little. The crude wooden boxes of the enemy, our nicely turned gray metal disks. But theirs defied the detectors. Mines. A foot misplaced, a leg missing. Mines. All sizes: big ones, some wired to set off a whole field, little ones, hand grenade size. Booby traps to fill the head with chunks of metal. Warren tried to shake off the jumble of his fears by looking at the sky. It was dark. Prevot had said that the searchlights would be bounced off the clouds at 2230 hours, "which gives us time to get settled in position."

Because they were new men and to be sure that they didn't get lost, Prevot had placed Warren and White in the center of the patrol as it filed out. His eyes now fixed on White's solid figure, Warren could hear behind him the tread of another. He could also hear the stream which he had seen from his position. They were going to follow it for part of their journey. "It's safe," Prevot had said, "and it provides cover for our noise."

Soon they were picking their way along the edge of the stream which glowed in the night. On their right rose the embankment covered with brush and trees. If a branch extended out too far, each man held it back for the next, and if they met a low overhang, each warned the other. Thus, stealthily they advanced upstream; then they turned to the right, climbed the embankment, and walked into the valley again. There was no cover here, only grass sighing against pant-legs. And with each sigh, like a whip in the hand of an expert, the grass stripped something from Warren. The gentle whir of each footstep left him more naked than before, until he felt his unprotected flesh tremble, chilled by each new sound. The shapes of the men ahead of him lacked solidity, as if the whip had stripped them of their very flesh. The dark forms moved like mourners on some nocturnal pilgrimage, their dirge unsung for want of vocal chords. The warped, broken trees in the valley assumed wraith-like shapes. Clumps of brush that they passed were so many enchained demons straining in anger to tear and gnaw on his bones. Looming over all, Papa-san leered down at him, threatening a hundred hidden malevolencies. Off in the distance a searchlight flashed on, its beam slashing the sky. The sharp ray was absorbed by a cloud, then reflected to the earth in a softer, diffused radiance. Somewhere over there another patrol had need of light. Warren thought of all the men out that night who, like himself, had left their protective ridge and—fear working at their guts—picked their way into the area beyond. From the east to the west coast of the Korean peninsula was a strip of land in which fear-filled men were at that same moment furtively crawling through the night, sitting in sweaty anticipation of any movement or sound, or shouting amidst confused rifle flashes and muzzle blasts. White's arm went up and Warren raised his own. The patrol was stopping.

Prevot came up. "Take that spot over there," he whispered, pointing to a small clump of blackness. "Give me your machine gun ammo." Warren handed him the metal box and Prevot quietly disappeared down the line.

Lying in the grass behind the brush clump, Warren looked about. The others likewise had hidden themselves in the grass and the brush. Over his shoulder he could see Prevot with the machine gun crew. Even at this short distance they were only vague shapes, setting up the machine gun on a small knoll so that it could fire above the heads of the rest of the patrol.

Warren eased his rifle's safety off and gently, slowly sneaked another clip of ammunition from one of the cloth bandoleers that marked the upper part of his body with an X. This he placed within quick reach. The walk and his fears had served to overheat him and his sweaty armpits cooled at the touch of the night air. Although the armored vest fitted the upper part of his body snugly, he felt no security. Figures seemed to crouch in the surrounding dark; in the distance he saw a band of men who seemed to advance and retreat even as he watched. Certain this menace was only imaginary, he yet stared in fascinated horror, his hand sticky against the stock of his weapon.

83

He was aware of insistent inner beatings, as if prisoners within sought release from his rigid body.

Above, the glowing ivory baton of their searchlight pointed at the clouds, diluting the valley's dark to a pallid light. Then the figures which held his attention became a group of shattered trees, standing like the grotesques of a medieval damnation scene. Even so, he could not ease the tension of his body; the rough surface of the earth itself seemed to resist every attempt on his part to relax. Sensing the unseen presence of the other men in the patrol, he felt mutely united to these nine near-strangers sharing this pinpoint of being with him. He sensed something precious in the perilous moment, something akin to the knowledge gained on his bicycle trip through the French countryside, a knowledge imprisoned in speechlessness.

——In France he had puzzled the meaning of the great stone monuments men had thrown up to the sky, and always as he wandered, he felt a stranger to their exultation. They were poems in a strange language, of which he could barely touch a meaning—enough to make his being ache with the desire for the fullness he sensed there. Brittany, that stone-gray mystery through which he traveled for thirty days, sleeping in the barns of farmers or alongside roads, had worked some subtle change in him, he knew, and it was in Brittany that he had met Pierre.

Pierre had no hands; they had been severed at the wrists. With leather cups fitted in his handlebars, he steered his bicycle. He and Warren had traveled together for four days. They visited the shipyards at Brest and Pierre had to sign the register, vouching for the integrity of the visiting foreigner. He took the pen in his stumps and began to write.

"Wait! Wait!" cried the guard who ran from the hut to shout to other men standing about outside. They crowded the small room and peered over one another's shoulders to watch the handless man write his name in the book.

"C'est formidable," they exclaimed.

"Mais, oui. C'est merveilleux."

And then the questions came, eager, interested questions, and many compliments on his having overcome his infirmity.

"Doesn't it ever bother you," Warren had asked, "to have people always asking you about your hands?"

"Oh, the French are a very curious people," Pierre had laughed. "They are also honest seekers after truth. Now the English are painfully silent about my missing hands. They refuse to mention or to notice that they are not there. The Americans, like yourself, take the fact for granted, try to be helpful, but don't ask questions. I'm used to all three, but I think the French have the healthiest attitude."

That was the day that Pierre had told Warren about the Abbey of Solesmes. "You are looking tired and there you can rest. It will be good for you. I think, too," he said, his dark eyes mischievous, "that you will find there some clue to the secret of the cathedrals about which you have spoken."

Within two weeks Warren was ringing the bell at the abbey gate. The monk who opened the door immediately calmed his worries about his reception: "I speak English," the old man said, "but I do not hear it very well." He smiled and stuck a large finger with white hairs sprouting on it into his ear as though that might help. Smiling at Warren's protestations, the old monk took his grip from him and led him down a corridor to a small parlor. "Will you please wait in here. I will get le Père Hôtelier." He disappeared in silence, leaving Warren in a parlor full of overstuffed furniture surrounding an oaken table.

Warren walked to the window and gazed out; it was November and the growing things were just beginning to realize it: ivy leaves clinging to the stone wall were only now turning rusty. It was embarrassing not to know whether a man was "père" or "frère." Some were priests and some were brothers, he knew, but which ones? He heard a slight movement and turned to meet a second robed and smiling figure. The handclasp of the man was light. "If you will follow me, monsieur." Le Père Hôtelier took his bag and held the door open for him.

They crossed a courtyard and the tonsured man escorted him into the chapel. Warren tried to imitate the monk, clumsily crossed himself with holy water, and knelt in the last pew. He did not pray; he did not know how. When the monk rose a few minutes later, Warren followed him from the chapel. Passing a cemetery, they returned the bow of an aged, white-haired monk who moved slowly past them, followed by an equally slow-moving cat. "Father has been looking at his grave again," le Père Hôtelier said softly. "He meditates there."

The bell of the abbey chapel sounded the hour and down the valley other bells sang out. As they walked through a garden, a young man paused in his trimming of a tree and bowed down at them from his ladder.

The two men entered a cottage at the end of the garden. "You will find our schedule here," the monk said, nodding toward a card tacked to the back of the door. "You are not required, of course, to attend any of the services, but you may if you wish." His hands disappeared into the wide sleeves of his robe. "At suppertime I will come and get you that I might show you where you will sit. Also where you will have breakfast, for we have breakfast very early and you will have yours separately." He smiled and then gave the room a last thorough glance. "If you have need of anything," he said, opening the door, "simply have one of the monks fetch me. I hope you enjoy a most profitable stay."——

Warren turned abruptly, hearing a sound behind him. Sergeant Prevot motioned him up and indicated that they were going to start back. Warren was surprised that time had passed so rapidly, for he had expected the hours to crawl. He followed the gesturing Sergeant Prevot and, half-crouched in the pale glow of the night, took the box of machine gun ammo that was held out to him. White stealthily approached. Prevot gave him the other box. The crew was taking apart the machine gun, others crept in from their positions. All accounted for, Prevot took the point position and the men began their return over the route they had followed out. Crossing the field, they moved quietly down the embankment beside the stream. As they picked their way down the stream, Warren saw White's hand shoot up in the signal to halt. He raised his own hand for the man behind him and the entire patrol crouched in the darkness, listening. The stream washed gaily over the rocks, its flippancy as out of place as giggling at a funeral. Warren's alert being was angered by the stream which frustrated his attempts to hear whatever had caused Prevot to stop. Warren could hear only the snickering of the water. Down the line came the signal to proceed and the men moved ahead with greater caution.

——Walking one afternoon in the garden with Le Père Hôtelier, listening to the old priest tell of his admiration for Shakespeare, the bells up and down the valley began to ring out with joy. The town bells had been the first to commence and their great melodious notes were answered by all the other bells in the area. When the usually sober monastery bell joined in the festive ringing, he had turned to the priest beside him and asked the reason.

"In the convent in the town, a nun has died," the priest said. "She had lived nearly all of her eighty-four years in the convent. She knew that she was dying and so she asked that upon her death the Te Deum be sung and that the children in the village be given candy. She was a great friend of the children and they loved her dearly. Also, she requested that the bells be rung in celebration as this was the day for which she had, all of her life, been waiting."——

The shout came from the rear. Warren wheeled even as White ran back to him; they dropped side by side as shooting began. "Up the embankment," White commanded and the two men lunged to the top of the hill and dropped flat. Rapid bursts of the BAR hacked the night air. Warren saw Sergeant Prevot with the machine gun crew at the stream and called to them. Prevot and the men with him clambered up the embankment. "They've pinned down our tail man, I think," White said, "but the other men must be holding them off."

The bru-up, bru-up of the enemy's weapons came in between the louder, more definite cracks of the M-1's. "Set up the machine gun here and cover the field," White ordered; then, remembering Sergeant Prevot's presence, he added, "I would recommend it, Sergeant. Warren and I can proceed across the stream and come up on their other flank."

"I'll go with you," Prevot said. Leaving the machine gun crew, the three men scrambled back down the slope. There was no need for silence now. They splashed through the stream and climbed the opposite bank. Crouched low, they ran a short distance and dropped to their stomachs to crawl around the area from which the firing was coming. Once on the other side of the firing, they hunched and ran again; then, turning to complete their half-circle, they crept down the slope and waded the stream once more. There they held a hurried consultation. Warren was to cover this end of the stream bed, while White and Prevot went up the bank to come in from the top. The two men rushed up the slope, breathing heavily, while Warren squatted in the darkness, waiting. The firing was accompanied by loud shouts; the machine gun rattled authoritatively. The enemy had attempted to cross the field.

In the brush down the stream a grenade crunched. Another followed. Then he heard grenades going off in the direction of the embankment and the machine gun rattled again. His breath was coming rapidly. Alerted by a new sound, he saw a figure splashing up the stream toward him. Impulsively, he leaped from his crouched position and the figure halted. They were not six feet apart. Warren froze for the split second that the burp gun was aimed at him; the gun fired one round and jammed. The man's finger clutched frantically at the trigger. Warren saw the look of anger turn to surprise as the slugs from his own rifle chopped into it. Then there was silence. Warren sat on the creek bank looking at the dead man who lay in the stream and his body shuddered as if chilled. Only the mocking voice of the stream as it chuckled past the fallen man's body scratched the silence. Warren turned his head and vomited.

"Hey, Warren! You all right?" Sergeant Prevot called as he slid down the embankment. "We cleaned 'em out," he said. "Let's get the hell outta here. I've called for covering fire." He spotted the body in the stream. "Search him; then come upstream. We've gotta get outta here."

Sergeant Prevot rushed upstream leaving Warren alone again with the corpse. He sat and looked at the body, remembering the face now hidden in the water. Trying not to think of what he was doing, he got up and dragged the leaden body out of the stream. He searched the soggy pockets of the man's pants and then his upper garment. The job was made difficult by the wet clothing. He patted the sides of the shirt and then looked for dog-tags. Finding nothing, he fled upstream to join the others.

White and the ROK soldier were carrying Martinez. The BAR man hung limply, one arm around the neck of each man. Warren could not tell whether the Mexican was dead. Someone else was being tended by two other squad members. The wounded man was sitting up, saying over and over again, "Oh, God, Oh, Mom, Oh, God, Mom, Oh, Mom, Oh, God."

"Get goin'," Prevot yelled and the two men helped the

moaning one to his feet and moved out. "Warren," Prevot shouted, "grab the BAR." Then, with earth-crushing strength, the artillery began to land behind them.

It was only when they reached their own lines once more and dawn was breaking that Warren realized that his hands and arms were covered with the dry scales of caked blood.

Later, Warren stared at the beams that supported the weighty sandbag roof above his head. He felt dirty. Although he had washed himself, using his steel helmet as a basin, he felt the blood still clinging to his skin. It was as if, invisible, the dry irritation of the brown flakes was yet upon him. Neither had he been able to wash the stain out of the sleeves of his fatigues. Although he had never been more restless, he lay motionless.

When he had asked to come here, he had not considered the killing. The vision on the train had so overwhelmed him that he had not thought that he, who would risk being killed, must first be prepared to kill. Now side by side with that image of himself in the rain, there was the face that had stared at him in surprise as it was shattered by his bullets. One vision negated the other, and he was uncertain of what he should do . . .

"All right," Sergeant Prevot poked his head in at the bunker door, "I'm going to the shower point. Come along if you want." His Adam's apple ran up and down his scrawny neck like a signal flag. "Only comes once a week," he smiled, entering the bunker. "Go tomorrow if you want, but I thought maybe you'd like to go today," he said, glancing at Warren.

White put his weapon together with swift dexterity and Warren rolled himself out of his bunk. Within a few minutes the three men were in Zikowlsky's jeep as it whined its way along the serpentine route to the rear. The heat was smothering in its dampness. "Gonna hit the

90

rainy season, soon," Prevot said. "Any day now and this road'll be mud up to your ears."

The rainy season . . . It was in the rain that he had been crawling, in the rain . . . It was raining, too, when he last left Jean.

——He had not told her of the vision, although meeting her had caused him to question it. While on the first three-day pass Lieutenant Ordway had shoved at him, he had found her at the circulation desk in the public library. At his approach she had lifted her wide, soft eyes from the book in front of her and he had gaped.

"Hello, may I help you?"

He did not answer. She raised one thin hand to her smooth cheek where the flesh was brightening under his gaze.

"Would you like to take out a book?"

Her question awakened him. "Yes," he said, "these." He placed the books on the desk, no longer interested in them.

"Do you always stare like that?"

"You've the loveliest voice. Say something else."

"You work fast," she said, taking the books.

"Oh, believe me. I'm quite sincere."

"Your card," she asked without looking up at him.

"Oh, forget the card," he said impulsively. She looked up at him. "Forget the books," he went on, his eyes looking into hers. "I won't have time to read them anyway. Not if you'll come to dinner with me this evening."

Neither of them spoke nor moved. The silence was filled with the urgency that his voice had given his request. There was no struggle in their mutual gaze, no laughter either, but something akin to that wonder bred of contemplation. Slowly, almost tentatively, he put his hands on hers where they rested on the books and she, just as slowly, withdrew hers.

"I don't even know your name," she said, almost in a whisper, and he knew that a barrier had fallen.

"And I don't know yours."

They continued to look at one another as if neither had spoken. He gazed at her in much the same way he had gazed upon countless quartrocento madonnas, touched by a sort of reverence before her guileless eyes.

"Thomas Warren," he said at last.

Her eyelids lowered slowly and her head dropped in a slight, graceful movement, like the Virgin in Donatello's "Annunciation," at once modestly demurring and accepting the message.

"Jean . . ." she said quietly, "Jean O'Brien."

Later, when they had gone out together often, he had told her about the Italian madonnas and of how she had despoiled them of their heritage, making them all Irish in his mind. And they had laughed together. But his imagination, his memory or his intuition had not played him false in one regard: she was a Catholic. The rock of the Church was thrust between them.——

"I don't know why I have to take a bath, Sarge," Zikowlsky said. "There ain't no women around here."

"At home I'll bet your mother used a baseball bat on you," Prevot said.

"You bet your life. Or threw apples. I remember the day I hid from my little old mom and her baseball bat in an apple tree. There was Mom at the bottom of the tree waving her bat and shouting at me to remember the fourth commandment. I wasn't coming down, not on your life. Then she began to throw apples at me. A whole lug box of apples she threw before she got tired and went back to the house. Boy, they stung," he said in a voice full of admiration. "She's got quite an arm, my mom has."

——At eight o'clock he called at her home where she introduced him to her father, a bushy-eyebrowed man with a knobby briar root of a face. "Ye wouldn't be want-

92

ing a little bit of whiskey?" the gray ridge of hair raised above the brown eyes.

"Oh, now, John," Mrs. O'Brien protested. "Don't detain the young ones." Her face beamed pleasure. " 'Tis late enough as it is and they probably starvin' to death."

"No," the eyebrows dropped, the gnarled briar of a face dropped also, "I suppose ye wouldn't."

Warren had asked about the photos on the mantelpiece just before leaving, and Jean lifted each of the three portraits and held it for a moment as she named a sister.——

"Apples," Prevot sighed, "I could go for a nice, juicy apple right now. An apple just out of the refrigerator, cold as ice."

"Aw, cut it out," Zikowlsky pleaded.

——He had taken her to an Italian restaurant where he had often gone alone. It was an autobiographical evening; he wanted to know everything about her. Her parents had come to America just after the birth of their second child. Her father was a retired policeman. She, their youngest, had been educated by the nuns until the ninth grade and then had gone to public schools, there being no nearby Catholic high school. Bridesmaid at all her sisters' weddings, she loved to sit with their children. She had thought for a time that she had a vocation to be a nun; she did not think so now. Swimming she liked—tennis, music, and reading, too. She was working in the library for the summer vacation. An English major, perhaps she would become a teacher. "You see," she said, "the Autobiography of Anybody."

He delighted in her slightest movement. When her arms reached for her purse, he thought he had never seen so graceful a gesture.——

"Tasmania. Ever been to Tasmania?" Prevot turned his head, his Adam's apple trying to break through his turkey's throat.

"No," White answered.

93

"There they have apples," Prevot said reverently. "Tasmanian apples are the biggest, firmest, juiciest apples . . ." His voice faded into respectful silence. "I was there once in the merchant marine," he added.

——They decided to walk home. It would be a long walk, but she had accepted his suggestion with immediate enthusiasm. Before they arrived at her home, he found himself telling her all sorts of reasons why he could not get married, protesting that he must not fall in love, why he could not . . .

"You sound as if I had proposed," she laughed at him and he felt foolish.

As they stood before her door, he cupped her small chin in his hand and tilted her face up towards his. "It's very pure this evening," he said and kissed her lightly on her smooth forehead.——

"Thought there'd be a line," Prevot said as they pulled into the shower point: a group of squad tents arranged in a connecting series alongside of a stream. The sound of the pump motor could be heard from the rear of the tents. The parking area was crowded with dusty trucks and jeeps. A few men sat in the trucks, smoking cigarettes, waiting for their companions.

"Just hit it right," Zikowlsky said as he backed the jeep into a space between two other vehicles. "Hope they've got some clothes my size this time. For the last week my crotch has just been squeezed to death."

——The most innocent parts of his being seemed to respond to her presence. He had experienced something similar in the abbey when, walking along the dark cloister to the dining hall, monks had dropped to their knees as he passed, reverencing Christ in him, their visitor. Only then, he had been humbled by the experience, while with her he was exalted.——

Just inside the door, Warren found himself in the midst of a crowd of pushing, naked men, shouting their clothing sizes to three slow-moving and apparently deaf attendants behind the counter.

"What d'ya mean, ya ain't got no size eleven socks? Dammit, ya ain't never got no size eleven socks," a flabby, pale-fleshed man was yelling. "When in hell does a guy have to get here to get a goddam size eleven pair of socks anyway?"

"Come on," somebody moaned, "I've gotta get outta here today."

"This bastard place ain't no damned good," a voice said in Warren's ear as he edged his way between the press of the damp skinned bodies and into the dressing area.

Finding a place on a bench near one wall, Warren began to undress, hanging his rifle and web belt on a nail above his seat. He stuffed his wallet and pen into his combat boots and shoved them under the seat amidst a litter of foot powder cans.

——There were many such moments of happiness, evening after evening they were together and in the days when they were apart, he found himself elated by every thought of her, eager for each new meeting with her. They continued to spend their evenings very simply: walking together, dining together, holding hands and laughing. It was as though she had liberated him from all darkness, from the memory of his mother's sufferings, from the burden of his vision and the melancholy days he had spent before meeting her. The alchemy of her presence mixed with questions brought him out of himself and she had him recalling and laughing about things in his past which his loneliness had always made less than happy. As if by unspoken arrangement, they did not talk about his departure and not since that first evening had they hinted at the possibility of their marriage. Yet somehow he knew that if ever he were to marry, it must be to her. Their evenings always ended like that first one, with a single, gentle kiss on her forehead. He sensed that the moment he went

95

beyond that something would be lost, their childlike joy, perhaps, and that what would be gained would be a whole new commitment, a commitment that frightened him. There seemed at that time two futures before him, the one illuminated on the train ride and still so vividly present to his memory and the other present to him whenever he thought of Jean. He wanted to choose Jean's, but he was already committed to the other. The date of his departure was drawing close, and one evening he sought to change the course of events.——

"Let me read you this," a harsh voice nearby was saying. "I wrote her and ast her if she was still a virgin an' she wrote me this. You gotta hear it." The voice assumed a falsetto tone. " 'Hello, Hon, I got a letter from someone I like very much. That means you, of course. It was mailed on the . . .' "

——Returning from an evening out, they entered the house and, without turning on the lights, sat down on the sofa, still talking.——

" '. . . tenth and arrived on the eighteenth, which isn't bad, is it? No, Hon, I won't get mad at you for asking that question. It's only natural for a boy and a girl who like one another to ask things like that. Yes, girls discuss sex and boys just like men discuss sex and girls, but in a different way, I think. It's only natural for girls to think about things like that just like boys do . . .' "

——As she was speaking, he leaned forward and kissed her on the lips for the first time. She pulled herself away and stood up, turning her back on him.——

"Now we're coming to the good part," the voice dropped to its normal tone for a moment. "Get this!" Then, resuming the falsetto tone, it went on: " 'I could of lied to you, Hon, and said I was still a virgin, but I won't do that because I like you very much. Hon, it's only . . .' "

——"Jean . . ." He touched her shoulder, placing an

96

arm around her. "I love you." Her arms flew to his neck and bent his head to her lips.———

" '. . . natural for a girl to let herself go when she gets all worked up and have an intercourse.' "

———Then, quickly, her head dropped to his breast. He stroked her hair. Pulling herself away from him, Jean walked over to the fireplace. "What are we going to do?" In the darkness she was but a small child's shadow.———

" 'She's just like a boy in that she can't help it.' "

———"What do you mean?" he started to go to her.

"Don't come near me," she said. "I'm not myself when you're near. Not any more."

He stopped where he was.———

" 'I don't know any of my friends who hasn't had an intercourse.' "

———Her voice was shaky, "I'm in love with you. You know that?"———

" 'You show me a girl of eighteen who hasn't had an intercourse and I'd like to meet her.' "

———"But do you know what it means? Oh, why did you meet me?"———

" 'I'd like to know what's wrong with her, because it's only natural to do it when you get all bothered . . .' "

———"Why did you? I love you and . . . and . . . I'm afraid."

"Afraid?" He put his arm around her and turned her to him, his right hand gently lifted her face toward his. "Afraid of what?"

She moved away from him, returned to the sofa. He followed, taking her once again in his arms.

"Please don't," she said firmly, turning away from him. Reluctantly, he dropped his arms.

"You see," she said, her voice husky in the dark, "one of my sisters married a non-Catholic. That may not seem much to you, but it nearly broke my parents' hearts." She paused, still looking away from him, into a dark corner of the room. "My sister and her husband were married in the Church, but when my sister got pregnant, her husband divorced her. He didn't want children, it seemed."

"What's this got to do with us?" Warren asked.

"I don't want to end up like her! I don't want to be raising a child without a father. I don't want to spend my days in the sort of misery she endures . . ."

"But this is different."

"Don't say that!" She turned on him, her eyes on his. "That's what she told us." Jean began to weep. "Oh, I know how she felt—I feel it now too."——

" 'So you see, Hon, I've been honest with you. Now please write and tell me all about yourself. Are you a virgin? I'll bet not. Ha, ha! Well, so long for now, Write soon, Gail.' "

——"Do you want to stop seeing me?" he asked hesitantly.——

"And ya know," the voice drawled, "I didn't expect an answer. Didn't give a damn either way."

——"Yes," she sobbed. "And no! Oh, I love you, I love you and you can hurt me. You're hurting me now . . ."

"Look, sweet." He dropped to the sofa beside her and took her warm, shuddering body into his arms again. "Soon we'll no longer see one another anyway." He began to stroke back her hair. "In another week I'm being transferred. Please, let's forget tonight and carry on as if this never happened."

She dropped her head onto his shoulder, her hair brushing against his face. "But it did," she said, "and it won't be the same."

They did carry on as before and she was right; it wasn't quite the same; their silences bore the burden of that night.——

Warren entered the shower tent. Spotting a free nozzle near the far end of the tent, he picked his way along the soap-slimed floor toward it. On either side of him men, their naked bodies twisting under the water, shouted at one another in order to be heard above the general din.

"Are ya gonna marry her?"

"Hell, no!"

"Why not?"

"If she let me have it, how many others got it, eh?"

"So I says to this bitch . . ."

"It was a forty-eight Merc, a real beaut . . ."

"That was the most chickenshit outfit . . ."

"Oh, this one," White was saying, looking at a small scar on the calf of his leg. "That was from an officer's Luger. He got me there just after I shot him."

White was standing between Zikowlsky and Prevot. Warren's shower spigot was opposite White.

"You've had some close ones," Prevot said, soaping himself under the arms.

"What was your closest?" Zikowlsky asked as he allowed the water to run over his broad shoulders.

" 'C'mon, babee, take one,' she whines to me." *A giant Negro on Warren's left mimicked the voice for the benefit of someone on his own left.*

"See this," White pointed one thick finger at a scar the size of a fifty-cent piece near the base of his throat.

" 'Hell, no, bitch,' I says." *The Negro growled.*

Zikowlsky looked over at the scar. "Uh, huh," he grunted, getting busy with soap.

" 'Other GI takee it. Come on, babee. Take one . . .' "

"And these," White pointed a finger to his wrist as he turned his palm toward Zikowlsky. "One on each wrist."

" 'Hell, no, bitch, I ain't playing that horse . . .' "

"And one here and here," White indicated the scar tissue on the inside of each thigh.

" 'Bitch, that horse'll throw you . . .' "

"Yeah," Zikowlsky was now paying full attention, gawking at the wounds.

"That bitch took five shots that night. She was an old

hand at it. Had five hypos and about five hundred bucks worth of the stuff. It's cheap over here, you know . . ."

"What happened?" Prevot asked.

"She'd take that little tube of white stuff and break the top off and put some in the needle and then a little water, and then, man, she'd find that vein in her arm . . ."

"I was with a small recon outfit. We went behind the enemy lines and established radio contact with our unit. We set up in a little farmhouse with German units all around . . ."

"You know, man, she'd draw blood into that needle to mix with the junk and then put it back and shoot her-self full of it . . ."

"We had tied up the farmer and his wife, they were harmless . . ."

"Man, that bitch was really gone on it . . . Why, man . . ."

"One day the Germans came to call. They had been having milk delivered by the farmer's wife and . . ."

"I woke at three in the morning and she was making paper flowers out of scivvie paper . . ."

"After three days without milk, they decided to see what was the matter."

"Paper flowers all over the place."

"I was at the radio when they kicked in the front door and sprayed us with submachine gun fire."

"I said, 'Bitch, c'mon on back to bed,' but she didn't even hear me."

"Left only two of us alive. Even the farmer and his wife were killed."

"So I got outta bed and slapped the crap outta her."

"Then these men, not regular German soldiers, mind you, but a special corps . . ."

"Man, it's the only way to treat 'em."

"Special even for the SS . . ."

"They ain't got no feelings, man."

100

"Decided to do something very special with us . . ."

"They ain't human, man." The giant black man left his shower and strolled, sure of foot, along the slimy planks.

"So they got spikes," White said, "and nailed us to the floor."

"It should of killed you." Zikowlsky was wide-eyed.

"That was not the point of it." White smiled cynically. "The point was to make us suffer. Dying was incidental."

"How'd you get out?"

"I was able to pull my hand free. It took me three hours to do it, but I worked the spike out of my right hand and then was able to use it to loosen the others and get up. My friend was dead. They hit his jugular vein, or an artery, I think."

Warren could feel the pulsing of his temples. Hurriedly, he ended his shower and was in the jeep when the others came out.

"Hey, you got through in a hurry." Prevot approached the jeep.

"Yeah," Zikowlsky added, "you must not a been very dirty."

"Sweet smelling as a lily," Warren replied.

"What'd you think of White's story?" Prevot asked, settling himself in the front seat once again.

"Interesting."

"Interesting!" Zikowlsky cried out. "Will you get that. It's more than interesting. For my money it's amazing. Why the guy could've been killed."

"Yet," Warren responded, "that wasn't the point. The point was that he should suffer."

"I'll bet he did," Prevot commented.

"More than most people," Warren added.

"God!" Zikowlsky exclaimed. "Scars all over him."

White came out of the doorway of the shower tent and strode over to the vehicle, his face wreathed in smiles.

"Feels good to get cleaned up." He threw one short leg over the side of the jeep and pulled himself in.

"And I got a pair of pants that don't pinch the family jewels," Zikowlsky said. "Must be my lucky day." He started the jeep, backed out of the space they were in and wheeled out to the road once more.

"Now we get dirty all over again," Prevot sighed.

Lieutenant Fregni, his dark skin oily with sweat, came out of the company C.P. as Zikowlsky braked the jeep. "Got a new replacement," he announced to Prevot. "He's up at their bunker." He nodded at Warren and White. "Take the place of the psycho."

Tom Rickley, the new replacement, had clear blue eyes; a grin accompanied his strong grip. After introductions were over, White took him forward to explain the situation. Upon returning to the bunker, Rickley offered to take the first shift of duty, which meant going out immediately. "Get the lay of the land," he said, "while it's still daylight."

"An intelligent fellow," White said after Rickley had gone out to the position.

"Yeah," Warren agreed, "I can think of worse people to share a bunker with."

"Duke, for instance?" White laughed. "That hero did not last ten minutes."

Warren said nothing.

"You do not approve of my treatment of the Duke," White said stiffly, "but it was correct. He was going to crack up, anyway. I knew it on the truck. I preferred that he do it here, rather than out there." He waved his hand in the direction of the enemy and walked from the bunker.

Warren got accustomed to life along the line with an ease he earlier would have thought impossible. The enemy seemed lethargic, but while no major action took place, the days were never free of at least one mortar barrage—

102

complacency was not allowed. One day, sitting on the slope of the hill beside the field kitchen, Warren heard the characteristic hiccough of the tubes as they spat up the shells being dropped into their open mouths. The men about him scurried, dropping their trays or huddling over their food as if to protect it from the explosion to come. Like many around him, Warren instinctively hugged the ground and waited. Tense moments he measured by the beat of the blood in his temples. From where he lay, he could see a group of men walking up the road; apparently they hadn't heard the warning sound. Watching them stroll up the road, he felt the inevitability of what was about to happen; even as his throat tightened, one explosion followed another up the path of the road, a monster bellowing up the hill. Warren thrust himself to his feet and ran. The medic fell in beside him, shouting for stretchers. Together they reached the fallen men.

All were badly gashed up, none killed. The most seriously wounded man, his side full of shrapnel, his left arm hanging limp, his leg a stump, sat quietly, his eyes wide as though witnessing some wondrous ritual while the medic tore away his clothing.

The others were dragged off the road, into the commo trench and a nearby bunker. It was there that Warren recognized Rutledge among the wounded. Outside the medic shouted for someone to alert the helicopter.

"Helluva note, this is," Rutledge said, throwing a freshly lighted cigarette away.

"Where you hurt?" Warren felt Rutledge's legs.

"Some goddam war. Some crazy goddam war," Rutledge said, shaking his head. "Police action, hell! I ain't got no billy club."

"Are you hurt badly?" Warren began to unzip the armored vest from which jagged chunks of shrapnel jutted out.

103

"How should I know? Some crazy damned war. I need a cigarette."

The medic hurried in. "Start walking those guys," he waved to the outside, "down the hill. The jeep's at the C.P. . . . or damned well better be." Swiftly he unbuttoned Rutledge's shirt.

"Can't take any more losses," Sergeant Prevot said to Warren when the wounded had been evacuated. "Just can't. If we do—well, we may as well quit."

At night, standing in the forward position, Warren could hear the rattle of a machine gun far off down the line: *rat—rat—rat-a-tat-tat,* somebody would sound off with a drummer's beat. The next gunner would pick it up, the sound coming closer, finally passing and going on toward the other coast, the friendly communication of men to one another unknown. Sometimes, an inventive gunner would provide a variation on the theme: *tut—tut-a-tut-tut—tut-tut.* Tracers would arch through the night sky, winging like great fireflies to plummet into enemy land. Each tracer meant five rounds wasping to the target, for between each tracer were four regular slugs. Such random firing, Warren knew, served to harass and impede the enemy's night movements.

Sometimes a voice would call out in the night, some Texan bellowing out over the dark valley: "H . . . e . . . y . . . J . . . o . . . e . . . you . . . no . . . . . ho . . . ck . . . ing . . . good . . ." The words would echo and reverberate like those shouted in a cavern.

The regular patrols had been quiet, with one exception. That action had taken place so rapidly and in such dark confusion that Warren retained no clear picture of it. Two furtive shadows had slipped into his vision, moving quietly forward without a sound. They squatted, remaining still for so long that Warren began to doubt that he had ever seen them move. His doubts fled when one edged upwards and scurried back into the dark area out of which both had come. Within moments the night seemed alive with the dread shapes moving about and Warren, tensed to the snapping point, was gripped in the sweaty fear that no one else had seen them. The wild notion seized him that he was alone, somehow had been deserted in the vast night to face this ordeal in naked singleness. He dared not move and the panic rising in him was snuffed out only when it had reached the pitch of an unuttered scream. Then the sound of Prevot's carbine off to his left came as a relief. Burp guns sounded sickly as they returned the solid cuts of the M-1's. The air was punctuated by a hundred sounds, the dark flared up in scattered spots of hot color, shadows darted, men shouted, grenades trembled the earth. Warren fired rapidly, sighting at the nearest points of flame, rolling a few feet to a new position and finding another burning target. Grenades began exploding behind him, earth pelted his neck and hands, something cut his cheek, adding to the moist stickiness already there. Then came Prevot's call—and the thunderous crush of artillery which, when he had first crouched to run, pushed him back to the earth.

It was only later, when Warren heard Prevot's report, that he understood all that had happened. The enemy had entered their field of fire and had been pinned down. But the enemy patrol had either forked in two at some point further up the valley; or there were two patrols following parallel routes, one on either side of their own position. In any case, as the first group was pinned down and fire was being called in, the second group hit from the rear and forced withdrawal. Aside from Warren's facial cut there were no wounded, but Lim, the ROK, had been killed by a grenade which had torn away his head. As Prevot said, they were lucky to get out. But then, Warren thought later, his test would come on a rainy night.

Duty on the line became routine. Now Warren, White

and Rickley took two-hour shifts in the forward position, with four hours off.

Rickley's constant good humor, which in other circumstances might have been contagious, was disconcerting to Warren. Above his bunk Rickley had built a shelf on which he had placed his girl's picture—enclosing the photo in an acetate envelope to keep it free of dust. He seemed forever working on a letter.

"To the girl friend?" Warren asked one day.

"Not this one." Rickley shook his blond head. "This is to the folks; them I write every other day. On alternate days I write Mary. The one to the folks has to satisfy the whole family." He grinned. "Otherwise, I'd never be through. Here's my family . . ." From his leather writing-kit he pulled a snapshot and handed it over. "Eleven. Count 'em," he said. Warren saw a crowd of laughing faces. "The little ones are all my nieces and nephews. There's been another one since that picture was taken and three more are on their way. The folks, you see them there in the center, have twenty-two grandchildren as of now."

"Quite a clan," Warren said.

"Still growing, too. Gotta start making my own contribution to the family one of these days."

"Aren't you a little young to be thinking of that?"

"Nineteen," Rickley said. "Old enough to be here."

"Aha," Warren said, "then you do know this isn't just any place?"

"What do you mean by that?"

"Well, you've been acting like you don't know you can die here."

"You can die anywhere," Rickley said. Taking the photo Warren was holding out to him, he replaced it in the leather case. "It's up to God just when or where you die."

"God will keep you from getting killed?"

"From getting killed?" Rickley looked at Warren and shook his head. "No. My job is not to worry about things like that . . ."

"I don't know whether I should envy you or feel sorry for you," Warren said, getting up. Putting on his steel helmet, he zipped up his armored vest and slung his M-1 over his shoulder. "But I think I envy you," he said quickly as he left for his turn at the forward position.

A few days later, Warren was alone in the bunker when White, having been relieved by Rickley, entered.

"Damn it," White said, throwing his helmet onto his bunk. He stalked back and forth across the small floor, his M-1 still over his shoulder, his fist white in its clasp on the strap. "Damn it. I thought he had more brains than that."

"What's up?"

"What's up?" White stopped his pacing and stared angrily at Warren. "I will tell you what's up. He is a fool!"

"Who?"

"Our friend Rickley." The name was twisted into a sneer.

"What's wrong with him?"

White hurled the words, "He is a Catholic!"

"I gathered that."

"A Catholic!" White announced, pacing again.

"You liked him before—"

"I can have no respect for anyone who accepts such absurdities." He stopped again and turned on Warren. "You have no need to tell him that. He is a good worker and there is no need to upset him." Then, he hung up his weapon and threw himself on his bunk.

"How'd you find out?"

"Why, before I left the position he had taken out a rosary. I asked him what that was for. He said he prayed while he watched. He has no shame! Do you know what

107

he prays for? He prays for peace. Ha!" White turned his face to the wall. "For peace."

As for White's suggestion to the colonel, nothing had come from the colonel's direction for three weeks. Warren hadn't decided whether he would go with White. The prospect repelled and attracted him, appealing as if something very fundamental to his being stood out there to be touched if he could only go forth. He let the matter rest at the bottom of his mind, always a possibility, one of those choices one may make or not make, but for the present suspended.

Then, on his next inspection tour, the colonel stopped. "As you were," he said. "White, you made a request about a month ago?"

"Yes, sir."

"I'm afraid I can't grant it just now," the colonel smiled. "Fox company got a prisoner. They got him in a rather unmilitary manner, but they got him, so there's no need for you to go out. I want to thank you for volunteering, though." He extended one browned hand and White took it. "Glad or sorry?" the colonel asked, his eyes twinkling.

"Sorry, sir."

"Well, maybe something will come up," the colonel said.

When the lanky frame had disappeared down the line, White exploded: "Damn! Damn! Damn!" He spat the word like command. "I will rot here!" Turning, he entered the bunker. "Sentry duty, that is all it is!" Warren followed him in. Striding up and down, White continued, "Stand guard in the trench, stand guard in the valley, stand guard, that is all we do!" His whole frame shook with wild energy. "This is not action!"

From that day, Warren watched White grow more and more restless. Unable to stay in one position, he would

108

lie on his bunk smoking cigarettes with a furious intensity, then jump up and stalk outside to pace the road. When Warren went out to the forward position, he would find him poised there as if about to bound over the embankment and throw himself at the enemy.

Prevot told them of the "rather unmilitary manner" in which Fox company had taken its prisoner. The fellow had walked up and into their lines one night. "I tell ya, Fox company's got as few men as we have," Prevot said, "so you can see what happens when you've only got nine men on a platoon front." The enemy soldier had, it came out, rapped on two or three bunker doors; the occupants shouted for him to come in, but, not understanding what was being said, he had patiently moved on to the next bunker. Finally, some energetic soul got up, opened his door and found the man, a nervous smile on his face, standing with his arms high above his head.

When White heard this story of the capture, he was furious. "What were they doing?" he shouted. "They should court-martial those fools!"

"And who would fight the war?" Prevot asked.

"War! You call this a war?" White snorted in return. "These people are playing games. They do not know what war is!"

More replacements came into the company; they could be spotted for the first few days by the anxious look on their young faces, the meekness induced by fronting the unknown. Warren knew that he himself must once have looked like that, but it was not long before each was one with his fellows manning the line. One afternoon Prevot came in to say that the ammunition bunker next door would house another man who would share their duty. He was a ROK soldier and White was to instruct him in the use of the machine gun. Behind Prevot stood the Korean soldier—who, Warren thought, looked like Lim.

"Lim," Prevot said, "this is Warren."

"Pleased to meet you," said Lim in faltering English. "My English is not good, but I will please to try."

Warren asked about the name.

Lim smiled broadly. "Oh, yes. Lim common name. Like Joe in America. Many Korean named Lim."

Warren learned that Lim's home had been in North Korea, in a town now destroyed. His parents were probably dead, he was not sure; his little brother was killed by an artillery shell, American.

"He gets three thousand hwan a month," Prevot told Warren later. "That's about fifty cents. A PFC gets thirty-four hundred and a corporal, which is what he'll be if he lives through his stay with us, gets four thousand. Ya know what a houseboy in reserve gets?"

Warren didn't.

"A minimum of forty-five thousand a month. Hell, a broad in Chunchon or Pusan gets four thousand or so for a half hour's stint."

The additional man on their post meant that Warren, White, and Rickley were left together in the bunker whenever it was Lim's turn to go forward.

One evening Rickley came in, hung up his weapon, and took off his armored vest before sitting down on the edge of his bunk. He took out his leather writing-case and opened it up. Suddenly, he turned to Warren and asked, "Are you in love?"

"I think so," Warren replied.

"Don't you know?"

"Well, then, yes."

"Love!" White stood up in anger. "It does not exist. You are too intelligent for such rot," he said to Warren, "or I thought you were."

"If you experience it," Rickley said, "you know it exists."

"Love! A word!" White said derisively. "No more than

110

a word men use to cloak their lusts. I refuse to hide behind a word. I do not believe in love and I say so."

Rickley asked, "Why?"

Ignoring the question, White turned to Warren. "This is an irrational world, Warren. There is no meaning in it. Life is full of stupid tortures. The delusion of love is only a more subtle torture. I found myself by admitting that," he said softly. "You will find yourself when you recognize it."

"The world," Rickley said, "is only irrational if you don't believe in God."

"God!" White swung to face Rickley in disgust. "What has belief in God done for the world? The Mayans offered human sacrifices to the gods; they killed young virgins, the purest of their race, to keep the sun up in the sky; they flayed the skins off of living sacrificial victims and danced in them to keep the gods happy. It is no different today. Gods have been changed, but virgins die here, and at Buchenwald they made lampshades of human skin."

White's face, red with anger, was contorted as he threw out the words, and when he fell silent again, it was as if he had been wrestling an adversary and finally thrown him. His whole frame, a moment ago wildly animated, was now drawn in upon itself, contained and waiting for the next onslaught.

"What's all the hullabaloo?" Prevot poked his head in the door.

"Having a little discussion," Warren answered.

"Well, can it for tonight and hit the sack. Gonna pull a big one off tomorrow night. You'll need the rest. Briefing's at ten hundred hours." With that, Prevot's head was withdrawn.

"At last." White dropped to his cot and began to unlace his combat boots. "At last."

111

Warren got up to go to the latrine and as he stepped outside the door, he felt the tentative drops of rain.

The next morning from the forward position, Warren was scanning Sniper's Ridge, to the left of Papa-san. For the last few days it had been worthy of its name. Someone was machine-gun sniping at them, pulling off four rounds at a time. Warren could see nothing on the brown surface of the hill and the mist still hung over the valley from the night's rain. The dusty earth had been transformed into an oozing mass; Warren could feel his socks, spongy with water, inside his cold, slime-covered boots.

Prevot came up. "The rain's late," he said, "but it'll be pretty constant from now on in."

An artillery round landed on the crest of Papa-san.

"Rain makes it sound funny, doesn't it?" Prevot asked.

Warren had noticed before that the usual slam of an exploding shell and its impact on landing was softened and diffused by the mud and mist.

"Briefing's at ten," Prevot reminded.

"Yeah," Warren said. "Same deal as the one they called off?"

"I think so," Prevot replied, lighting a cigarette and turning his brown eyes toward Sniper's Ridge. "He active?"

"Not so far this morning."

"The mist'll slow him down a little. Deadly little bastard, isn't he?"

Warren nodded his head in agreement. Two men had been wounded by the sniper in two days. One, a beefy Texan due to rotate, had lost his jaw.

"Do me a favor?" Prevot asked.

"Sure. What?"

"Well, we've gotta turn in our valuables and wallets

112

to the C.P. before going out and . . . well . . . I'm not certain I'm coming back . . ."

"Who is?"

"Yeah, but I'm worried about this one." A note of urgency underlined the words. "I'm due to go home next month and I always figured I wouldn't come out of this alive . . ."

"You stand a better chance than any of us."

"I'm beginning to feel my luck can't hold." Prevot's brown eyes contemplated Papa-san. "Anyway, I've got no home and I've something I'd like you to have if . . . well . . . in case this one doesn't come off right for me."

"No relatives?"

"Yeah, I guess so, but they don't know me from Adam. My folks were killed in a car wreck and my brother and me went to live with an aunt, but she's dead now."

"What about your brother?"

"Him? You never saw such a kid. Had everything I didn't. Why, girls calling him up all the time. Top man in his fraternity. Class president. I don't suppose anybody was so popular. Bright, too. I worshiped that kid. Then I came home one day—I was working in a plant then—my aunt was downtown shopping, and I found him on the front room floor. There was a .22—I gave it to him for Christmas—lying beside him." Prevot took a long drag on his cigarette, his damp fingers squeezing it tightly. "I couldn't believe he'd do a thing like that. I told the cops somebody must have murdered him . . . but the inquest said suicide. Some broad said he wanted a home. Damned cops." He looked at Warren. "Everything to live for, everything." He took a last drag on his cigarette. "Couldn't stick around there. Went and joined the merchant marine." The sodden cigarette, flicked into the mud, was nudged with his boot. "Anyway, I don't have a family," he said, "so I want you to keep something for me

113

and, if I get it, you can have the thing. If I rotate, I want it back. Okay?"

"Sure."

"I've got it here," Prevot's bony fingers nervously fumbled at the zipper of his armored vest.

"But," Warren added, "what if I told you that I don't think I'll come out of this one?"

Prevot's eyes focused on Warren's. "You feel it, too?"

A 155 went off behind them and both men looked toward Papa-san, waiting to watch the shell hit. It came down on the spine of the ridge, cracked and spilled over like an egg splatting on concrete. "White Phosphorus," Prevot said. "Poor devils." His hand came out of his vest; in it he held a small, thin parcel wrapped in brown paper and enclosed in a polyethylene bag. "You got a family?"

"No."

"Oh." The pause bulged with meaning. "I'd give it to Rickley," Prevot said quietly, "only I don't know him so well. He and you are the only guys who might appreciate it." Mud sucked Prevot's boots as he moved over, still gripping the parcel, and plopped down upon the seat. "Funny, isn't it?" A wry smile touched his lips. "I don't know you none too well, I suppose, but I feel I know you better than most of these guys. Well enough to want you to have this." He gestured with the package. "And so what happens? You turn out to have no family, just like me. You turn out to feel the same way I do." He shook his head, the corners of his mouth still turned up in an unhappy smile, his Adam's apple buried deep in his throat. "Now I don't know what to do with the thing." Meditatively, he stared at the package, tapping it slowly against his leg, and then looked up at Warren. "I told you once about a girl in Hong Kong?"

"The Russian princess?"

"Yeah. She gave it to me."

"Then you'd better keep it."

114

"But, don't you see, man? I can't."

"Send it back to her. Tell her you don't want to lose it here."

"I can't! She said when I understood this, then I could come back to her."

"What is it?"

"You'll see. Only if I send it back, she'll think I've given up."

"Makes it difficult."

"Impossible. I've never felt about anyone in my whole life, not my brother or anyone, like I feel about her." Prevot stood up, the mud grasped after his boots as he moved to the front of the position. "She's the most beautiful woman, a kind of electricity jolting you all the time making you realize . . . and sad . . . with a kind of deep love for everybody who was sad . . . maybe that's how we got together . . . Anyway, I love her—she said I didn't, not really. I only know that . . ." He broke off. "Well, anyway, she gave me this the last time I saw her and said we couldn't get married unless I understood its meaning." His brown face turned toward Warren. "And I don't. Not yet. I don't know what she meant or what this," he lifted the package, "means. Now I won't have time to figure it out, but I just can't mail it back—taking the chance it would get there—and have her think I've given up all thought of her. God," he moaned, "I think of nothing else."

"She know you're here?"

"I told her when I left I'd probably go into the army, but she doesn't know I'm in Korea."

"Don't you write?"

"No. It's like I said, I'm not to see her again or write unless I can say I understand this . . . this thing."

Neither of them spoke for a long time. Warren took out his cigarettes and offered one to Prevot; side by side, the two men stood looking out over the hazy valley at Papasan which sat awaiting their next attempt to take it.

"I wonder," Warren said, "if that hill is any more valuable now that so many men have died for it."

"Not worth a damn," Prevot exclaimed. "That's what gets you. Even if we take it, we start the same thing for the one beyond. Makes you wonder what in hell it's all about."

They watched the shifting haze, wafted like the smoke of incense around the base of a great idol.

Prevot asked, "You got a girl?"

"Sort of. We don't write either."

"You could address it to her and leave instructions . . ."

"No. I think you should hang on to it. You don't know her and besides you'll probably come through this . . ."

"I could say the same to you."

"Well, I'm certain. Maybe not tonight, but one of these rainy nights."

"Tonight for me. Certain!" Prevot said firmly. "So take it." He thrust the package forward.

"We're in the same boat." Warren shook his head. "Think it over. There must be somebody else."

At 1000 hours Warren and White went down to the briefing. Prevot assembled the platoon near the C.P. and outlined substantially the same plan of attack as the earlier canceled one. "You'll turn in your valuables, as usual," he closed, "at the C.P. Test-fire your weapons this afternoon. Get what sack-time you can but be ready to move out at 2100 hours." He sounded as he had at every other briefing and he said nothing to Warren about the package.

About 1300 hours the artillery began in earnest to lob shells at the enemy. "They're using a lot of T.O.T.," White announced when Warren relieved him at the forward position. Then he hitched his weapon onto his shoulder and left Warren to watch the Time-on-Target shells alone. Timed to burst before they hit the ground, the shells exploded in the air, spewing shrapnel all along the ridge.

The hot meal was moved up from three to two o'clock that afternoon, since the enemy had lately begun to throw mortar rounds in at the regular chow time. Even then the meal was interrupted by a couple of small mortar bursts on the top of the ridge. "Starting early today," said Rickley, who was sitting near Warren. They hurried their meal and slogged their way through the commo trench. Rain, light as mist, was coming down before they reached the bunker.

When they passed Lim in the forward position, he smiled, waved at the enemy. "Tonight," he grinned broadly, "tonight, we kill many, eh?"

Warren forced a smile and the words, "Yes, tonight will be fun."

"Tonight we have fun," White rejoiced, rubbing his hands together happily, as Warren followed Rickley into the bunker. "The rain will be good cover, but not so good for trying to get up the hill."

"Your turn for chow," Warren said. "Better hurry it, they're starting early on the harassing."

White put on his poncho.

"I'll relieve Lim so he can go down with you," Rickley said, following White from the bunker.

Warren, sitting on the edge of his bunk, began to dismantle his M-1, laying the parts on his sleeping bag. He oiled a cloth and was wiping the bolt clean when he heard the mortars crunch; the bunker shifted, earth rained down from between the beams in the ceiling. He felt the debris particles pelting his neck as he put on his steel helmet. An entire battery had apparently been fired at once, for the company front was shuddering with the crunching explosions. He thought he could hear voices yelling down the line, but they were indistinct. Then he stood up—a sound, a voice near his own bunker—somebody calling his name. He zipped up his vest, waited at the bunker door, listening for a break between the incoming rounds; then, hearing the voice again, hurled himself out of the bunker. Near the commo trench opening on the road a man rolled about in the mud. Warren ran over, grabbed his feet and dragged him into the trench. Then, not pausing to examine him, Warren ran, sliding, slipping, until he reached the Forward Position. "Call the C.P.," he shouted to Rickley. "Get the medic. Got a casualty up here." Hurrying back to the man who lay twisting in the mire of the trench, he took out his handkerchief and began wiping the mud away from the face. The fellow's helmet had been blown away; the flesh of his face was deeply gashed.

"Get Warren. I can't see." It was Prevot.

"This is Warren."

Prevot twisted in a furious agony. "The package," he cried, "take it! Take the package! Oh, I can't see."

Warren unzipped the armored vest, put his hand inside, but found nothing. "Where is it?" he asked.

"Out there." Prevot's body stiffened with pain. Warren looked about but saw no package. "Get it!" Prevot said. "Get it!" Warren, reluctant to leave the wounded man, stepped away for a moment and looked around the mouth of the trench. "Got it?" Prevot asked.

"Yes," Warren lied. Once again he took Prevot's head in his hands and began to wipe the mud from the wounds.

"Keep it!" Prevot said, breathing heavily and bracing himself for another spasm of pain. "Keep it."

The medic, his poncho sleek with rain, arrived with two stretcher bearers. They rolled Prevot onto the stretcher, strapped him down and started back. "Can't take the trench," the medic said, "gotta take the road." Warren

118

watched as the men began their dangerous trek down to the C.P. The mud dragged at them: the forward stretcher bearer slipped, horselike, to his knees and then—with the medic's help—got to his feet again. The men sloshing down the road were perfect targets. Tensely Warren watched, hoping the rain obscured the sniper's vision. One burst could catch them all.

When the group had completed its journey to the bottom of the hill and the stretcher was being secured to the jeep, Warren returned to the commo trench and searched for the package. In the mud he knelt and felt with his hands wherever he thought it might have fallen. The sticky earth clung to his fingers, the rain seeped coldly down his neck; his whole body trembled with chills as he prowled about near the mouth of the trench. There was only mud and, in one spot, Prevot's helmet. The chin strap had been severed and a piece of shrapnel was imbedded in the side of the green metal.

Finally, exhausted, he returned to his bunker, poured some water into his helmet; stepping outside, he washed his hands and face. After scraping most of the mud from his clothes, he went to his cot and, pushing aside his sleeping bag, stretched out on the canvas beneath it.

White came in and said, "Prevot got it."

"I know. He was bringing me something."

"Oh? . . . What?"

"A package. But he didn't make it."

"Killed delivering a package." White shook his head.

Warren sat erect. "He dead?"

"He died on the way down the hill."

Rickley entered the bunker. "Somebody lose this?" He held up the package.

"Yes. Prevot was bringing it to me." Warren held out his hand. "I couldn't find it out there."

"Lying right in the trench," Rickley said, handing it to Warren. "Too bad about Prevot."

"He knew it was coming," Warren said.

"He did?"

"He told me this morning. He expected it later . . . to-night." Warren lay back on his cot and closed his eyes, wishing the discussing, everything, would end.

"Strange . . ." Rickley murmured, "that he should . . . sense it . . ."

"Not strange at all," White said. "I have had many of my men tell me they were going to get it on a certain day or in a certain action. Most of them did."

"No kidding?"

"One does not 'kid' about such things. Of course, it may be because they want to die at that time. They take chances . . . they just give up."

The weight of the parcel in Warren's hand was heavy, heavier than he would have imagined. He did not look at it, but merely held it in his hand as he lay on the cot and tried to blot out the words being spoken around him.

"Then, others," White went on, "they want to live, but they know, they get a premonition."

"That must be a terrible feeling," Rickley said. "I mean to be certain of the time that you're going to die."

"As for myself, there would be a relief in knowing." White laughed. "With that knowledge, think of what a man could do!"

Warren turned his head to see White's back as he left the bunker to relieve Lim. "Prevot thought of giving this to you," Warren lifted the package toward Rickley. "So if something happens to me, you'll find it in my sack."

"What is it?"

"I don't know." Rickley looked at him openly and Warren felt he should explain. "Prevot just said it was important that one of us get it. A White-Russian girl gave it to him. A princess, he said. I don't quite get the whole story, but she told him that unless he understood this," Warren lifted his hand, feeling again the weight of the object,

120

"that he wouldn't understand her and couldn't marry her."

"You going to open it?"

"I guess I should," Warren said, sitting up and looking at the parcel. It was strangely heavy. From the plastic bag he took the package which, less than six inches long, about four inches wide, was a little thicker than a pack of cigarettes. Slipping the twine off the paper, he placed it neatly, deliberately, on his cot. With tentative fingers he removed the outer wrapping paper only to find another sheet underneath. That removed, he discovered a blue velvet bag. Opening the draw strings, he slid the contents of the bag into his hand.

Rickley quickly moved over to sit on the cot beside him. Together they gazed at the golden square which had slipped out of the velvet pouch.

"An ikon," Rickley said.

"The most beautiful thing I've ever seen."

Two faces, two pairs of slender hands, showed through apertures in the golden case. The robes of a Mother and Child, hammered out of the gold itself, rippled with gems of many shades. With large compassionate eyes set in a Byzantine face, the Mother gazed downward at her Child, whose hands stretched to touch hers. There was an awful sadness in the maternal gaze—as of profound sorrow accepted, already transformed into quiet dignity. And the Child, as if to console that lovely brow, put tiny fingers forth in a gesture that was in itself a caress.

"What did she mean by saying Prevot had to understand this?" Warren asked.

"Who knows?" Rickley shrugged. "Perhaps . . ." His voice trailed off and he did not go on.

Warren's eyes returned to the treasure in his hands. "What am I going to do with it?"

"Puzzle it—like Prevot."

"What do you mean by that?"

Rickley shrugged his shoulders, "An old proverb says God writes straight with crooked lines."

"Maybe," Warren said, "but Prevot offered me this earlier and I turned it down because I felt . . . I feel . . . the same way he did."

"That you're going to die tonight?"

"One of these nights."

"I don't think so."

Warren was startled by Rickley's definiteness. "Why not?"

"I just don't believe you will."

"What about Prevot? He felt the same way."

"But he gave you this."

"What's that got to do with it?"

"Idiotic as it may sound, I feel that perhaps this was given to Prevot so he'd give it to you."

"Prevot might've given it to you."

"I doubt that. He passed me in the trench on his way up—bringing it to you." Rickley stood up. "I've gotta get my ammo for tonight, coming along?"

"No. My shift starts in a few minutes."

"Right," Rickley said. "See you later."

Warren settled back on his cot, holding the ikon before him, and thought of Prevot. The ikon was a paradoxically beautiful monument to Prevot's dread certainty; how long had the awful secret clawed at him? What an intense pitch it must have reached to force his telling of it, to make him hurry up the hill, racing against death, to put the precious treasure safely in another's hands. Safely? Warren shifted about, sat on the edge of his cot, the unfamiliar thing still in his hand. Prevot's death proved Prevot's thoughts were not imaginings; White's talk of similar experiences were but a pale shadow of proof beside Prevot's gashed face. And what did that make of his own thoughts? Perhaps it was true—what he had told the boy on the river bank—that he would die this winter. Wasn't that what he had come to believe during the long journey here? Yet, back in the States, he had been restless, even troubled, until he had volunteered. At the time, he told himself that he would not live out his life as a coward, even if it was a secret cowardice, a cowardice that hurt no one else. And if the choice was such cowardice or death—had he seen the choice like that? Or hadn't he colored it, looked upon it as a challenge, felt that in the confrontation with fear he would discover himself . . . or God? For Bernhardt had said that God would be found here. To find God did one have to die? The ikon pictured God as a child of distorted proportions contemplating the delicate face of a woman, a face elongated to a sorrowful beauty. As he looked, the beauty of the ikon sent a pain through him and a chill, like anguish, shook him. "Not yet," he blurted out, and the sound roused him. He slid the golden square quickly into its velvet pouch, dropped that into the plastic bag and buttoned it inside his fatigue pocket.

A few minutes later, having hurriedly assembled his weapon and put on his vest, poncho, and helmet, Warren was treading uneasily through the muck of Prevot's death couch, brushing against the muddy sides of the commo trench.

"Wondered if you would make it," White beamed.

"Dozed for a minute."

"I must rest, too," White said, turning the muzzle of his M-1 downwards so that rain could not enter the bore. "Want to be in shape," he added, slipping the sling over his shoulder. "It is going to be a good one." He looked out at Papa-san and rubbed his hands together. "Tough."

Warren watched White make his way up to the turn in the commo trench, his slick, shiny poncho cloaking his whole body, his dark helmet bobbing low on his head. He was all helmet and poncho, looking like some strange armored beast—an enormous beetle—boring a path along the surface of the earth.

Tonight? Warren wondered, turning to confront the ridges before him. Or would he, like Prevot, endure many nights before the final one? What would it be like, dying? A swift agony like Prevot's? Better that than his mother's, lying in bed feeling the growths moving within her as they pinched off her life a little at a time. Later, the body, his mother's, had looked nothing like her, stiff and painted, when the body . . . was just a corpse . . .

Like dark waves responding to a turmoil in the depths, the ridges before his gaze heaved their sharp edges skyward.

Larry believed in heaven, in hell; so did Jean. The old monk meditating over his grave-to-be thought it was so. They were all so certain. He lit a cigarette and looked above the restless ridges into the threatening sky.

——"Bodies don't marry bodies." Jean's eyes penetrated his. "Persons marry persons." Then she touched the edge of the table with her finger, smoothing its white linen edging. "I always thought that I could never marry a non-Catholic . . . until you came along." The finger went back to press down a wrinkle that had been missed. "Being with you is as natural as breathing, but, on the other hand, it frightens me. It frightens me," she repeated slowly. "It's like standing on the edge of a dark cliff and looking down at the sea foam below. I've done that. You're tempted to jump, only you don't—you get frightened and you back away. Because it seems a small thing, to step forward—and the temptation is usually that way —it's not 'jump,' but 'another little step.' But when you take it, you can't go back—you're falling." She turned her eyes to where her fingers played with the edging. "That's why I'm afraid. If I let you hold me in your arms, if I take that little step, I'm through, I'm not going to be able to step back. I'll be yours always." She looked up. "That's the way it was with my sister—only he didn't want her always."

124

Perhaps it was because it was their last evening together that she spoke so frankly to him.

"You've been good to me, by not trying to seduce me. Because I don't think if you'd tried, that I could have resisted. I love you and everything in me tells me that I belong to you—everything but the memory of my sister."

At the front door of her home, she turned to him and touched his face. "You can't come in tonight. I've admitted too much to you and to myself." Suddenly her lips were on his, her hands clutching at his hair, her whole body seeming to be thrown at him in one burst of passion, but only for an instant. Before he had sufficiently recovered, she was closing the door upon him.——

"You'd think they had a grudge against the earth." Rickley's voice broke the silence beside him. Warren had been staring with such intensity at the smeared ridges in front of him that he had not heard the other come up. "Maybe they do," Rickley went on with a grin. "Starting with Genesis and 'by the sweat of thy brow.' Still," he shrugged, "much as they do violence to it, they have to make peace with it if they're to eat. Have you been praying?"

"No," Warren said.

"You should be."

"I'm not very good at it."

"Maybe you're better at it than you know. Got a cigarette?"

"I didn't know you smoked," Warren said, after he had lit the other's cigarette.

Rickley grinned broadly and plucked at a piece of tobacco on the end of his tongue before answering: "I'm not very good at it."

Warren laughed. "That makes us even." He turned to scan the uneasy ridges in the distance. Their sharp edges rose out of the mists of the valley and dropped downward, like the lines on some graph registering the contractions of the heart or the waves of the brain—a continuous irregular line of jutting peaks separated by gaps shallow or deep. Rickley stood silently at his left shoulder, looking out on the same scene. Under a darkening sky, the mists shifted silently around the impenetrable hills.

"My prayers," Warren said, watching the slow movement of the swollen black clouds, "always seem to stop about three feet above my head. I get the feeling that they're not prayers at all, just me mumbling to myself."

He had spoken quietly, almost as if enunciating the thought to himself. Rickley's response came with the same quality, as if merely completing Warren's thought: "But feelings don't count," he said.

The wind, working with redoubled vigor to move the heavy clouds, pressed hard on Warren's cheeks. "What about Prevot?"

"I mean in prayer."

In the valley the wind was shoving the gray masses hard against the jagged walls, herding them up ravines, stuffing stray whisps into crevices, getting them out of the way.

"God hears," Rickley said, "no matter what *you* feel, God hears."

"Yeah," Warren said, surprised by the tone of his own voice. "And when does He answer?" He turned to look directly at his companion.

Rickley dropped the cigarette into the mud of the trench and with deliberate care put his booted foot upon it. "At least once," he said slowly, "usually more often, but at least once to each of us."

"Well, I haven't heard Him." Warren turned abruptly away from the other's gaze and looked again to the hills and sky. In the distance to his left the sky was smeared with the downward spill of rain.

"What about the ikon?"

Warren's hand touched his breast pocket. "What about it?"

126

"Doesn't it tell you anything?"

Warren's eyes were still intent upon the distant streaks of rain. "It tells me that Prevot's premonition was correct. He died as he said he would."

"Is that all? Doesn't it tell you somebody else died as He said He would?"

Warren was silent for a moment, then: "Doing some convert work, Rickley?" The wind on his cheek carried moisture, the gray smear in the distance was widening. A chill hunched his shoulders momentarily and, at a sound, he turned to see Rickley walking away. "Wait a minute," he called. Rickley turned and Warren saw that the usual smile was gone from his face.

Without a word Rickley returned and waited.

"Don't give up on me," Warren smiled, trying to return the other to his less troubled, more normal state. Rickley scuffed his boot in the mud, looked at it, scuffed it again. All at once Warren saw him as a very young boy clad in a costume that didn't fit. "Have another cigarette," he said, offering the pack.

Rickley looked up, smiled. "I've given 'em up."

"Well, I'll have one. Don't go away. I want to talk to you. I've got some things on my mind." Warren felt the first drops of rain on his hands as he cupped them around the match. He stared at the raindrops gathering on his hands until the match burned his finger and he threw it aside.

"You might not believe it," he said, looking not at Rickley but at the distant hills now being pelted, as he was, by rain, "but I'd give anything to be in your shoes. Things, even life, makes sense to you. And once when I was in a monastery—I never told you that, did I?—I found that even death made sense to the people there." His words came rapidly, flowing with the increased tempo of the rain. He spoke what was in him at the moment, holding nothing back.

127

"I want what you've got and I came here to find it, whatever it is. And yet, I'm not going to have time. I may not live through tonight. Don't ask me how I know, I know —like Prevot. And if I live through tonight, I'll get it some other night. Sure, you'll say I've just got to have faith, to make up my mind to believe, but I can't. Maybe I'm after some proof. Even the Apostles had proof, loaves and fishes, the dead brought back, the blind made to see. I came here, I think, looking for something as definite as that, and I don't need anyone to tell me that that's crazy. It's no crazier than the fact that while I'm in love with a girl back home and could have stayed there, I came here feeling damned sure I'd never leave alive." He stopped, turned to Rickley who was standing a few steps behind him. "Now I've spilled my guts. Anyway, I feel better."

Rickley looked at him with wide eyes, the rain running off his helmet and down his cheeks. "Pray," Rickley blurted out. And with that he spun about and hurried clumsily down the trench.

After Rickley turned out of sight, Warren looked up and down the line of fortifications. Here and there a tenuous curl of smoke betrayed the charcoal fire being lit. In the crude little structures dotting the M.L.R. lived men knowing the same feelings as himself. All they wanted was to be away from this place, to be laughing with a girl, to be . . . anything but sitting here. But like himself, they could not escape, and no words would take away the ache they felt.

"Pray."

The monks prayed at all hours of the day and night. He had heard their chant, sitting as the only person in the nave of the chapel while their voices traveled up the slender nervures of the arches and they bowed humbly . . . but he had not been able to pray.

The aged monk meditated at his grave and the bells rang out in celebration at the death of a nun.

"The world is so beautiful . . ." Warren had experienced its beauty piercing him like an arrow when he had traveled through the French countryside. He had wanted to reach out and enfold the earth as if it were a delicate child, something to be nurtured, cared for, protected with infinite love. Even now he felt that tender yearning mixed with his deep loneliness.

Lim came squashily down the trench and Warren took one more look at the hulk which tonight they were going to attack. Involuntarily, with but the slightest passage of sound between his lips, he said: "Please God . . ."

Outside the bunker, gray men with dull green helmets filed by: the squad from further up the ridge going down to the C.P. Warren heard the slosh of their feet as they plodded heavily, dumb and patient, through the night. There was a note of inevitability about the sluggish forward motion of the men. He lit another cigarette and moved away from the doorway back to his bunk.

Warren wished now that he had told Jean exactly why he was coming here. Out of fear he had hedged about, mentioned the thought contained in Bernhardt's letter, but not the greater reason. He had been more honest with Rickley today, had communicated to him that fear from which he had shielded her. But if he had told her, he would not be facing this alone. She would be writing to him and he to her, and that would give him some contact with a cleaner world than this, help to free him from his confinement in this land without hope.

"All ready?" White asked heartily. "We will be going down in a minute."

"I'll get Rickley." Warren put on his helmet and stepped out into the gray blackness.

The night was cold. The soft chill rain was silent in its descent. As he waded through the wet darkness, he heard his own feet echoing the plodding, unenthusiastic sound

129

that had marked the passing of the squad. The commo trench was treacherously slimy and he shuffled through it feeling defeated by mud, rain and night.

"Halt, who goes there?" Rickley's voice overcame the darkness.

"Warren."

"Password?"

"Rotten."

"Bananas."

"Time to go." Wearily, Warren approached the position.

"Right with you."

Warren heard the rustle of the poncho as Rickley moved about the position. Coming closer to the other, Warren said, "I want you to take the ikon."

"No thank you."

"Well, then, take it to send a friend of mine, will you?"

"Not necessary." Rickley shook his head, his face a bright circle in the gray mist.

"Pretty damned confident."

"Ask and you shall receive," Rickley said. "Did you ask?"

"No."

"Well, I did." Rickley shrugged. "Shall we get moving?"

Rickley took the lead as they traveled up the black, wet trench. Before leaving the trench, he stopped, half-turned about and said, "That's what's dangerous about prayer."

"What?"

"You get what you ask for . . . and sometimes it's not what you expect." He started walking again.

"Well, we must go," White said impatiently as they entered the bunker. Lim stood grinning beside his tutor.

"Just a minute," Warren said, "there's something I want to take care of."

"We will go down," White said. "See you there."

The three men left the bunker and, once more alone,

Warren searched in his bag until he found a sheet of paper. Quickly, he scribbled a note asking that the package be sent to Jean, printing her name and address in large letters on the page so there would be no mistake. Folding the paper, he put it in the bag with the ikon and buttoned it inside his breast pocket before zipping up his armored vest. Then, grabbing his weapon, he extinguished the candles and left the darkened bunker.

The three men were vaguely discernible about halfway down the road: at intervals, waves of heavy rain blotted them from his vision. Mechanically, Warren picked his way through the mud. Was it only this morning that Prevot had been carried along this same road, the forward stretcher bearer buckling to his knees at just about this spot? An ugly place to die. But Prevot had not been able to see it. What *did* he see at the last? Warren looked about, as if to fill his memory with images, storing them up against the moment when he himself might not see again, but all was lost in shadows.

Small groups of men stood about the C.P. There was some whispering, but it embedded itself in the swish of the rain. The faces of the men themselves were cloaked in gray and they waited, their figures swaying in the mist.

"Damn, damn, damn!" Warren heard White's voice and saw the man himself charge past, the face, for an instant visible, glowering anger. He turned to watch White rushing back up the road.

"Warren." Lieutenant Fregni's voice brought Warren about. "Get your things. You're not going out tonight. Been transferred. Here are your orders. Jeep's waiting."

"Have you read them?" White stormed when Warren entered the bunker. "Counterfire! Tonight of all nights! They should have waited until morning! What's so urgent about getting us, now, tonight?"

Warren had been too dazed by the reprieve to even look at the damp sheet of paper in his hand. Now he unfolded it and, while White still swore and began savagely taking out his vengeance on the items he was throwing into his duffle bag, Warren sat on his cot and by the pale light of the candle read the orders. They were special orders, assigning the men listed to the counterfire platoon as of that date. Beneath the standard paragraph of army abbreviations he saw their names, ranks, and serial numbers.

"We will go back there and sack out for the night," White fumed. "Damned fools. They could have waited." He continued his commentary on the stupidity of the whole affair until they were well on their way down the hill, lugging their belongings and weapons and trying to maintain a steady footing on the road, which ran like an enormous slide into a pool of blackness. At the bottom of the hill near the C.P. a man jumped out of a jeep.

"Here you go," he said. "Got everything?"

Warren answered affirmatively and the driver helped them get their stuff into the jeep. "Betcha you're glad I came when I did," the driver said, but neither Warren nor White replied. "I was supposed to pick you guys up earlier, but I had to make some runs up to Able and George companies. Got held up. Lucky I made it when I did."

The area was deserted and quiet. Along the forward ridge three shadowy shapes loomed for a moment and then descended over the other side. "Colonel's up there," the driver said. "Saw him come in a few minutes ago."

"The colonel?" White asked.

"Yeah. In the C.P. Guess he'll be here 'til the show's over."

"Wait!" White commanded and rushed off toward the C.P.

"Where's he going?" the driver asked.

"To see the colonel, I guess."

"Well, I'll be damned. What about?"

"Oh, they're old buddies."

"Really? Well, why can't he see him tomorrow?"

"Because he wants to go out tonight."

"Christ! He crazy or something?"

Warren did not reply and both men sat in the silent darkness, the mist washing around them as they stared at the C.P.

Shortly, White stamped out of the bunker and over to the idling jeep. "Let's go," he said. The driver shifted and the jeep started down the hill towards the rear. "The needs of the service," White hissed, his head dropping low to his chest. "The needs of the service, hell!"

Warren sat quietly as the jeep whined along the muddy road. From both sides of the road distorted shadows beckoned to him. The familiar countryside of his trips to the shower point had been transmuted into a cemetery of ghostly figures roaming the hills in the night.

The road guards challenged them, the men standing, weapons ready, ankles rooted in the mud, waiting for the word that would mean friend, the word that would open the route. The word. What was the word?

——One night staggering with drink he had reeled up to a priest in the town outside the post. "Father," he had said. "You've got it! Give me the word! Tell me the word that opens the gates! The word! That's what I'm looking for, the golden word, speak it to me and I'll be happy forevermore."

The priest's face had been startled, had looked at him wonderingly, then said, "Christ is the Word, my son."

"Christ," he had tittered drunkenly. "Oh, but, Father, Christ is a swear word!" And he had staggered back into a bar.——

"Bananas," the roadguard gave the countersign and the jeep, swearing at the encroaching mud, pulled itself forward.

Warren felt the ikon press against his chest. For a moment he imagined himself as carrying a rich treasure to some distant monarch.

The night air was tense, the rain itself seemed not so much to be falling as to be standing like tall stalks of gray wheat awaiting the scythe of their passage.

Rickley had been so damned confident that this evening was not to be it. Prayer, Rickley had said, prayer. He had not admitted it to Rickley, but he felt that, somehow, this afternoon he had prayed for the first time in his life.

"Halt!" The voice threatened like the strange night itself. A few minutes later they were stopping in the regimental headquarters area.

Here, during that night which seemed so long ago, they had brought Duke, trussed and weeping, his eyes wide with fright. A "coward" White had called him. How thin was the line between cowardice and not being cowardly, between Duke and himself! One thing only was certain, that he had been acquiescent, going out, going out against himself. The fear of facing the challenge had been overcome by the fear of not facing it. That he would die, he had felt certain, but to try to escape dying seemed futile in the face of that certainty.

The driver led them to the bunker, down a flight of burlap-covered stairs hacked into the dark earth. "Careful there," he whispered, "damn near broke my back the other day." He flicked on a flashlight, showed them where to put their bags, and indicated a couple of empty bunks upon which they could put their sleeping sacks. He put the flashlight on a workbench near the entrance way and its beam cut down the center aisle of the bunker between the rows of bunks and onto a cot at the far end.

The bedding on the cot moved restlessly. A muffled voice said, "Cut that diddling light out, will ya?"

"Turn over," the driver said. "Ain't no place else to put the light."

"Might have known," the voice grunted. "Damned Folger again." The speaker raised himself on one elbow and blinked in the direction of the light. "Always Folger, late-

134

again Folger, wake-a-man-up Folger." With what seemed a tremendous effort, the blankets endured an upheaval and the speaker turned his back to the light. "Remind me to bury that light tomorrow," the voice mumbled. After a few more grunts the figure was still.

"All ready?" Folger whispered.

"Yes," Warren replied after a glance at White who was in his sack, his hands under his head, his face scorched with resentment.

The light was snapped out.

"Sure nice to be in the sack and not out there," Folger sighed in the darkness.

"Can it!" a cold voice commanded.

The bunker was silent.

"You both requested the line," Lieutenant Held said the next morning, "and that's what you'll be getting." He was leaning against his jeep as he spoke; the gray sky behind him was threatening more rain. "You'll get more of the line with us than in a rifle company. Rifle battalions pull into reserve. We don't, not unless the whole regiment does."

Lieutenant Held was young, younger than either White or himself, probably about twenty-two, Warren figured. He wore tailored fatigues with a combat paratrooper's insignia on his breast.

"We don't pull any patrols, but you've probably found out this war has boiled down to an artillery duel and counterfire's the best way to wipe out enemy artillery." His face was boyish but sharply cut, his eyes metallic. He spoke in a brisk, officious tone. "I specified you men out of a batch of six files the S-1 sent me. I wanted men with high I.Q.'s and above-average background. Can't afford to have a slow learner. The equipment's not too complex once you get the hang of it, but you've got to get the hang of it fast! On line!" He paused.

Warren thought there was something of White about the

135

young lieutenant, but his tight-fitting fatigues sheathed a lithe, well-proportioned body more polished than White's; this one was marble, the other granite.

"Since we don't pull into reserve like the riflemen," Lieutenant Held went on, "you'll come down off the line one day each week for a shower, a rest, a little beer. You'll spend the night here and go up the next morning." He stopped. "Are you buddies?"

"Yes, sir," White answered.

"I'm going to have to split you up. Can't have two new men in the same squad. Maybe we can reshuffle things later." He stopped again and turned toward the hole leading down to the bunker. "Folger!" he shouted.

Folger barreled up the stairs. A slight man with downy, yellow tufts of soft hair on his cheeks, he peered through his glasses at the lieutenant. "Yes, sir," he said breathlessly.

"What time you going up today?"

"I was gonna wait for the mail, sir."

"Fine," Lieutenant Held said. "Take White here up to Able company and Warren up to the hill. Try to get them there before midnight."

"Yes, sir," Folger said, scuttling down the stairs again.

"Slow, but dependable," Lieutenant Held smiled. "Your platoon sergeant is on R and R; he'll be back in a couple of days. I take it you've met the others."

"Yes, sir."

"We're losing another man to rotation next week. If you know of anyone who'd be good for our type of work, give me the word. We're below strength now. And one more thing: keep your position sharp. The colonel thinks we're the most valuable unit he has in this situation. We've got a top-notch reputation, so let's keep it that way." He climbed behind the wheel of his jeep. "You had breakfast? Well, I haven't. So long, and good luck."

Back in the bunker, Corporal Nevers, the disgruntled sleeper of the night before, was reading a comic book. He

136

put it down as they entered, "He give you the pep talk?"

"Yeah," Warren responded.

"He's a sharp cookie. Talks tough, but he'll work for ya. He tell ya about the railroad guns?"

"No."

"Ah, them railroad guns made us, boy. Ya know nobody knew what in hell counterfire was. When we was in Japan, we didn't have the junk to work with; on maneuvers we just picnicked while the infantry ran its tail off. Only when we came here did we get any real stuff to work with and then we had to learn to use it from the field manuals. Anyway, we kept getting these damn azimuths pointing clear off, damn near to Manchuria. Didn't know what to do. Thought we were all fouled up, ya know? Even figured it was the equipment and sent it down to be repaired. Finally, Lieutenant Cutter—he was our lieutenant before Held came—he goes to the colonel and tells him where those azimuths are always pointing and the colonel calls an airstrike. Air Force reports six whopping big railroad guns, three destroyed, three probables. Maybe they're bullshitting, ya know? But anyway we can do no wrong now. Ya oughta hear them guys on line when the rounds start coming in. 'Hey counterfire, got that?' or 'Counterfire, get them bastards!' Real nice." Corporal Nevers lifted his comic book for a moment, then dropped it again on his chest. "Say, what outfit he sendin' ya to?"

"I'm going on the 'Hill,'" Warren said, "whatever that is."

"Oh, baby, that ain't no company. All alone up there, and nothing 'tween you and the enemy. 'Course you got a company on the ridges on either side of you, but they ain't really next-door neighbors. No hot meals for you, just C-rations. Where you going?" Nevers asked of White.

"Able company." White did not look up from his packing.

"Now *there* you get a hot meal. Good bunker, too. Only

137

at night Joe Chink comes in mighty close there. You'll get a lotta work, they're concentrating on Able company lately. What outfit ya come from?"

White did not answer, so Warren told him.

"Baker company! You just got out in time. They really got it last night."

"How do you know?"

"This is regimental headquarters, boy. Guys here know everything."

"What happened?"

"They didn't make it. Seventeen KIA's, fourteen WIA's and two missing. You were lucky to get outta that mess, boy."

"Where can I find out who got hit?"

"That's right," Nevers said. "You maybe got buddies there, eh? C'mon," he said, swinging himself down from his bunk. "We'll go over to the S-2 bunker."

"Want to come along, White?" Warren asked.

"No."

Warren followed Nevers out of the bunker and across the track-streaked mud. They entered a sandbagged passageway that jutted out of the side of the hill. The passageway made an abrupt right turn, bringing them to a wooden door which Nevers opened. They entered a room paneled with wood from ammunition boxes. Electric lights hung down from the ceiling and a long map table extended along one wall. In the center of the room at high drafting tables sat three men tracing lines on acetate with colored crayons.

"This guy's just down from Baker company," Nevers said, introducing Warren to the three men. "He's a new man in counterfire. Wants to see if any of his buddies got it last night."

A man Nevers had introduced as Lefevre ran a hand through his black, wavy hair, walked over to a board on one wall. "There's the dope on the number," he said, shaking his head and turning away. Warren saw the same figures

138

that Nevers had announced. "And here's the list of names." Lefevre handed him a sheet of paper. "Only came in about an hour ago."

Warren recognized many names, men he had spoken with, nodded at, but he passed over them, searching for particular names. Under 'wounded' he saw Lim's. "Thanks a lot," he said, handing the list back. Rickley's name was not on it.

A telephone rang. "Not for that," Lefevre said, picking up the phone.

"They're all-right guys," Nevers said when they were outside once more. "That Lefevre's a real brain, but doesn't act like one, ya know what I mean? I drop into their bunker when I come down for a rest, like last night I did. I like to listen to those guys talk, real brainy type talk, ya know what I mean? Last night they got on God. Can ya beat that, talking God when you're here? But they're good guys anyway. Did I tell ya we're pulling into reserve soon? That's the scuttlebutt."

In the bunker, White had finished rearranging his gear and was lying on his cot smoking a cigarette. Warren decided not to bother with his own gear until he got back on line. "Lim was wounded," he said to White.

White nodded and continued to stare at the cot above him as if resenting its presence.

"Rickley's all right," Warren added.

White's throat vibrated with a sound of disgust. "Should have been the other way around. Lim is the soldier!"

That afternoon Folger jeeped the three men up to the line. Nevers and White were dropped at the turn-around point at the base of Able company's position; carrying mail and a new microphone, the two men commenced their walk up the steep and muddy road toward the ridgeline.

"Use'ta drive right up there," Folger said, motioning with his head, "before the rain. Now I'd never make it." The jeep churned the mud as he slipped it around and started

139

back to the main road. "Got one more call, Easy company, before I drop you off."

Along the road behind Easy company, a large, smiling Texan was waiting. "Good to have another body aboard," he said to Warren. "Where ya goin'?"

When told, a grin spread across his broad face. "Know it well. The lonely outpost. C-ration hill. You'll be lucky if ya can wade through the C-ration cans up there. Got a strong back? You'll need one to lug batteries up that damned hill. Straight up, isn't it, Foggy?"

"Almost," Folger replied. "Here's your mail, Tex. Latch on to that battery. I wanta get back tonight."

"Foggy, you're always in a hurry, but you never seem to be on time." Tex hoisted the green battery box out of the jeep and strapped it onto a pack-rack. "Foggy's nervous in the service," Tex explained to Warren. "Doesn't like it up here so close to Joe Chink." Resting the load on the hood of the jeep, he slipped his arms through the straps and eased the weight onto his back. "Off with you, Foggy," he ordered, "and here's a list of things we need." He pulled a list from his pants pocket and thrust it at Folger. "See ya," Tex said, beginning his hike up the road toward the company.

The jeep passed a mortar company where men puttered around the silent tubes. A sign near the road said, "We deliver."

The road followed the base of the ridgeline, curving like a blacksnake behind the dun hills. The jeep growled along the winding route for another ten minutes before Folger brought it to a stop. "That's it," he pointed.

The small hill sat like a cone in the center of a valley. The ridgeline, which everywhere was a bulwark against the enemy, had been breached here by nature. As if a section of wall had been torn out, the ridge gapped open; in the center of the gap stood the small hill, a lone sentry at the break.

"It's not so bad," said Folger. "There are tanks in the valley in front of ya, 'tween you and the enemy. Them guys on the ridges are too far away to be company, though." He handed Warren a batch of mail. "For Red. He's up there. Just follow the steps." He pointed to the notches that ascended the slope in a direct line to the top. "Can't miss it—only bunker up there."

Folger whined away as Warren started up the hill. The steps were slippery and he climbed cautiously, pausing now and then to rest and to look over the country. The day was darkening. The ridge to his right, the only one he could see from the path, was quiet; he couldn't make out its defenses. Above him the slope seemed deserted. At the halfway point in his climb he was able to see the top of the bunker. Below him, like a relief map, spread Korea, its ridges green and brown, its valleys hiding in the gray mists that obscured the horizon. There was no sound.

"Can I give a hand?" a voice called from above. Looking up, Warren saw a man descending the steps. "Name's Cox, call me Red. Heard you'd be comin' up." A good-natured grin creased his freckled face as he grabbed Warren's duffle bag and slung it over his shoulder. Warren followed him up the steps to the bunker squatting just below the crest of the hill. Logs jutted out from under the layers of sandbags on the roof of the rugged shelter; the doorway was protected by a sandbag wall that stuck out and made a right angle in front of it.

Inside were three bunks, a wooden desk made of ammo boxes and a large table with a Coleman stove squatting on it. C-ration cans, candy bars, and full packages of cigarettes littered the table. From the ceiling hung a Coleman lantern, and at one end of the room Warren saw a battery box like the one Tex had carried to his position, and from it black cords extended to a green machine. The machine was narrow and long, propped up at the front end by two spindly legs, while its base rested on the bunker floor. Putting the

141

duffle bag down, the redhead flung his helmet on his cot and walked over to the instrument. "Ever seen one of these?"

"No," Warren answered.

"Me neither 'til I came here, and I hope I never see another one." Red waved at the two empty cots. "Get settled and I'll show ya how it works. Been handling the whole show myself for the last three days. S'posed t' have three men here. Never have. Usually two."

Warren tossed his gear on the bunk and went over to the machine.

"Simple enough gadget," Red went on in his friendly twang. "The box has a recorder in it. When ya pick up the sound of an enemy weapon, ya stop the machine and then ya begin to work these knobs here. I'll handle that for a while 'til ya get it down. Then ya end up with two numbers here," his stubby finger tapped a dial face, "and here." He got up, walked over to the desk, and picked up a computing disk. "On this ya work out the two numbers. That gives ya an azimuth to the weapon. One azimuth wouldn't be any damned good, though, so ya've got another squad up on the ridge over there." He waved out the door to the ridge on the right. " 'Cordin' to the manual they shouldn't be so far away from us, but it works okay." He lifted an acetate-covered map from the desk. "Ya plot your azimuths here and then they call their azimuth over to ya and ya plot theirs. Where the two lines intersect, ya can bet your life there's a weapon. Ya call the coordinates in and in a few minutes," he shrugged, "no more weapon. C'mon outside a minute."

Warren followed him out of the bunker.

"Those are our mikes up there." Red pointed to the crest of the ridge which shielded them from enemy view. Warren could just see the small shapes. "That," Red indicated a sandbagged position about thirty yards away, "is where the stop button is. We always miss the first round or two while

142

we're starting the machine and getting to the stop button, but when ya press the button, that stops our machine and theirs," he nodded at the ridge to the right, "at the same sound. Then ya got 'em by the balls," he said cheerily. "That is if you make it to the stop button and back."

The two men stepped back into the bunker. "The first few days just follow me around 'til ya get the hang of this. Next barrage I'll let ya play around with the sound on the machine, after I've gotten the coordinates. Ya hungry?"

Warren said he was.

"C-rations. Got more C-rations than the army could eat. Take your pick. Candy bars, cigarettes," Red waved his hand at the table, "all over the place." He flipped the lid of a cardboard carton on the table, and inside Warren saw a great jumble of brown and white packets. "Powdered coffee, powdered cream, sugar . . ." Red continued, "All ya need and plenty of it. Could buy all the whores in China with it. Make yourself at home. Nothing to do 'til Joe Chink gets active."

"Is that often?"

"Often? Too often t' suit me. Those damned tanks down there in the valley are A-number-one targets. Joe throws somethin' at 'em every day. I think we've had it for today; they lobbed ten rounds in this morning. Wouldn't be so bad, but when they overshoot, they land on this damned hill. Well, gonna read my mail," he said, tearing open one of the envelopes. "Ya married?"

"No."

"I was. She sent me divorce papers t' sign about two weeks ago. Some mail. Hell, I don't blame her, though, she waited nearly a year."

"Been here a year?" Warren asked.

"Part of it in Japan. Take it from me, though, don't rush t' get married. Women are like streetcars—one comes along every five minutes."

"You going home soon?"

"My last week. Four more days 'n I go down that hill for the last time. That's why I want ya to know the machines by then. Ya may be up here alone—like I been." He returned to his letters. "Here's a hot one." His arm thrust out of the jacket sleeve, exposing rusty-red hairs, as he held the letter out to Warren. Warren took it. "There's a good laugh there," Red said.

The thin rice paper had delicate pink flowers in the upper corner; the handwriting was like that of a child, the words scrawled carefully in jet black ink:

. . . Oh, my belove, when with you I was not like a girl in business, but was like ordinary girl of female sex for three days with you. Now you are gone and I am sad. Is feeling like was lost alone in desert when you left. I am trying as you ask to be good girl but need money to repair bed and furnishings so will catch one GI unwillingly. Please forgive. I know we can never be normal couple— but please to consider me your wife until someday you marry . . .

"Just a Jap whore," Red said taking the page back. "I told her t' be a good girl," he smiled, his face shading more deeply. "She was a sweet little tyke." Crumpling the letter in one hand, he threw it into a wooden box near the door.

Red had been correct in saying that the machine was not difficult. Within two days Warren was taking turns with Red at the machine and at the outpost. When the one at the forward position had pressed the button on the sound, the other in the bunker would begin to work the machine, his eye pressed to the little scope in which the sound-picture appeared while he rotated the dials to bring the "blip" into the proper shape and then note the numbers—a procedure followed twice for each sound.

"Ya learn fast," Red said.

"You're a good teacher."

"I'm glad ya got it down pat. They may just leave ya

here alone and it'd be hell if ya didn't know how t' run the damned thing."

Warren had previously learned to recognize different weapons by the sound of their firing, but Red added to his knowledge. "Seventy-sixes," he said, "can be wheeled away after they fire 'em. They do it, too. For that matter, they must lug those mortars of theirs all over hell and gone just t' keep away from our return fire. We play hell with 'em, 'cause if they're in the same spot five minutes after they've fired, we've got 'em. They didn't know how in hell we did it 'til the damned marines lost a counterfire unit to 'em. Guess they know now."

Each afternoon a radio check was made with the platoon sergeant back at the regimental bunker. "Normally use the phone, though," Red said, " 'cause they monitor our radio just like we do theirs. Radio's for emergencies. Then it probably won't work." He grinned boyishly, slapping the green metal. "SCR-300, the most undependable radio in the world."

"Been good knowin' ya," Red said happily the day he was to go down. "I was right. You're gonna be here all alone for a while. Sergeant Claypool says there ain't nobody to send up." Red had just hung up the phone after a talk with the platoon sergeant. "They'll relieve ya the day after tomorrow to go down for a rest. Looks like this is gonna be a one-man post for a while."

That afternoon, still cheerful, the redhead left the bunker and started down the hill. "I'd run," he laughed, "only I'd slip in the mud an' get killed. Just be my luck." He waved and Warren watched him down the hill.

Alone, Warren turned back to the bunker. He housecleaned, arranging the C-rations in rows upon the table, clearing the litter from the floor and burying the garbage on the rear slope. While cleaning, he found the letter which Red had casually crumpled and tossed aside. He smoothed

145

it out on the table top and reread it slowly. "Just a Jap whore," Red had said . . .

———"Avez-vous une cigarette?"

He had strolled up the Champs-Elysées in the early evening, when the traffic and the crowds are thickest, and car headlights are being turned on. The late workers, the clerks, and the shopgirls were going home, and the early diners were just beginning to show up at the restaurants. Footweary from long hours spent in the Louvre, he had taken a seat on one of the benches that faced the broad boulevard. When he turned to reply to the voice at his shoulder, his eyes were met by the soft gray of her eyes.

"Mais, oui," he said.

"Vous êtes anglais?" she asked, taking the cigarette between her pale fingers.

"Non, américain."

"Ah," she smiled, raising the cigarette to her full, well-shaped mouth. "Do you have a match?"

"Surely." He struck a match and held it to her cigarette as she puffed, then inhaled with deep satisfaction. Her lips parted, formed an oval that seemed to caress the smoke as it left her mouth. For a moment she watched the smoke's languid movement toward him, then arching the thin black line of her high eyebrows, she asked: "Would you like to sleep with me?"

"I have no money," he said.

"But you are an American. All Americans have money." She arched her neck aristocratically and looked down her Modigliani nose at him.

"Not this one."

Her neck relaxed a little, she put her hand to her cheek, her cigarette still between her fingers, and her large eyes engulfed him. "Am I not pretty enough?" The question was meant to sound seductive, but it struck him as a curious blend of sensuality and fear.

"Lovely."

146

"But you don't want me?" Now her nervousness was more apparent and he felt uneasy. How could he tell her that in his loneliness he probably wanted nothing more . . . but not as a business proposition.

"Three thousand francs?" she said tentatively, but not without a certain haughtiness.

"No."

"It is not much." Again she tilted her head back and looked down her elongated nose at him.

"More than I can spend."

"You are cruel," she said, but her voice lacked emphasis. As her hand raised to bring the cigarette to her lips once more, she announced with royal finality: "Two thousand francs."

"No."

She dropped the cigarette to the ground, and threw herself on the seat beside him. "Please," she turned her wide eyes upon him in a look of open supplication, "I have had nothing to eat all day. Please . . . for one thousand francs."

"I haven't eaten yet," he said. "Come along. Do you know of a place nearby?"

"Mais, oui, monsieur." Linking her arm in his she began to lead him off. "But, no," she stopped. "That would not be good. You would not like that place and besides I owe them much money and—seeing you—they would ask me for it."

"Then I know of a place," he said, turning them about.

"It is funny that you do not have much money and that you are an American. But then it is funny too that you do not want me," she chattered on. "Americans never say that they do not want to sleep with me. After the war, many Americans . . ."

"Talk of something else."

She stopped talking and they crossed the Place de la Concorde and walked along through the Tuileries in the quiet dark, hand in hand. This was the way it should be, Warren thought, and not the other . . . but her words broke into his thoughts.

"Maybe you are good, eh?" She stopped and shot an accusing look at him. Her high cheekbones were pale circles under her wounded eyes. "I was good once, too." Her whole face was once again a mask of nobility, defying challenge. "But one must eat. One must live," she insisted. Then, in a gentler tone she said, "Good people don't understand things like that."

They continued their walk, crossing the Pont Royal; her high heels clicked beside him. How many nights had he crossed this bridge alone, leaned on the railing gazing down at the green water below, and thought of how good it would be to be in Paris with a woman, with a woman one loved. He stopped and she with him and the two of them looked back from whence they had come; the bright lights of the Champs-Elysées made the sky glow. Down the river Notre Dame basked in the light of its nighttime illumination, a green and silver monument. The girl beside him turned to look at it, too. But there was in him no joy with her. She was sad . . . and she did not belong to him. Still, it was that very atmosphere of sadness about her that attracted him. They were together in their loneliness.

He took her to the Chez François on Rue Sabot. He had often eaten there and the waitress took them to his usual table in the upstairs dining room. When he removed her coat, he was surprised by her smallness. Her narrow shoulders sloped away from a slender neck, elongated even as her nose was elongated. Her black hair was long and straight, curving inward as if to encircle her face before dropping across her white collar to her shoulders where it blended with the black of her dress.

After they had ordered, they did not speak; they ate as if the meal were some silent ritual they were performing. If she was famished, she did not lose her poise, but ate slowly

148

and with easy grace. When he refilled her wine glass, she merely nodded her thanks, her shaded eyelids opening more fully, her eyes meeting his in a gaze which made him turn his own to his plate. The silence was natural to him; he had often eaten here alone and in silence. Now the silence seemed richer, the woman sharing it seemed to be at home in it.

Out in the street again, she took possession of his arm and said, "You are very nice." They cut across to the Rue du Dragon and walked up to Boulevard St. Germain, passing the small church on the corner of Rue des Saints-Pères. "And you do have money."

"It must last a very long time."

She laughed for the first time, a quick brief laugh. "I will not steal it."

"Where are we going?"

"Why, to my room."

He did not protest. Indeed, he was reluctant to leave her. They passed a wine shop where the merchant was just putting up his shutters. "Buy some wine," she said, and he bought two bottles of the man's white.

Her room was not much different from his own. When she had turned on the single bulb that hung from the flaking yellow ceiling, he saw a heavy, wooden bed and beside it the inevitable night table with a lamp. He took her coat and his own and dropped them across the back of a wooden chair with padded seat and arms that sat near the window which opened out into the dark of night. The room was cold as his own was always cold and he knew that the radiator framed by the chipped and cracked marble of the imitation fireplace was also cold. She went to the washstand and took two glasses from the shelf beneath the mirror. As she washed the glasses in the basin, he opened one of the bottles. While waiting for her to finish, he glanced around the room. It could be his room, anyone's room in a hotel anywhere; only the bidet and the large wardrobe

149

closet with brass fittings marked it as a room in Paris. There were no marks of her presence here, no pictures on the walls, nothing. He had often felt the pang of his own homelessness and he now experienced the same ache upon recognizing hers.

She brought the glasses and he poured the wine. Kicking off her heels, she sat on the bed, her back against the high brown headboard, her legs stretched in front of her, one slightly on top of the other. Raising the glass, she said: "To love."

Silently he drank and as he drank, he continued to gaze at her. She did not seem to mind, but looked intently at her wine. "Once I loved a boy," she said after a while. "Would you care to hear about that?"

"All right."

"I loved him and the war killed him," she said flatly. "That's the story."

There was another long pause; he turned to look out of the window. It was dark out there and the street offered up no sound. A chill breeze struck him and shivering he got up to close the window. The girl shifted on the bed behind him. He threw the bolt on the window, picked up the wine bottle and went toward the bed; but she had put her glass on the nightstand and was now stretched full length on top of the covers, her hands under her head, her eyes closed. He returned to the table, poured himself another glass of wine and sat down.

"Shut off the light," she said and he got up and pulled the string, making the room as dark as the outside. Sitting down in the chair again, he sipped at his wine. From the bed he heard her move; the small lamp on the nightstand snapped on and she was sitting up, looking at him with her wide, surprised eyes. "Aren't you going to take me?"

"I don't know," he said.

"You are so strange," she said, standing up and removing her dress. She dropped it to the floor and in a few minutes her slip fell in a soft pile on top of it. She sat on the edge of the bed and undid her stockings, carefully rolling them down her slender legs and placing them in a drawer on the night table. He watched as if at some ballet while she moved about and the girdle and brassière fell on top of the slip. Her liberated body glowed golden in the yellow light of the tiny lamp and she faced him, arms outstretched.

No desire stirred in him, no emotion save pity. Mechanically, he lifted his glass and drank.

Her eyes widened, almost in horror. She elevated her chin in a gesture betrayed by the tremble in her voice. "Am I not beautiful?" She ran her hands down her flanks over the full curve of her buttocks and up her inner thighs, widening her fingers as she passed over the gentle fold of her stomach and finally cupping them under her breasts. Her body undulated gently, she closed her eyes and swayed, humming as if in ecstasy. Then, with a quick sob, she collapsed to the bed and wept.

Her weeping brought him to the bed. He took her head on his lap and began to stroke her hair. She turned her eyes to him, eyes rapid with fright. "Why don't you want me? Is it because I am no longer pretty?"

"You are . . ." he paused, "very beautiful."

"Then why?" she pleaded, her eyes full of tears. "Is it because I am a . . ." The fright grew larger in her eyes. "Are you worried because . . . about your body . . . about disease?"

"No."

"Maybe then it is your soul. Perhaps you are religious. Then it is your soul." She scanned his face wildly. "I will take care of your soul. Oh, what am I saying?" She turned her head away, pushed her small fists to her eyes, and wept uncontrollably.

He stroked her forehead with the palm of his hand, brushing the hair back and allowing it to tumble through his fingers. What, indeed, held him back? He had desired women he had only glanced at on the street more than he now desired this one who offered him her body. But the very emotion she roused in him was contrary to passion. She was too like a child; it would be difficult to guess her age, eighteen, twenty-eight, somewhere in between. She was a child now. She had quieted under his stroking and her eyes were closed. He pulled the covers back from the bed and lifted her onto the sheet, then gently covered her. Switching off the lamp, he filled his glass at the table and dropped into the chair once again.

They were total strangers; he didn't even know her name. Why was she so insistent? Perhaps she wanted to pay for the meal, but that thought in itself was repugnant to him. If only she had not mentioned money, if only she hadn't tried to sell her body; yes, that was what hurt. He didn't want just a body, he wanted a person. That was what was wrong on the bridge, what was wrong from the start to the finish. In a way he knew the sort of person she was, and it was that very recognition of her as a person that made lust impossible. She should be cared for, not used. He roused himself. His glass was empty and he had begun to doze. Standing up, he separated his coat from hers and started for the door, but stopped to look at the bed. She had cried herself to sleep. He didn't want to hurt her any more than she had already been hurt. Dropping his coat on the back of the chair, quietly, slowly, in the darkness he undressed and got into bed. She turned on her back with a sigh as if to welcome him.——

Neatly, he folded the page and set it to one side. He did not know what he would do with it, but he could not destroy it; that was too much like destroying a person. That, he now realized, was what bothered him about Red's remark. A Jap whore is an object, but the person who wrote the letter was a woman. How had she put it? He opened the page once more and sought out the words: "like ordinary girl of female sex." If you thought of her as a person, then

152

you couldn't just throw her aside, casually destroy her . . . And he began to see that this was what bothered him about that girl, about the enemy soldiers, about Prevot, Duke, and all the rest. He was not able to make objects out of them: "the enemy," "the psycho," "the whore."

As it had each day, the rain came for a few hours, just enough to keep the ground soggy, the sky dismal. At four o'clock he called in the radio check, then prepared his meal: heating a can of stewed chicken and making a cup of coffee. Sitting at table, sipping the coffee which he had gotten too hot, he heard two mortar rounds crumple in. Grabbing his helmet, he flicked on the machine and started out; as he ran from the bunker, he heard another round vomit out of the tube and he threw himself into the forward position in time to see the shell burst below him, halfway up the forward slope of the hill. He clutched the stop button, waiting, ears probing the silence for the next sound, but none came. When he returned through the rain to the bunker, he tossed the cold coffee out and lay down on his cot to smoke a cigarette.

The smoke curled above him and he turned slightly, shifting his body on the rude cot. On his breast he felt in an unfamiliar way the familiar pressure of the ikon. Unbuttoning his pocket, he brought out the package and unwrapped it, laying first the plastic, then the velvet sheath on his chest and finally holding the ikon above him. Lovelier than he had remembered it, the golden image seemed to focus a spear of light upon him. The delicate face, serene and yet imbued with a profound sadness, gazed at the Child nestled in the right hand, the Child with face upturned toward its mother. The mutual contemplation of the Mother and the Child touched a wound within him.

He had visited Chartres. The cathedral was all airiness, as if the granite defied its very principles to leap toward heaven in a surge of joy. Inside, Notre Dame de la Belle Verrière reigned from her radiant window-throne, the Child

153

at her center, His hand raised in benediction. Angels arched around, wafting incense of praise. The stones denied their weight and danced beneath her gaze. The sun itself bowed to her, putting on robes of blue, red, orange, gold, all the tints of joy, as it entered that holy place.

In contrast, the ikon, though richly clad in gold and painstakingly embellished with gems, conveyed none of that joyous lyricism. The artist had delineated a face of contained majesty, of compassion, a face calmed by sorrow. The Child's upturned face was expressive of a like compassion, the tiny hand stretched out to console His Mother.

Restless, Warren laid the ikon on the cot and walked to the door. Outside the rain sloshed heavily at the already pulpy hillside. He lifted his poncho from its peg on the wall and tugged himself into it. Then, settling his steel helmet firmly on his head, he stepped outside; the rain splattered against his poncho. He slogged through the earth, gummy as treacle, to the highest point of the hill. Hidden were the tanks in the valley ahead; the valley itself was lost in a wash of gray rain as were the hollows behind him and the mountains, too.

In silence heightened by the sweepings of the rain, Warren contemplated the scene; it was like a watercolor, the harsh elements softened by the fluid medium, the spiny ridges dissolved under the blur of rain.

——One wintry day, the rain pouring down, he was standing with his father and mother at a back window watching the storm. His father couldn't work when it rained and his mother had paused in her cleaning of the house. He was too young for school. They stood side by side, listening to the rolling thunder and watching the lightning and thick gray rain. The wind screamed about the house and then a great shimmer of lightning flashed nearby, there was a shudder of thunder: his father turned about and dashed

154

to the front of the house, his mother following, and he scampering after.

When he reached the front room, the door was open and outside in the alley a thick wire was lashing about. Over the wind, over the thunder and through the rain, his father's voice boomed, "It'll catch the house on fire." His father was leaping over the twisting wire and darting about in the mud. He saw his father stop and clutch at the sputtering snake. He heard his mother scream and he saw his father stiffen, falling backwards with the wire in his hand. His mother was still screaming when a man appeared out of the rain and pushing them aside ran into the house, tracking mud over the linoleum his mother had just mopped. His mother stopped screaming and was crying when the man, running from the house with a broom, shouted to her to telephone an ambulance. She ran off through the mud of the alley and disappeared in a cloak of rain. He saw the man using the wooden end of the broom to push the wire from his father's hand. Moving from the house doorway, stepping into the wet, he edged closer to the man with the broom. The man called to him to get out of the way, but when the man began to push the wire farther down the alley, Warren tiptoed over and looked down at his father's face: it was blue and his mouth was flecked with foam, the eyes, wide open, were staring up at him. Large drops of water were hitting his father on the cheeks, the lips, even the eyeballs, but he did not move. Warren stood and stared at his father, his father in the mud, on his back, with strange blue face, bulging eyes wide open, thick lips, foaming mouth, and the rain drenching him.

His mother returned and carried him away from his father and a few minutes later the ambulance, that had come to take his father away forever, splashed through the puddles.——

Now, remembering, he felt again that pang, a sudden conviction of his own isolation. The world seemed to be

155

sliding away from him. At his feet a chasm gulfed wide; his father taken from him, he had been a stranger to his mother, unable to respond to the desire to communicate that had gripped him often, most of all on her deathbed. After her death, he had sold the house and gone to France seeking—consciously, painfully—some meaning to life, to his existence on the earth. But he had come to no conclusions. Between all other men and himself had been that same gap, and now he was gripped by the awful image of himself as a stranger on the earth. He wanted to reach out and caress the shifting hills, to draw them unto himself, to take care of them—but they were alien and separate. Now that desire to communicate crested in upon him like a strong wave which, while thundering above, exerted a powerful undertow sucking at his destruction.

Oh, for a word from Jean, for the flavor of her speech, her smile. Slender, bright-faced, she had entered his life and her presence had given hope, her wide eyes lived in his mind and he could almost touch the strands of her hair.

They had agreed not to write.

"Because," she had said, "we must think this out. It's important to discover God's will for us . . ."

But his own will had brought him here.

Had his refusal to unmake the decision been rooted only in the fear that such a turning away from the test would convict him of cowardice? Or wasn't there another fear, unrecognized at the time, a fear of that other realm, that unknown land that opened before him after he had met Jean?

He moved restlessly, forced his thoughts back to his father's death. That act, so heroic and unnecessary and even stupid, also had been freely chosen. He smothered, as he had smothered so often in the past, the reproach he felt welling up in him toward the man who had left his mother without a husband and himself without a father. For he must have been thinking of them when he chose to

156

do that which brought him down, flat on his back in the mud, the rain pelting his face, dead.

A shift in the wind sent a spatter of raindrops under the edge of his helmet and into his face. He turned and plodded back to the bunker. Hanging his helmet on its peg, he pulled the dripping poncho over his head. After changing his muddy boots for a dry pair, he bent over the metal canister that did duty as a heater and built a charcoal fire. When the black sticks were glowing, he brought the ikon near the stove and sat down to look at it.

Most of the ikons he had seen were larger than this, but he had seen small ones, too: little paintings on wood, encased in brass, in the antique shops of Paris—probably sold by *emigrés* down to their last franc, or taken by the concierge raiding the ikon altar after death ended the exile of a roomer—none of them had been as richly embellished as this. Prevot's White Russian must, indeed, have been a princess to give him such a precious gift; sad, nut-brown Prevot, his Adam's apple bobbing in his throat, had been loved by a princess. But she had placed a charge upon him and he had not met it, had died before he could slay the dragon.

Warren looked about the bunker before getting up and going to the shelf above the desk where he cleared a space and empedestaled the ikon. Then, pulling a box over to the desk, he sat down, elbows on the map board, chin in his hands, eyes fixed upon the ikon.

——"I'm trying to find out why I'm alive," he said one day to the old monk as they walked in the garden. He was nearing the end of his two-week stay and that morning he had decided to tell the monk of his reason for coming.

"You are trying to find out why there is something rather than nothing," the old monk commented, "and that is the greatest question one can ask." He paused beside a rose bush, lifted its single wilting flower between his fingers, and gazed at it a moment. "All creation," he said, as if speaking to the dying rose, "is an act of love. We exist because God loves us." He took his hand away from the blossom and the flower drooped once more. A single petal fell to the earth. They walked on.

"But Father . . ." Warren began, "I don't . . ."

"Let us sit here," the monk indicated a small stone bench alongside the walk. "This time of year, autumn, winter, always make me realize how old I am." His smile creased his entire face, bringing a lively glitter to his brown eyes. "The years have gone by so swiftly." He sighed, put his hands inside his wide sleeves and looked out over the garden toward the great stone monastery building. "You see life as a problem to be solved, a question to be answered," he said. "But life is a mystery. A mystery is to be contemplated, meditated upon, experienced, but it cannot be solved." He looked at Warren and smiled again. "We can only understand and live with the mystery of ourselves if we love . . . everything is wrapped up in that mystery of love. Because God loves us, we exist. Because God loves us, He became man born of woman and He came to dwell with us and in us . . ."

Warren was uneasy whenever the monk spoke of Christ, but he said nothing. He looked at the dying leaves and the cold stones and listened.——

Only much later did he stir, rummaging through the papers on the desk until finding some dirty stationery with a Red Cross letterhead. "Dear Jean," he began, wishing he had something other than a pencil to write with. "I love you," he wrote on. "Something you don't want me to say, but something I have to say at this time and from this place. I must hear from you. Something we agreed not to do, but something we must do—you must do—if I am to retain any sort of hold upon myself. Please write. I need you." He paused, unable to write any more. When he raised his hand, the paper followed; he shook it loose and it dropped back to the desk; sticky, where his hand had rested, soiled like

158

himself by its existence here, the note begged for destruction. As he hesitated, his eyes raised to the ikon. As if by command, he signed his name to the page, boldly printed his address at the bottom and stuffed the note into a coffee-stained envelope. After addressing the envelope and putting it into his jacket pocket, he got up and prepared a cup of coffee.

All the next day the rain continued to fall. There was no firing. The other position called over and asked him to push the stop button so that they might check their equipment, but otherwise he spent the day in the bunker. He cleaned his weapon, scrubbed the mud from his boots, washed his socks: routine actions which left his mind free to digest the swallowed whole of those past weeks . . .

He had killed a man. Faithful to the teaching received, he'd killed . . . a human life ended in one quick movement. An encounter of a moment for each of them, the killer and the killed, a moment testifying to life's fragility.

Unlike White, who attacked life as if it were an enemy to be throttled, Warren realized that he had become open to all things; allowing things to happen to him, he accepted each new imposition of men and events without struggle. Looking back, he could see but two events initiated by himself: his being in Korea and his relationship with Jean. The first move made, he had allowed the action to carry him along without attempting to direct it. The killing had been more of an event happening to him than an act precipitated by him—although his eye leveled along the barrel, his finger triggered a weapon he had cleaned and loaded. His hands itched with dried blood, the same hands which had lifted Jean's face that evening when he had kissed her forehead, saying, "It's all very pure . . ." Could purity survive here? The letter Red had shoved at him, the letter which still rested on one corner of the table, had seemed intensely pure. ". . . is like lost alone in desert without you . . . but . . ." and then it lost its poetry . . . "but must catch one GI unwillingly . . ." The girl trying to "be good" would stand on a streetcorner screeching, "Me hot to go, Joe," take into her arms, open up her body, allow to penetrate her womb a man of no-name, a "joe" who will—after pouring into her his momentary heat—call her "bitch."

What anguish in life—for the girl acquiescing to the violence done her person, for all who try to "be good," for men deserted by wives tired of waiting, and young girls who find fornication "only natural," and for himself. Perhaps he had come here secretly desiring the end envisioned on the train ride—an end to anguish—and not Bernhardt's God. In a way, that was true, but the day he had thought was his last he had prayed; Rickley would probably say his prayer was answered, but was it? How reconcile this broken world with Rickley's affirmations, or Jean's, or the monks of Solesmes, or that of the nun who, dying, rejoiced? Was it the same world they looked out upon?

The next morning Sergeant Claypool phoned to say that Tex would come up to relieve him for two nights. Warren was to bring all of his gear down with him because it was uncertain whether they would send him back up to that position. While packing, he slipped the ikon into its protective covers and put it in his pocket with the letter to Jean. He sensed a harmony between the two, but did not pursue the thought as he prepared to go down.

On the way down the hill, he passed Tex.

"Say," Tex said, "Foggy'll break his scrawny back with that water can. Would ya mind totin' it up here?"

Down the steps Warren saw Folger buckling under the weight of the five-gallon can lashed to the pack rack on his back. It hadn't rained for a few hours, but the steps remained dangerously slick and Folger staggered as if at any moment he would tumble to the base of the hill. To maintain his balance on the treacherous stairway, Warren took each downward step almost sideways. "I'll take that,"

160

he said upon reaching the puffing Folger, "if you'll haul this junk down to the jeep."

"Gladly," Folger wheezed, struggling to free his shoulders from the cutting straps. Warren helped him to get free, then handed over his own gear. "Heavier 'n hell," Folger grunted, boosting the pack onto Warren's shoulders.

Warren heard the water sloshing within the can as he climbed back up the slope, carefully choosing each footing to avoid a slide that could break his back. Tex at the top of the hill started to come down.

"It's okay," Warren called, "I've got it."

Tex waited where he was and then walked with Warren to the bunker.

"Well," Tex said, "what d'ya think of C-ration hill?"

"Not so bad." Warren relaxed as Tex relieved him of the can and dropped it to the ground near the bunker door. "Nice and quiet."

"Aw, you hit it lucky. Just my bitchin' luck to have 'em clobber this place for a week. Just as well. I don't like it none too quiet up here. All alone. Nothin' to do 'cept think. My God, a man could go crazy up here."

"Nice place to meditate on your sins."

"Sins. Ha!" the Texan roared. "That's a laugh! You're a real joker." He pounded Warren on the back with a beefy hand. "Man, we're more sinned against than sinnin' here. Ain't had no good piece of tail in nearly three months."

As Warren began the descent once again he heard the Texan bellow, "Meditate on your sins! Ha! That's a good one!"

In the jeep Folger seemed morose. "They're thinking of putting me on line," he said. "Ain't got enough men, so they want to put me up there."

"It's not so bad."

"Not for you guys. You've done everything. I've not done

161

everything yet. I don't want to go getting killed without having done everything."

"What's everything?"

"Oh, you know . . . everything!"

"Nobody has done everything."

"Oh, you know, women and all that." Folger faltered over the admission. "You may as well know, I ain't had no woman yet. Everybody knows. They all razz me about it. I can't help it. I *want* to," he wailed. "It isn't as if I didn't *want* to. Those guys act like I'm—" The voice cracked. "Well, I'm gonna. Before I get home, I gonna." A grim line of determination seized the weak mouth, then the chin wavered again. "Anyway, you can see I shouldn't be sent on line before I've done everything, can't you?"

"The needs of the service . . ." Warren left the sentence unfinished. "Virgins die here," White had said, but how much of a virgin was Folger? Warren looked sideways at his companion. What fitful dreams of fornication devoured this little man? Warren scanned the face; the weak eyes could easily be imagined devouring the obscene pictures some of the men carried with them, the wobbling lips wet with expectation. Tex, the colored man in the shower, Red, all of the narrators of sexual experience seemed healthy in comparison with this impure virgin. Warren turned his gaze to the mud of the road. The suck of the tires escaping the downward drag of the muck hummed loudly in his ears, almost drowning the words of the man beside him as he spoke again.

"I tried once," Folger implored. "I ain't told nobody that. Don't you tell, please, they'll razz hell outta me. They don't think I'm as much a man as them. But I am!" The whimper was lost under the determined statement, then it returned. "I went to a place in Sasebo when I first got over, but I couldn't do it. I got in bed with this gal and nothing happened. We tried, but nothing happened." He turned

162

his wide eyes beseechingly at Warren. "It ain't like I haven't tried."

Warren wanted to be away from the whine of that voice, away from the pleading eyes. "Maybe you're impotent," he said, knowing it was cruel.

"Oh, no," Folger said. "It ain't that."

"How do you know?"

"I just know," Folger said guiltily. "I think I just got scared. I read in a sex magazine about it. It was psychological, that's what. Anyway, 'til I get a chance to . . . to do everything, I don't want to get sent up on line."

"When will that be?"

"I get my five days R and R next month."

"So you're going to spend it in a brothel?"

"You mean a whorehouse? Sure."

"Why?"

"Why? 'Cause they razz the pants offa me all the time, that's why."

"Why don't you tell them to mind their own business?"

Folger cast a bewildered look at Warren and then said, "You crazy? You gotta do it sometime."

"When you get married."

"You *believe* that?" Folger's eyes grew large.

"Sure."

"Nobody thinks that any more."

"I know some who do."

"Ah," Folger said, "religious guys, maybe, nobody else." He swung the jeep into the regimental area. "You won't tell anybody what I said, will ya?"

"No," Warren said. "I won't rat on you."

A short, heavy sergeant watched the jeep park and then came alongside. He pulled a juicy cigar from his loose lips and spat. "So you're Warren, eh? I'm Claypool. How'd you make out up there?"

"Fine, I guess."

"Wasn't much going on."

"Which was fortunate," Warren added.

"Yeah." Sergeant Claypool scrutinized Warren with the air of a butcher eying a side of beef. He rubbed his red sausage fingers along his chin and put the cigar back into his mouth. "Yeah. You did all right," he said. "I don't know if I care to put a green man up on that position alone, though." He continued to appraise Warren with his lazy eyes. "Damned S-1 isn't giving us any bastard replacements. Then they ride our cans for not getting every weapon the enemy fires."

Warren hauled his pack out of the rear seat of the jeep while Sergeant Claypool looked on, his small eyes almost malevolent. Under the sullen gaze, Warren became conscious of each of his movements.

"When you get your gear stashed in the bunker, you can eat," the low voice rasped. Then, plunging one of the sausages in Folger's direction, Claypool announced: "Foggy's taking some guys to the shower point after noon chow, so you can go along. Ain't that right, Foggy?"

"First I heard of it," Folger said. "I gotta work on the vehicle."

"The hell you do. All you gotta do you can do when you get back." Sergeant Claypool spat again. "Might take a shower yourself," he added in an ugly tone, "a cold one."

Warren lugged his pack to the bunker. Nevers was coming up the steps, cramming a helmet down over his shiny black hair.

"Chow time," Nevers said, "chop-chop. Come along. I'll wait." Warren tossed his gear on an empty cot and joined Nevers. "I got down yesterday," Nevers said, "go back up tomorrow. How'd you like the lonely outpost, C-ration hill?"

Warren told him.

"If we don't get a few more men, Claypool's gonna put Foggy on line and drive the damned jeep himself. Says he

164

could do it in half the time Foggy takes. Probably could."

"Folger told me about it."

"Oh, he's so scared he wets his pants thinking about it. Might do him some good, ya know? He needs something." Nevers turned his sharp face to the sky. "Damn, it's gonna pour this afternoon again. Look at the sky."

Each man grabbed a tray and moved through the short line. Nevers' commentary on his last week's activities was chopped into fragments by his comments to the cooks and K.P.'s who ladled out the warm food.

"Anyway," he said, as they turned from the serving line and carried their food-heavy trays over to a log that had just been vacated, "take a word from me and be careful of Claypool."

"What do you mean?"

"I mean, play it cool. Don't cross him . . ."

"Well, I don't think . . ."

"He's a sonafabitch when he's crossed. I . . ." his voice trailed as Folger approached with his tray.

"Going to the showers in fifteen minutes," Folger said in a voice as sallow as his face.

Back from the shower point, his body refreshed and warmed by water and clean clothes, Warren nearly collided with Lieutenant Held as he came up the bunker stairway.

"Say," the lieutenant stopped him. "You know Lieutenant Ordway?"

Startled, Warren replied, "Yes, sir."

"I thought you might. Saw on your record that you were at the same post with him—on Division Faculty. I knew him at Psycho Warfare School. God," his head wagged from side to side, "he's a genius, a real genius."

"Yes, sir."

"I got some letters from him a while back, but I guess

he's getting busier all the time. He still holding a captain's position?"

"Last I heard he was, sir."

"God. I don't understand it." The young face registered honest pain. "If anybody deserves promotion, Ordway does." The head moved again in puzzlement. "Top of his class at the school and didn't even half try."

Warren waited while Lieutenant Held, the paratrooper's badge glistening on the breast of his tightly tailored fatigue tunic, looked at the muddy steps as if the answer to his problem might be found there.

"How'd the men like him?" The lieutenant's smooth face was lifted for the delivery of the question.

"Not too well, sir."

"Why not?"

"They felt he harassed them too much."

"He's a perfectionist!" Lieutenant Held declared. "But he doesn't ask anything he won't do himself!"

"Yes, sir."

"People just don't understand him. They say he's too military, but, by God, you don't rack up silver stars and bronze stars with clusters for being civilian." Indignation gave way to softer tones as the lieutenant continued, "He's a lonely man, you know. It's funny, a man as brilliant as Ordway has so few friends. I may as well tell you, I was the only officer at the school who liked him. The others thought he was . . . well, anyway, they were jealous of him. One night we went out and he had a few drinks too many and he told me he has no real friends, not one. Can you imagine that? A man as brilliant, as much a genius as Ordway is and he has no friends."

"Genius is like that," Warren said.

"Yes." The lieutenant snapped a look into Warren's eyes. "By God, you've got something there. And it's because of envy. People are jealous of a man as brilliant as Ordway.

166

Well, I'm not. I admire him. I try to follow his example. That's the only way to improve yourself, isn't it?"

"Yes, sir."

"I'm going to write him another letter one of these days. He's probably too busy to answer, but, by God, I intend to write him anyway. He's still there, you say?"

"As far as I know, sir."

"Fine." The lieutenant took another step up the stairs, then turned. "Remind me to show you the letters he wrote me."

"Yes, sir. And by the way, where do I mail a letter, sir?" At the shower point Warren had found the letter to Jean still in his pocket.

"I'll take it," the lieutenant said. "I'm going to the orderly room."

Warren handed him the letter. Looking at the address, Lieutenant Held smiled. "To the girl, eh?"

"Yes, sir."

"Ordway had a fiancée once. He showed me her picture. A school teacher. Intellectual, just like Ordway. Funny thing, though, about them. He told me that even they weren't what he called good friends. Now doesn't that sound crazy?"

"Yes, sir."

"Well, that will be all, Private Warren. Oh, yes, how did you like your first taste of counterfire work?"

"Fine, sir."

"Too bad we had to leave you up there alone. We're short, you know."

"Yes, sir. I've been meaning to ask if you'd be interested in another man from Baker company."

"It'll be difficult to raid another one from them, but if he's good, we can probably work it. What's his name?" The lieutenant pulled a small leather notebook from his pocket and uncapped his ball point pen.

"Tom Rickley. He's a rifleman now, but I think this is right down his alley."

"Does he want to come?"

"I don't see why he wouldn't. He's a very bright boy, sir."

"Good, good," Lieutenant Held said. "Tom Rickley, Baker company, rifleman. Got it." He flipped the notebook closed. "I'll want to talk to you some more about Ordway. Show you his letters."

"Yes, sir."

"It was a privilege for you to meet that man, you know."

"Yes, sir."

The lieutenant gazed at the black book in his hand. His head semaphored bewilderment. "I just don't understand it. Still a lieutenant." He walked off to his jeep.

After chow that evening as Warren stood in line to wash his tray, someone behind him touched his arm. "I don't recall your name, but mine's Lefevre." Turning, Warren recognized the man he had met for a few moments on the day of his assignment here. "You were interested," Lefevre said, "in your friends at Baker company. If you'd care to come up to the bunker, I've got a report on a couple of them."

As they walked toward the S-2 bunker, Lefevre said, "Did you know a fellow named Rickley?"

"Has he been hurt?"

"Oh, no. I was just asking if you knew him."

"He was in my squad."

"He tell you he'd been in a seminary?"

"No."

"He was; we were there together. Got out for different reasons, though. Funny that we should both wind up in the same regiment here."

"He might get transferred to counterfire."

"That would prove interesting," Lefevre said as he entered the sandbagged passageway and opened the wooden

168

door. They stepped into the warm, brightly lighted room.

A lone man, working at his acetate-covered drawing board, glanced up only briefly and then returned to his work. "You're off duty, Lefevre, why don't you take advantage of it?" he asked, bowing over his tracing board.

"I'm getting out as soon as I check on something," Lefevre said, spreading some papers on one of the tables in front of him. "Here we are," he tapped one, "Warrant Officer Wise, Private Zikowlsky. Know either of them?"

"Both."

"See you later," Lefevre said to the man at the desk.

"Roger." The other did not look up from his work.

Lefevre held the door open for Warren and the two stepped out into the cold passageway again. "My bunker's up the hill," he said, "I've got some cognac there. Come on."

Warren followed Lefevre as he led the way up the slope. The sky had darkened rapidly, night was only a few moments away. About ten feet ahead of him, his poncho-clad guide, already becoming an indefinite blur against the hillside, stopped and waited for him to catch up.

"They were riding in a jeep," Lefevre said when Warren reached his side. "Coming down from the line. A direct hit from a .76 round." Then, abruptly turning to the left, Lefevre led the way along a narrow path to a bunker door. "Careful of the doorway here," he said, "it might be too low for you. In fact, you better wait until I get the light on or you'll break your neck in the dark." Lefevre went inside, closing the door behind him. A moment later he called, "Okay," and Warren opened the door, stepped into a dark chamber, and closed the door behind him. Then, pulling aside the shelter-half that separated him from the main bunker, he entered the room.

"You'd think we were getting hit all the time, from the precautions they make us take around here," Lefevre said, pulling his poncho over his head. "Of course, they're

169

right," he went on when his rumpled black hair again made its appearance. "What is it? The light from a match can be seen for how many miles?" He hung his poncho on a peg in the dark passageway.

"I forget. They ever get hit back here?"

"Oh, a round or two has come in. If you ask me, it's just an accident; they overshoot. Sit down, make yourself at home," Lefevre said, doing so himself. "Now, I've got that bottle here." He brought the bottle from beneath his pillow as Warren sat down on the cot opposite him. "Valuable stuff, this," he said. "Hennessy, no less." Putting the bottle on the wooden box beside his bunk, Lefevre stooped to reach into the box itself. "Voilà," he said, holding up two brandy snifters.

Lefevre poured the cognac, handed a glass to Warren and raised his own in a silent toast. The cognac brought a biting warmth to Warren's chill lips. He sipped slowly at the rim of the glass, savoring the liquor's taste. After a while, Lefevre lifted his glass up to the light and peered at its color appreciatively. "Good stuff." Warren was struck by the sharp line of Lefevre's profile. His nose, a little too long, his chin jutting forward, his wavy hair thrown back away from his sloping brow, gave him the air of an aristocrat or a poet.

"Why did Rickley leave the seminary?" Warren asked.

"Met a girl on vacation," Lefevre said, turning the glass slowly about to watch the effect of the light on it. "Fell in love; decided it wasn't his vocation."

"And you?"

Lefevre brought the glass down, leaned forward to peer directly at Warren. "You a Catholic?"

"No."

"Then why ask?" He dropped his gaze to the cognac once again. "You wouldn't understand anyway," he said in a softer tone, at the same time setting the glass on the box beside him. He got up and took some matches from a small

170

shelf above the oil heater; he knelt and adjusted the thermostat. Warren tasted his cognac, thinking of Zikowlsky and his little mother who had chased him with a baseball bat and thrown apples at him when he fled to a tree. Zikowlsky was gone and with him was gone the quiet Warrant Officer, that middle-aged man whose comment on Duke still rang clear in Warren's mind: "The poor damned kid." Prevot, too, and Lim. And here he sat with the tang of cognac on his lips, the heat of it in his mouth . . .

The tin stove was beginning to warm the room while Lefevre held his glass, now nearly empty, between his two hands and peered into it. "If you've never had the Faith," he said, "you don't know what it is to lose it." He drained his glass and put it on the box. "If you don't mind, I've got to get some sack time in." He began to unbuckle his boots.

Within a few minutes Warren was making his way back down the slope, through a slow-falling rain, to the counterfire bunker. As he passed the kitchen-tent, he could hear the sound track of a movie, accompanied by whistles and catcalls. As he expected, he found the counterfire bunker deserted.

The next morning he awoke to see Nevers reclining on the cot across the way, reading a comic book. "Decided you might want the sack time," Nevers said. "Breakfast wasn't worth the effort of chewing. Noon chow pretty soon anyhow."

"Thought you were going back up today," Warren said.

"Ah, Foggy's piddlin' around in the supply room, trying to get some stuff. He takes an age."

"Where's Claypool?"

"Over the orderly room with the lieutenant, filing reports." Nevers returned to his comic book. "Right with you," he said, "almost through." His brow furrowed as he studied each colored box before snapping his small eyes eagerly to the next one. Reaching the end of the story,

171

Nevers sighed and put the comic book to one side. "Where were ya yesterday evening?"

"With Lefevre."

"I thought you and he'd get along. I can spot your type. A brain like him. Bet you read a lot, too."

"Not a thing since I got here."

"I do. Not just this stuff, ya know. I read the classics."

"Oh."

"Yeah, but wouldn't ya know it, I ain't been able to find one of them here. Just these." Nevers pushed at the comic book with a distasteful expression. "These guys ain't got no real taste, ya know, not for the good stuff. I wrote my mom and asked her to send me a bunch of the classics."

"What ones?"

"Oh, any she can find. I know they brought out a whole lot of 'em since I been gone. Told Mom to get what ones she could. Then I won't have to read this crud, ya know." He waved his hand at the comic book again. "Tenshun," he called, leaping from his bunk.

Lieutenant Held had entered, followed by Sergeant Claypool. "At ease," the lieutenant said, "as you were." Then turning to the workbench near the door he put his hand upon the sound-locator that lay there. "This the one?"

"Yes, sir," Claypool said, pulling the cigar from between his large lips. "Can't do a thing with it. Had it apart twice and nothing comes of it."

The lieutenant took his hand off the machine and pushed his helmet back from his smooth forehead. "Nothing to do but take it to division then. I wasn't going today, but I can if Folger can't make it."

"Like I say," Claypool said, "that guy'll never get it there. Takes him all day to make the trip to the line and back. Today he's got Nevers to deliver and tomorrow the new guy."

"Well," the lieutenant sighed, "I'll run it down." Then looking at Warren, he asked, "Drive?"

"Yes, sir."

"Good. We'll leave after lunch."

"Yes, sir."

The rain had not ceased when, with Lieutenant Held beside him, Warren geared the jeep up on the Main Supply Route; green-robed M.P.'s left their cubicles at intersections to salute the lieutenant as the vehicle passed.

"I think we'll get your friend down," the lieutenant said. "I requested him yesterday, after I left you. We'll see."

"That's good news, sir."

"Be a break for him to come off the line. Or did he ask to be there, like you?"

"I don't think he did, sir."

"That's okay. I like the idea of having men with rifleman's experience." He paused. "Baker company a good outfit?"

"Good men, but short handed. Only one officer now."

"I don't understand the snarl," the lieutenant said slowly. "They've got plenty of men at the rear, quarter-master, artillery, all of them fully staffed. Division's bursting at the seams with typists." He shook his head.

"They nab them on the way through," Warren commented.

"Sir," the lieutenant reminded quietly.

"Sir."

"It's enough to disillusion a man," the lieutenant said, then added hurriedly, "I mean a man not devoted to the army."

"Yes, sir."

"Ordway's devoted to the army," the lieutenant continued as if it hadn't been a full day since they had last spoken of Ordway. "He really loves it. A real soldier, Ordway. I don't understand what's holding his promotions back. Then, there's all that business about a freeze on promotions for EM. It's tight for officers, too. Ordway ever tell you about his Korean experiences?" Lieutenant Held

173

looked up brightly, a note of enthusiasm in his voice. "No, sir."

"They gave him a heavy weapons platoon in Japan the night before it was shipped here. Most of the men were in sorry shape from the soft life in Japan, none of them really trained in their weapons. The moment he took command, Ordway put them on a schedule of calisthenics and weapons drill. He only had the three days on the boat over here, but by God he worked them. He told me about it. They hated his guts. Everybody else was laying around on the ship, loafing, while his men were either doing P.T. or practicing with their weapons. If anybody griped, and he heard about it, he gave them more drill. He knew they didn't like it, but when they hit Korea, he had a *team*. Some of them owe their lives to that training, don't you agree?"

"Yes, sir."

"That's the sort of soldier Ordway is: a perfectionist." Lieutenant Held meditated on the word for a while, then said, "I've got those letters to show you when we get out of this rain."

At division, Lieutenant Held directed Warren to an ordnance area where large green trailers were parked, their green metal stairways extending tonguelike into the mud. Warren carried the sound locator into one of the trailer workshops and Lieutenant Held discussed it with the repair man. As they left, Lieutenant Held told Warren to drive over to the Replacement Depot. "I've got a friend over there I want to see. Maybe he can do something about getting us some men."

The side trip took them through the town which Warren had viewed only momentarily on the hot, dust-clogged day nearly two months before. Robed figures huddled around small pots of fire inside the shops. Tiled roofs were washed of their dirt and showed rich red through the haze of the rain. Stray, stooped figures were on the sidewalks. A Korean policeman in black uniform saluted smartly as

174

they passed and smiled, showing large, flat teeth. The jeep approached a slow-moving stack of faggots from behind, and the sound of the vehicle caused the stack to hurry to one side of the roadway, exposing to view the short, bow-legged man bowed under the burden. His legs were bare and the mud clung like leggings to his calves. He stared at them as they drove by, Warren pulling the vehicle far to the left in order to avoid spattering the laborer. At one house, a man was feeding a fire that glowed in a tiled hole under the side of the building.

"Indirect heating," Warren explained, noticing Lieutenant Held's passing interest, "they had it ages ago," then, remembering, "sir."

The gate of the replacement company was reached and the Korean sentries ran from their boxes to open it. Warren followed the lieutenant's directions until they arrived in front of the orderly room.

"I know someone here, too, sir. Mind if I go see him?"

"Not at all. Get back here in a half-hour, though. We want to make it back to regiment in time for supper."

"Yes, sir."

Warren walked through the tent area; the earth that was anvil hard before, jarring the body with each step, now sucked at his feet, flowed over his boot tops. He could hear the talk of men in some of the tents, raucous sounds, a radio blaring out cowboy music. Above some of the tents smoke curled out of the tin chimneys, but many of the chimneys were dead and the rain fell on hollow canvas.

Opening the screen door of the quonset hut, Warren walked in. The front office was empty, the desks neatly arranged. The fan was gone from the top of the bar; instead a new tin stove, installed in the center of the room, gave off a warm glow. He walked through the opening in the partition.

Lesley was lying stomach downwards on his cot, his slippered feet in the air, his weight resting on his elbows while he studied a piece of paper on the clipboard in front of him. "Well, I'll be damned. Warren." He grinned cheerily, his snout wrinkling in glee. He swung about, plopping his feet to the floor, and stood up. One hand rushed to shake Warren's and the other, pen still clutched in it, swatted him on the back. "I knew you'd come down. Changed your mind after a taste of it, eh?"

Warren let his hand drop from the flabby grip and shook his head. "Social visit," he said, wondering now why he had bothered to come by.

"Oh." Most of the joy left the porcine features. "Well, let me know when you've had enough. Maybe I can do something for you."

"You can send me on R and R when my turn comes up."

"Pride, that's what it is," Lesley said petulantly. "You're just too stubborn to admit that you're wrong."

"Oh, can it, will you? I've come by to see how things are going with you."

"Great. Not much work, safe as a bug in a rug, warm bed, three hot meals, plenty of liquor, library." He waved his hand at the rows of books. "You just gotta play it wise. Here I am on permanent Rest and Recuperation and the folks think I'm a hero."

Lesley's leer caused Warren's stomach to knot. "A hero?" He dropped wearily on the nearby bunk and gazed at the bookshelves.

"Sure," Lesley affirmed, "listen to this." He picked up the clipboard and read from the attached page. "As we slog wearily through the mud, moving past the wounded who are moaning by the way, I think how fine it is to be fighting for freedom. When the rounds come crashing in and we fall on our faces in the slime, our bodies soaked with this filthy mire, I simply think that it is you that I'm defending and I feel strong, strong enough to live through this hell. I'm not sure I will, though, as many of the men who came with me are dead now or maimed. I feel my luck cannot hold out. If I should die, think only that it was for you—"

"Cut it!" Warren sprang to his feet, his hands clenched, blood pounded in his ears. "Tear that goddamned thing up!" He lunged for the clipboard. Startled, Lesley jumped back, the clipboard behind him. "Tear it up!" Warren commanded.

"Who in hell do you think you are?" Lesley moved away. "You've no right to talk to me that way." His lips wobbled, his whole face twitched. "I can write what I please to whom I please." His voice was high pitched, the spoiled child's voice. "Don't come near me! Get out of here. I didn't invite you in. Get out."

Warren dropped his hand, turned his back on the other. As he started to go through the partition, he stopped and, standing in the narrow aperture, turned. "Tell me. What do you gain by sending that filth to your parents?"

"There's nothing wrong with this!" The clipboard was waved in the pudgy hand. "You're just jealous because you don't have anybody to worry about you."

"I wouldn't want anybody to worry about me."

"Well, my folks *like* to worry about me. It makes them happy to feel their son loves them enough to die for them . . ."

"Do you?" Warren asked between tight lips. "Do you?"

"What business is it of yours? You're awful damned nosey now that you think you're a hero." Lesley's lips curled in a sneer. "A combat man. Glory happy, that's what you are. You've no right meddling in my life. I read you this because I thought you'd appreciate it. Why," the voice quavered, "why, it's almost poetry, it's so beautiful. But you can't see that. You're always trying to boss me around. Who do you think you are? Go back to your goddam line and don't come whining back to me when you want a soft post. You're no friend of mine any more."

The petulant wail was snapped off as Warren slammed

177

the screen door of the quonset hut behind him. At the jeep, he slid into his seat and his fingers tightened around the steering wheel not to relax until sometime later Lieutenant Held came down the wooden stairs from the orderly room.

"It's stopped raining, I see." The lieutenant held out his hand. Warren noticed for the first time that it had.

On the way back up the Main Supply Route, Lieutenant Held pulled out Ordway's letters. "You'll understand the man better when you hear these," he said. "I'll read them to you." The papers rustled as Lieutenant Held straightened them in his hand. "The first one isn't much, just a note telling me of an appointment we had broken; but this one he wrote when I told him about my promotion." The paper flapped in the wind. Lieutenant Held clutched it firmly by the edges, tilting his head to make out the words.

"Dear First Lieutenant Held: Congratulations, boy. But don't let it go to your head. Remember that I've got date of rank on you—ha, ha. That's what I like most about the army. You always know who is your superior and who is your subordinate. I'm still your superior, lad, and you're still my subordinate. Unless you make captain before I do, which is unthinkable, I'll always be ahead of you. That is if this new army doesn't do away with rank altogether. What with all this poppycock about asking instead of commanding, etc., it borders on anarchy already. Don't get carried away on all that baloney. Remember, you're not one of these lousy reservists or ROTC lieutenants, but a real officer of the Regular Army of the United States. Keep up the good work, lad, and I'll write you when I get those two bars so you can feel free to work for a couple yourself—ha, ha. Keep those bars polished, Lieutenant, they've got to serve for a long time. So long . . ."

Lieutenant Held folded the letter carefully and put it back into its envelope. "I told you he was a great man. A real officer. He eats and sleeps the army. This one," he said,

178

extracting another letter, "he wrote one night after he had been drinking. He drinks too much." Lieutenant Held's helmet rustled against his poncho as he shook his head. "But you can understand why when I read you this." He held the paper closer to his face.

"Dear Second Lieutenant Held," he read. "I was only a second lieutenant then," Held explained, "and Ordway wouldn't let me forget it." He chuckled and returned to the letter. "I write you this under the alchofluence of inkohol. I've something to tell you. Even if you are only a second lieutenant, we've hit it off well. We both love the army, that's why. You tried to talk me into not drinking that night you had to put me to bed and the next day. See, I remember. Well, Second Lieutenant Held, I've been thinking this evening while drinking—ha, ha,—that you'd drink, too, like me, if you had to forget what I've got to forget. What have I got to forget? Murder, that's what. I have bad dreams about the whole batch of people I murdered. Not soldiers, mind you, but people. I was moving with my patrol into a little village in North Korea and I got the feeling that we were being followed. I sent the boys on ahead and ducked into a doorway. The whole town seemed deserted, everybody indoors, and we didn't know whether the enemy was still there or not. We were taking no chances. I stood in this doorway and, sure enough, I heard the footsteps of somebody running, in short little runs, after my men. I got ready, then when he went by the doorway, I grabbed him by the throat. He wrestled free. I chased him and grabbed him again, this time in a space between two buildings. I held him against the wall and swatted him around a bit. Just then a board moved in a nearby fence. I fired one round into the fence. The boy I had been holding started to run. I cut him down. Then an old couple came running out of a house. The old man had a white beard, I remember it clear as day and he was shouting at me and waving a hoe.

179

I shot him. The woman screamed and came at me with a stick. I shot her. Then around the corner came two of the local cops and I shot both of them. Then it was quiet. These civilians were lying all around me, some of them not quite dead. My boys came back and I looked behind the fence. There was a child there. I had hit her right between the eyes. I had killed six people, and all because of some foolish boy who was curious. Count them, Second Lieutenant Held, six. A child, a boy of about fourteen, two old people, and two policemen. Sometimes I can convince myself that the policemen don't count, especially when I drink I can convince myself of that, because those policemen were all untrustworthy. But even then, I can't convince myself that the others don't count. I'd give all my ribbons away not to have killed those four. I tell you because we understood one another at the Psycho school. Remember . . ." Lieutenant Held paused to scan the rest of the letter. "That wouldn't interest you," he said. "It's about people you don't know." He slipped the letter into its envelope. "Right there!" Lieutenant Held said emphatically, "You can see why the man is so much above others. He *feels* things!"

The jellied road gave the wheels little traction and Warren concentrated on maintaining speed while keeping the jeep under control, but the lieutenant's words had projected a phantasm, clear and hard, into his consciousness . . .

———"I never made you happy," his mother had said weakly one evening, her body a skeletal frame, the skin on her face opaque, drawn tightly across the bones. With an effort she raised her hand to prevent his speaking. "We've been strangers." Her limp hand dropped of its own weight onto the white sheet. "Don't think badly of me. You're so much like your father was." Her eyes, dilated by pain-reducing drugs, looked out of their gray sockets, two luminous spots in the dead flesh. "You feel things deeply."———

180

Back at the regimental area, Warren spent the few minutes remaining before chow time in the counterfire bunker. Sergeant Claypool was bending over a sound detector, his thick fingers fumbling with the intricate mechanism. "Damn it all anyway." He picked up the stub of his soggy cigar. "They rotated our repair man. Can you beat that? Rotated him and they ain't replaced him. Got one bastard school at Benning teaches this stuff and I ain't yet had a man who's been there." He looked into the machine with disgust, then swung his beefy frame away from the table. "Almost chow time, ain't it?"

"Yes."

"What do you think of our outfit?" The sergeant plunged the ragged butt of the cigar between his lips.

"Not bad."

"It's a deal, that's what it is." Sergeant Claypool chomped. "But we'll be out of business if we don't get some men soon." His round eyes rested lazily on Warren. "You and the lieutenant have a nice joyride?"

"Fine."

"He's young." The sergeant removed the cigar from between his brown teeth and went to the bunker entrance to hack a gob of juice into the mud. "Too damned young, I'd say. Younger than most of the guys in the outfit."

"Seems to know his stuff, though," Warren ventured.

"Yeah, he's okay. Only, ya know, he doesn't take his whiskey ration. Four bottles a month he's allowed and he don't take it. Now Lieutenant Cutter—we had him before Held—he used to take it and give it to the boys, but Lieutenant Held won't do it. Says it ain't 'proper.'" Claypool looked at the used butt and ground it out in a tin can near his elbow, rubbing a fat thumb and forefinger together afterwards to wipe away the juice. "Proper," Claypool mimicked, pursing his thick lips. "Sounds like a Boy Scout." He looked at his watch and announced, "Chow time."

After chow Warren found himself confronted by Lefevre. "Can you come up for a shot?" The tone was meant to be casual, but Warren sensed a certain urgency.

"Sure."

"Sorry about last night," Lefevre said as they climbed the path to his bunker, "I was tired."

"Forget it."

Lefevre did not speak again until they were inside the bunker, their ponchos hung up, the heater lighted, and the cognac poured. For Warren the silence became a period of tense expectancy. He was intrigued, even fascinated by the other. Lefevre's sharp features seemed made for dramatic expression; the furrow of his sloping brow seemed more noticeable than such lines might be on another; his hands moving quickly to the glasses or through his wavy hair seemed alive with an excitement, or a tension, of their own.

When Lefevre finally leaned forward from his perch on the edge of his cot and with open anxiousness asked, "What's it like on line?" Warren laughed.

"I mean it," Lefevre insisted, "tell me."

"It's hard to describe."

"Are you scared?"

"Sometimes."

"Not all the time? What about the times when you're not?"

Warren sipped at his cognac, hoping to slow the pace of questioning, then said, "Well, there's always that tension, you know—but as for being really frightened . . ."

"Some people crack up," Lefevre interrupted. "Do you think I'd crack up?"

"I don't know you that well."

Lefevre's features sagged, his worried eyes lost their aliveness and dropped from Warren's face to the cognac in his own hand. In his eagerness, he had caused some of the liquor to spill over the rim of the glass and his fingers

182

were now sticky. Warren watched the thin fingers nervously tap the glass before Lefevre put it down on the box and, his elbows on his thighs, clasped his hands in front of him.

"I'm thinking of volunteering for the line," he said, his eyes darting to Warren's face.

"Why?"

"Because . . ." Lefevre hesitated, his gaze fixed near his knees where his fingers struggled, pulling and twisting against one another. With a sudden wrench his hands parted and he stood up. "Because if Rickley can do it, I can. If he can take it, I can."

Lefevre sat down again, he leaned forward and peered intently at Warren. "I used to throw Nietzsche at Rickley. I used to tell him that he had fallen for a sickly code of morality fit only for women . . . that I had chosen the path of men. Do you get what I'm driving at?"

"Somewhat dimly."

"Back in the seminary, when I first began to feel that there was too much that was human about the faith, I used to argue with Rickley—not Nietzsche then, but other things. I left before he did, but we used to meet and I would bait him." Lefevre's hands were once again writhing in sticky tensions.

"Why?"

"It wasn't hard to bait him, to tangle him in words, but I could never really get to him. You know what I mean?"

"Why try?"

"Because . . . because . . ." Lefevre stood up and faced the doorway . . . "I don't know. It's just that he's so sure of everything." His voice dropped. "So damned sure."

"What's that got to do with going on line?"

"You wouldn't understand," Lefevre said wearily, turning about to sit down on his bunk once again.

"Maybe not," Warren said, "but I'd like to try." Lefevre studied his glass, ignoring or considering the offer. "I've some muddled reasons of my own for being here." This confession on Warren's part brought Lefevre's eyes upon him and Warren went on to tell of the experience on the train in France, Bernhardt's letter, his eventual rejection of the stateside post.

"Bernhardt's letter really did the trick. It was, to me, a flat announcement that if I was serious in my seeking for meaning, for God, for call it what you will, I must come here."

Lefevre shook his head slowly, but said nothing.

"Anyway," Warren added, "I've got to believe that now. I've made my choice." He paused, then decided to tell the rest. "But I've begun to doubt because of a girl. At one minute I'm convinced I've got to face this; the next I think I'm just running away from her." Warren stopped, sipped from his glass and waited.

Lefevre was uneasy in his silence. He shot a glance at Warren and with an angry twist of his head said, "I don't know." He put his glass down on the floor before continuing. "I can't say anything about all of that. You could be fulfilling a death wish for all I know. The only thing that really makes sense is what you say about not wanting to feel cowardly forever. I understand that." He dug his fingers into his scalp and looked at the glass sitting between his feet. "Still, it's different for you. You could go ahead and volunteeer like you did . . . go on line . . . but I can't . . . I can't just go ahead and do it."

"Why not?"

"Because if I did," Lefevre stood up and began to pace the small room, "if I did . . . there's always the possibility that . . . I could . . . I might . . . die . . ." He stopped in front of Warren for a moment. "Don't get me wrong, I'm not afraid of that." He swung away and began to pace once more. "No. But I can't die right now . . ." He stopped at the far end of the bunker, his back to War-

184

ren, his gaze fixed on the wall in front of him. His voice came weakly, almost inaudibly, "Not the way I am."

That night Warren did not sleep immediately. As he lay in the darkness pondering, it was as if other things and people did not exist, but only his passive temper lay at the center of this space of musty burlap, while the soft breathing of his fellow humans blended with the respiration of night itself. The oppressive bulk of the dark pressed close upon him, as if his body were pulpy beneath it. He sensed himself suspended over a black emptiness by some invisible line, the void below hidden in impenetrable darkness. A heightened sense of his peril filled him with dread. Then, onto the screen of his memory flashed the scene witnessed that wintry evening in France on the train: again he saw himself wearing combat garb, crawling along the wet earth, then stopping, thrusting himself upwards, holding in his hand the sputtering grenade; again the muzzle flash of a weapon ripped the night in front of him, and he felt the fiery bite of pain and heard the sound thudding in his ears.

Turning onto his belly, Warren extended his hand under the pillow until his fingers came to rest on the soft plastic covering of the ikon.

In the morning Warren woke with the others. Claypool, fully dressed, was leaving the bunker as he dropped his feet to the damp floor.

"You go up today, eh?" Folger yawned, grabbing for his fatigues.

"Yes."

Folger pulled on his pants and pushed his arms into his tunic. "Beats rifle company, doesn't it?" Before Warren could reply, he added, "See ya at chow," and left.

But Warren didn't see Folger at chow. Instead, he was confronted by Sergeant Claypool who, having finished his own meal, came over and squatted beside him. Claypool's

185

blunt fingers stripped the cellophane from a fresh cigar. "Gonna send you up to Able company this shift. Your buddy White's comin' down from there today." The flaccid lips parted and he pulled the brown roll between them, moistening it. Biting off the cigar end, he spat it into the mud. "Folger'll start early if I have to dynamite him." The thick fingers snapped a Zippo lighter and he sucked at his cigar. "Lieutenant says we may get a new man, a guy you recommended. Sure as hell hope so." Sighing heavily, he pushed himself up and toward the bunker.

Folger, with only a modicum of profanity on Sergeant Claypool's part, did get started early and before noon was at the turn-around point where White was waiting.

"How'd it go?" Warren asked.

"Stupidly!" White was passionate. "Stupidly! Anyone can work those machines! I will complain! I am a soldier, not a . . . a telephone operator." He tossed his small pack into the rear of the jeep. "Now I rest up from my rest. It is ridiculous! 'I want men with high I.Q.'s and above average backgrounds,' " White mimicked Lieutenant Held. "Who is he kidding? Even Nevers can manage it."

"It can't be as bad as that," Warren said.

"Dull. Just a different kind of sentry duty, that is all! Some stupid way to win a war." His face muscled into a smile. "You and Nevers will have an interesting time, friend Warren. He just got a package full of 'Classic Comics.' 'Classic Comics,' prayers for peace, it is such a stupid—"

Folger revved the jeep motor and Warren stepped away from the spattering mud as the vehicle lurched forward.

Nevers was waiting at the top of the steep incline. "Whew," the thin-faced little man said. "Am I glad to see you. What's wrong with that guy anyway?"

"What do you mean?" Warren followed Nevers along the narrow path.

"He just ain't no fun, ya know what I mean? I ain't
186

never had such a miserable time, ya know. He's mad at the world, that's what he is, bitchin' all the time." They passed a group of men coming along the path in the opposite direction. The passing faces reflected the sky's gray gloom.

"Here's home," Nevers said, entering a bunker. "Careful of the stove there." Warren's leg brushed against the improvised stove near the doorway. "Got no stovepipe, so the smoke's gotta go out the door," Nevers said. "This place is sorta low for you," he went on. "Me and White fit nicely, but another two inches lower and you'd be stoopin'. Top bunk's yours," he nodded toward the two bunks at the far wall. Skirting the sound locator which squatted in the center of the earthen floor, Warren hoisted his gear onto the top bunk. "White left the desk all nice and neat," Nevers said. "God, did he bitch if I messed it up a little." He winced at the recollection. Warren examined the desk, a narrow board suspended from the ceiling timbers by commo wire and fastened to the wall by two pieces of two-by-four.

"This place is a bit cramped," Nevers said, "but solid as hell. Got a round dead center on the roof the other day. Right after the barrage, that guy White hustled out to patch up the hole. Real crazy."

"He knows his stuff. Maybe it was wise."

"Not then it wasn't. Come outside." Nevers stepped out the bunker door, Warren followed. "See that point?" Warren's gaze followed Nevers' pointing finger to a high knob that capped the end of a ridge off to their left. "That's The Castle. Every night Joe Chink takes it and every morning he's gone again. Only sometimes some gook stays behind and spends the day popping at us. That's just what some gook was doing the day White decided to patch the roof. Crazy, that's what he is, ya know?" Nevers' sharply pointed chin jabbed out. "Our other position is about two hundred yards up the line there." He waved up the path. "I'll take ya up there if ya want to go."

"No hurry," Warren said. "Where's the forward position?"

"Oh, yeah, along here." The shorter man darted into a trench beside the bunker and Warren followed. The trench was a short passageway which intersected with the company's forward trench. On the other side of the intersection was a door which Nevers held open. "The best F.O. position we've got." He ushered Warren inside. The bunker was small. A slit at about shoulder level gave a wide view of the terrain in front of them. "The window removes," Nevers tapped the plastic that covered the slit, "if ya can't hear the weapons too well. We share this position with the artillery F.O. That's his scope there." On the ledge in front of the window a twenty-power scope jutted through a hole in the plastic. "He's a colored guy, but all right. Lets ya use the scope if ya want to. He calls shots for the tank, ya know."

"I didn't know."

"Yeah. The tank's only a little way up the slope. They get a ration of about nine rounds a day of ninety-millimeter stuff they gotta fire, so he calls their shots for 'em."

"How'd they get a tank up here?"

"Oh, it's an old one. Great for direct-fire artillery. Bulldozed a road up from the end, I'm told."

"They'll never get it out in this muck."

"Who said anything about getting it out? It's here to stay."

Through the clear plastic, Warren scanned the spiny land; to the left, The Castle towered above them; in front, a narrow valley separated them from the opposing ridge; off in the distance the ridgelines were like the waves of a troubled sea.

"That ridge over there," Nevers pointed off to the right, "is where most of the firing comes from."

"They all look alike to me."

"Yeah, sure. Here's the F.O.'s map." Nevers took a

188

plastic-covered mapboard off the wall. "Right here," he indicated a series of red marks on the map.

Warren saw other circles and squares as well as x's, concentrations of mortars and artillery pieces, he supposed. "When's chow?"

"Lunch is C-rations. Hot meal at about three. The time's changed every other day, so Joe doesn't get wise, ya know? See that point there?"

Warren bent his neck to follow Nevers' directing finger. He looked beyond the sharp chin, the weak mouth, down into the valley that separated them from the enemy. "Yes," he scanned the general area.

"Got a listening post out there. Two riflemen go out every night, usually with the patrol, and sit out there, listening; they come in in the morning. Gives me the creeps just thinkin' about it. Glad I'm not a rifleman."

Warren took another look at the mapboard and spotted the location of the L.P. It was at the base of their ridge, where the valley of separation began.

Back in the living-bunker, Warren spotted a copy of *Stars and Stripes*.

"The F.O. gets it regular," Nevers said. "He passes it on to whoever wants it. Nothin' in that one but pictures of marines. They're in reserve and they get more write-ups about their damned reserve life than any of these outfits get about their activities on line."

"Good public relations."

"Yeah, I guess so," Nevers grunted. "Marine Corps squad," he recited the old line, "one rifleman, four photographers, four advertising men. Damned army doesn't know how to do anything."

"Better wear your poncho," Nevers warned upon his return from chow that afternoon. "Gonna pour again."

The dense rain washed against the ridges for twenty-four hours. Before it slowed, the downpour had turned the path into a muddy stream, rushing down to the base of the hill. Other, smaller streams poured over the edge of the path and flowed noisily down the rear slope. Neither Warren nor Nevers found it worthwhile to fight their way down the slushy path to the field kitchen for a warm meal; instead they heated C-rations on the metal ammo box that served as a stove. Brown cans of stewed chicken and sausage patties bubbled alongside canteen cups of coffee. The bunker itself was dry and warm from the heat of the stove. Outside there was no activity; all seemed content to wait through the rain. Nevers lay on his bunk and reread his "Classic Comics." For Warren it was as if time had come to a dead stop.

In silence and lassitude born of the rain, Warren lay on his cot and puzzled the backward and forward flow of happenings; what had begun as a test of his own courage had quickly mingled with his own desire for the Absolute and was now a confused medley of events and men. The vision had exercised a clear and definite pull upon him. He had seen his choice and made it. The brief note from Bernhardt had influenced him, too—but why had he not before seen that these could contradict one another: that dying and finding God are not the same? Prevot's death had killed any uncertainty about the truth of his own premonition, but it had also presented him with a new uncertainty —the ikon. For Rickley the ikon seemed to symbolize life, or at least to deny the vision of death. Did it? He could not deny that he had felt the pull of the ikon, was moved to seek the meaning which Prevot had not found, a meaning which Warren felt inextricably bound up with his past life and his present condition—especially with his feelings for Jean. Surely, if he could but understand something of the meaning of the ikon, the wall separating Jean from him would be down. And yet, what good would that do, if he never left this land alive?

But these thoughts were not untroubled by others which

pressed in upon him, thoughts of Duke, Zikowlsky, White, Lefevre, the living and the dead—and pressing most heavily upon his thoughts were the uncounted, unseen against whom he had aided in the hurling of artillery rounds: men whose faces, whose blood, he could not dissociate from the man he had killed in the stream. All the enemy he did not know became the one enemy he had known, and it was as if he had a hundred times over killed this same startled man.

The next afternoon the rain slowed and stopped. Restless, Warren went out to the forward position. Upon opening the door, he was greeted by a tall Negro.

"Hello, I'm Lieutenant Sweet."

Warren introduced himself and they shook hands.

"Not much going on just now," Lieutenant Sweet said. "Just lining up a little target for the tank crew." Warren stood to one side while the lieutenant focused his scope and glanced again at his map. His thin hand lifted the telephone that rested on the ledge. "Hello, Sergeant? You may fire that round for effect." A few seconds later the ninety-millimeter on the tank exploded in a roaring belch. Through the plastic window, Warren watched the shell burst soundlessly along the edge of a sloping ridge. "Right one hundred," Lieutenant Sweet said into the phone, "up one hundred. Make it W.P., easier to see. One round. Fire when ready."

There was the briefest pause before the weapon erupted again and this time the bubbling foam of the white phosphorus marked a spot at a point nearer the base of the ridge. "Fine, Sergeant. Right one hundred. W.P. One round. Fire when ready."

The next round foamed up in the valley between two ridges, a few hundred yards beyond a small grove of trees. "Fine, fine, Sergeant. Very fine. Now if you can be around at about 1730, we'll have something there for you. Oh, no, thank *you*, Sergeant."

The lieutenant turned to Warren, his lean face relaxed. "Want to see what we're aiming at?"

Warren looked through the scope at the spot where the last round had landed: a flat area, a few hundred yards beyond a small grove of trees, between the end of one ridge and the beginning of another.

"I've been watching that spot for three days now," Lieutenant Sweet said. "Every afternoon about 1730 hours a group of the enemy cross that spot, coming out from behind the ridge on the left and going over to the one on the right. Today, they'll have a surprise. Why don't you come up and watch the show?" He hung up his mapboard. *"Stars and Stripes*? Got it right here. All through with it. You may have it if you want."

Warren took the newspaper, thanked the lieutenant, and left the bunker. While wading back through the commo trench, he heard the pop of a mortar. He spun and dashed back into the forward position. The round crunched to earth down the line to the left near the tank.

"A little daredevil over there," the lieutenant pointed. "Don't need your little gadget." He picked up the phone. "Heavy Weapons platoon, please," he said. "Heavy Weapons? Got a target for the seventy-five. Forward slope of 402. You can see him. He's flopping mortar rounds in at the tank."

In a small depression on the face of the hill, the soldier could be seen. He had placed the tube between his knees and, with hardly a pause, dropped one round after another down the barrel.

"Tube'll be too hot to handle if he keeps that up," Warren said.

"Going to get warm there, anyway," the lieutenant said, and as if to bear out his words a .75 recoilless, firing from the right of their position, smashed a shell into the slope of the hill. The mortarman grabbed his tube and scurried up the slope just as another round landed, this time nearer

192

his first location. Warren could hear the snap of M-1's as riflemen spotted the figure clambering up the ridge once more. "Dangerous business, that." Lieutenant Sweet wagged his head.

That afternoon Warren decided to accept the lieutenant's invitation, and at the appointed time went out to the forward position where he found the lieutenant looking through his scope.

"You're just in time," Lieutenant Sweet greeted him. "They'll be coming along any minute." He returned to his scope. At his elbow on the ledge lay the sound-power phone that connected him with the tank. After a long watch through the black tube, the lieutenant groped for the phone, his eye still against the scope. "Sergeant, are you ready?" The words were like an ointment. "Now just be patient, please. They're coming into the field," the voice continued. "We'll let the first few pass. Here comes the main body now. All right, Sergeant, you may fire for effect."

The tank spewed fire, rocking the ridge with the weapon's backblast as round after round flamed from the ninety-millimeter tube. Warren could see the white phosphorus boiling into clouds at the point where the weapon had earlier been zeroed in.

"Beautiful, Sergeant," the lieutenant said. "Beautiful." He turned to Warren. "Like to see?"

The lieutenant shifted his position and Warren put his eye to the scope. The area was a cauldron of splashing white; he spotted a dark speck against the white: a man leaping up and running from the flow of white lava and stumbling, his arms clutching skyward as the searing liquid foamed over him. Warren stepped away from the scope.

"About fifteen, I'd say," Lieutenant Sweet was saying into the telephone. "Oh, about twenty-five of them, but I let five get by and you can figure five might have gotten away." He paused, "Oh, a beautiful job, Sergeant, a very

193

beautiful job. Yes, surely, Sergeant. Fine Sergeant. Oh, no, thank *you,* Sergeant."

"We oughtta have joy girls," Nevers said that evening. "Those gooks got 'em, ya know. Why can't we? Cook your meals for ya, give ya a little lovin'. Why, man, it would make life livable up here." He sighed. "They shot a woman leading a charge ya know?"

"Who did?"

"Oh, somebody in the early days. All dressed in white, riding a horse she was and waving a sword, crazy-like, ya know. They didn't know it was a woman until they shot her. That was last winter."

"I didn't hear about it."

"Naw, they hushed it up. She was a white woman, a Russkie. Same reason why the MIG's never come down below the thirty-eighth parallel any more. Them pilots are Russkies, that's why. An Air Force guy in Japan told me that he's been in dogfights with 'em while a whole group of Chink students just fly around above and learn from the Russkies how to do it."

"Do you believe everything you hear?"

"Don't you believe that? Why, it's the only reason anyone can think of for them not coming down. Lookit our layouts at the rear—most of 'em not even camouflaged. Joe could wipe out our supply depots, division headquarters, everything, if he wanted to. But he doesn't. Only people who ever hit our own positions by plane is the goddam marines."

"What've you got against the marines?"

"Well, they did, ya know. There I was, standing there shaving last summer. Then I hear this machine gun and this plane comes in low enough to chop off my head and where does it go? Right down on our own field artillery position and dropped a couple of bombs. I was there. Lieutenant Cutter told me later that it was the marines. The

194

only reason they didn't kill anybody was because the crews were at chow. They had an investigation and everything."

"Mistakes will happen."

"Ah, the damned marines probably did it on purpose. They're like that, ya know. Cut the army's throat every time."

White came by the next day on his way up to the other position. Not having visited the other bunker yet, Warren went along with him.

"I hear that you gave Lieutenant Held Rickley's name," White snorted as he stomped up the muddy path.

"Yes. I thought he'd make a good addition to the outfit."

"Why him? The only good thing about this transfer was getting away from that praying jackass. Zikowlsky would have been a better choice."

"Haven't you heard? Zikowlsky and the Warrant Officer were hit while riding in the jeep."

"Killed?" White asked, not slowing his pace.

"Yes."

"No more apples for him," White said. "Well, anyway, I do not want Rickley around me and I told Sergeant Claypool that. Just looking at that damned fool makes me mad."

"Not before you found out he was a Catholic."

"That is all I have to know."

White led Warren to a square blockhouse of a bunker, its top barely hidden by the ridge. "Did you meet Pedretti?" White asked.

"No," Warren replied.

"He manned this bunker. I passed him going down the hill. I came over here to get away from Nevers, but Pedretti is an ass, too."

"You alone here?" Warren followed the stocky White into the bunker.

"Yes. I prefer it that way, except maybe if you want to come over here. It is all one with me. Anything to be away from these idiots who whine about home, think of nothing but women, or pray for peace. What sort of soldiers are they?" White dropped his pack on a table and stepped out of the bunker again. "See that knoll?" He pointed to the rise which Nevers had called The Castle. "There was a sniper up there the other day. I gave him a chance to kill me." He smiled without mirth. "But he did not even try. I am going crazy with boredom! I requested a transfer back to a rifleman's post, but the lieutenant will not approve it."

"The colonel already turned that one down, didn't he?"

"Fools!" White snapped bitterly. "They are all fools! I will rot away here with nothing to do! I am getting old, Warren, twenty-seven. My stomach is thickening on me and I am slower than I used to be. I must get in more action or I will go soft!" He waved a short arm at the terrain in a violent gesture. "Look at it. Want to go for a stroll in the country? All we need is birds singing and we have a pastoral scene."

"Not very pastoral with all these bunkers and holes cut into the ridges."

"You know what I mean," White was impatient. "It is in action that you are most alive. In combat I am a man. Sitting here I will become a vegetable. I thought you were like me at first, but now I do not know. I do know that I must see more action and not just sit here twiddling my thumb on a little dial."

"Haven't you seen enough in your lifetime?" Warren braved the question.

"No. I am a soldier and this is my life. I cannot live without war."

"You like war?"

"Me?" White hesitated, looked quizzically at Warren. "Why not admit it? I hate war."

196

"I'm puzzled."

"So, you are puzzled." White shrugged his shoulders and turned toward the bunker with an air of finality. His stocky figure hesitated at the log-framed doorway for a moment, then turned around. "Would you be less puzzled if I told you that I have come here for a specific purpose?"

"Perhaps." Warren stared into the hard, gray eyes. "What purpose?"

The eyes did not flinch, the face twisted wryly. "Let us just say . . ." White's strong, solid shoulders squared themselves. "Let us just say . . . nothing." He turned and went into the bunker.

Warren stood for a moment looking at the doorway, then down at the muddy earth before beginning the walk back to his own bunker.

Dividing the night up into two-hour security guard shifts, Warren took turns with Nevers. While Nevers preferred to remain inside the living-bunker, Warren sat out his guard duty in the forward position, peering into the murky darkness, listening to the rain-streaked sounds of night. On evenings when the rain eased up, he could hear the sound of the enemy carried across the air damp and crisp as fresh lettuce; shovels clinked against rock, metal pinged against metal, as unknown men across the valley dug in for the winter.

"Hell, man," Nevers said one day, "they must have that whole ridge hollowed out by now. They do it, ya know. They make a little city in there, just like ants."

One night Warren thought he heard a voice raised for a moment of abrupt command, but the night swathed it in unreality. Then, early one clear evening, he did hear a voice. Amplified by a microphone, distorted by the distance and the currents of moist air sweeping up the valley, it was a voice nonetheless. "Come on over, Joe," it said in a tone meant to be persuasive but sounding only sickly. "We your friend, Joe. We no want war, Joe. Come on over. Many girl, Joe. Girl hot to go, Joe. Big party for all GI. Come on over. You friend. We give you girl, car, whiskey. Big party, Joe." The voice was interrupted by the squawking of a record as it screeched out a rendition of *China Lights*. Then, over the microphone came the wheedling voice again, repeating the same phrases. Warren strained to hear the words, but nearly each sentence was marred by the distance.

Behind him the door opened. Warren swung about to face Lieutenant Sweet, who removed his helmet and lifted the telephone to his face. "Polar pink, please," he asked of the operator. While waiting to be connected, he smiled at Warren. "Haven't seen you at the show lately."

Each day, at almost the same time, Lieutenant Sweet called the tank fire upon the group of men crossing the valley.

"No, sir."

"Hello, Sweet at Able. Would you mind giving me two flares at . . ." The lieutenant flicked a small penlight onto the mapboard and gave the grid coordinates. "Then stand by for a fire mission."

"Party, GI. Come on over, Joe . . . whiskey . . . girl . . . car . . . big party . . ." the voice fluctuated over the darkness of the valley.

"We're going to have a party," Sweet said quietly as he put his face against the plastic and waited for the flares.

With a soft pop, the canister opened in the air and a brilliant white orb, suspended by a parachute, appeared in the sky. A second pop, and a second small sun appeared above the first, casting over all the valley a pale, fluorescent light. "Don't shoot, Joe . . . friend . . ." The voice fought against the distance. "Girl, all hot to go . . . Come on over . . . whiskey . . ."

"That's where I thought they were," the lieutenant's voice was calm as he moved to the scope and peered

198

through it for a moment. "Yes, three of them there that I can see." The flares ceased their battle against the night and sputtered out against the force of darkness. He raised the phone once again and gave his fire mission to the mortars as the voice shrilled . . . "Come on over, Joe."

"Yes, Sergeant. W. P., please. Fire for effect." He put down the phone. "Did you see them?"

"No." Warren shook his head.

"Watch, then."

They watched. The phonograph had just begun to screech out a Bing Crosby recording of *My Blue Heaven* when the rounds landed.

Along the line a machine gun clattered, the tracers arcing gracefully through the night sky and into the boiling white phosphorus that churned up the area.

"That will do, Sergeant," Lieutenant Sweet said pleasantly. "You may cease fire. Yes, Sergeant. Three KIA's. A psycho warfare unit. Thank you very much, Sergeant." He put down the telephone and peered out the window again. The W.P. had ignited a few small fires which burned like melting candles in the midst of the simmering foam. "A nice job, that," the lieutenant clucked happily. "I like W.P., especially at night. It's so pretty." Picking up his helmet, he walked to the door. "I don't think you'll be disturbed for the rest of the night."

"You'd think them chinks'd learn," Nevers said. "Every day for a week they been getting it at the same spot and they keep on coming. That's plain stupid, ya know." Nevers had packed his bag and was studying a "Classic Comic" while waiting for the jeep. "That Foggy hasn't even left down there yet," he complained. "Wonder if Claypool is gonna send him up on line?"

"I don't know."

"Serve him right. But we're gonna pull in reserve soon."

"I heard that when I came to this outfit," Warren said.

199

"Yeah, I know, but we gotta. They can't keep us here forever, ya know. It wouldn't be fair. Gotta give the marines a chance to see some action, too."

"Why worry? You've got a deal here."

"Don't I know it? Up on line the company treats you like kings 'cause you're regiment. At the rear, they treat ya real polite 'cause you're combat. A real deal, ya know?"

"That's what I said. So why worry?"

"Well," Nevers screwed his face up into a pitiful smile. "Ya can still get killed up here."

A short while later Warren watched the small figure start down the path to meet the jeep.

Later, back in his bunker, he heard the cough of the enemy mortars. He flicked on the machine, grabbed his helmet and then paused, waiting for the first rounds to land so he could break for the forward position. The downward whine of the shells caused his body to tense for the explosion, but the familiar sound did not come and the silence slashed at his self-confidence. Again he heard the downward singing of the missiles, but instead of the usual explosion shuddering the earth, he could hear only the faintest pop. Sweat broke out on his forehead. Perhaps it was gas. He had no mask; no one had. Outside the door he heard the whine and thud of a piece of metal landing. He pressed himself against the far wall of the bunker. The sounds continued as before: the familiar whine followed by the pop. Finally, he edged himself to the door. There, he faltered before shoving himself outside. Hearing the whine of a shell, he disobeyed instinct and gazed upwards. The popping sound came again and in the sky appeared a cloud of papers which broke apart, caught upon the breeze and wafted out across the ridge and down the forward slope of the hill. Other men were coming out of their bunkers now, some were shouting, others pointed up to the floating leaflets. One man stood on top of his bunker, a perfect target for the enemy as he clutched at the bits of paper which drifted past him and out over the exposed land that lay between the armies.

Involuntarily, Warren broke into hoarse, dry giggles that scraped at his throat and would not stop. As he watched the falling papers and the antics of the men, his laughter increased; his body, so taut before, seemed shattered by relief.

"Deo gratias."

Warren felt a hand on his arm and turning, found himself confronted by Rickley. He tried to suppress his laughter, but failed; in wordless explanation he pointed at the last of the papers as they drifted earthwards.

"Inside, friend." Rickley took Warren's arm and led him to the bunker. "This *is* your bunker, I suppose." Warren dropped onto his cot and immediately began to regain his composure. "Somebody's whistling into the phone," Rickley announced.

Warren stretched for the phone. "Warren here."

"Where in hell have you been?" White snapped. "I have had the machine on and been waiting for you to stop it. Why didn't you catch them?"

"Didn't try."

"Why not? Machine out of order?"

"No. Me."

"What?"

"I was scared stiff."

"Scared? I never heard of such a thing! We could have gotten those mortars. Now they are finished and you say you were scared. I am disappointed in you, Warren."

"So you're disappointed." Warren looked over at Rickley whose pleasant features contrasted with the sharp voice barking out of the black earpiece. "Better luck next time." He put down the instrument. "Scared silly," he said to Rickley. "I didn't know what they were throwing— thought it might be gas. When I saw that," he waved his arm toward the outside, "I cracked up for a minute."

"Sure," Rickley said. "Now, what are we up to here? I'm told you put the bug in Lieutenant Held's ear, so here I am," he shrugged his shoulders. "What's the scoop?"

"Oh, you're so damned . . . eager," Warren smiled. "Well, may as well begin."

As Warren had been taught by Red, he now began to teach Rickley. While showing Rickley the forward position and demonstrating the stop button, he found a copy of *Stars and Stripes* which he carried back to the living-bunker.

That afternoon, while waiting for Rickley to return from chow, Warren lay on his bunk with the newspaper. On the second page his eyes skipped over, then darted back to a dark block of print. Carefully, he reread the headline and then the article, not allowing himself to leap ahead to the name that had first caught his attention. When he had finished, he let the paper flatten on his chest.

"Going down to dinner?" Rickley asked when he entered.

Warren shook his head.

"It wasn't half bad," Rickley said. "I think the foulness of army cooking is overestimated."

"Read this," Warren tossed the paper towards Rickley. "Second page, top of second column."

The paper rustled in Rickley's hands as he folded it over. "You mean this 'GI's Letters Kill Mother'?"

"Yes."

Warren scanned Rickley's face as the latter read the item; the features firmed, the lips pursed, the head began to move from side to side.

"The wrong one died." Warren sat up on the cot. "I know him."

"You do?"

"A mama's boy." Warren stood up, desiring movement. "That woman lived and breathed her only child. Now he's killed her, him and his damned letters." His long legs car-

202

ried him across the floor, back again, to and fro. "I saw him about two weeks ago and he read me one of those damned letters. Revolting . . ."

"But suicide . . ." Rickley stopped.

"It tells there," Warren pointed wearily and sat down on the cot again. "They quote her note—not able to stand the anxiety, knowing he was going to die any day. That bastard!" Warren stood again, paced to the door and looked out. "Sure, he'll feed his ego on the fact that somebody loved him that much."

"You don't know . . ." Rickley began.

Warren swung about. "He killed his mother! That I know—and none of your moralizing or prayers will change that!" He turned his back to Rickley once more. "Sorry," his voice dropped. "Get me off this subject."

"Some of the leaflets that came down today." Rickley extended a slip of paper. "Got 'em at chow. Some of the boys went down the forward slope for them. Wanted souvenirs."

Warren smeared his thumb across the cheap ink. "Stop this murder of innocent people," he read aloud. "The Korean People's Republic wants only Peace. The warmonger capitalists are using you and your buddies for their own imperialistic ends. They are lovemaking your wives while you fight against peace loving . . ." Warren handed the leaflet back.

"Look at this one," Rickley held out another.

On the leaflet was a picture of a prosperous-looking man sitting beside a pool in what appeared to be a Miami Beach hotel. A girl in a bathing suit was lighting his cigarette. Over his head was a balloon with the words, "And where is your husband, my little darling?" Over her head was the dubbed-in balloon with the reply, "Oh, he died in Korea, sweetheart."

"That might be effective." Warren returned the leaflet. "Met one in the platoon whose wife got tired of waiting."

"Lots of those around," Rickley nodded. "Our Warrant Officer, Mr. Wise, in Baker company was one."

"A little old for that, wasn't he?"

"Married fifteen years. Once he got overseas, his wife divorced him and married a twenty-five-year-old corporal."

"How do you know?"

"Lieutenant Fregni told me just after Mr. Wise got killed. Said she was having an affair with the corporal even while he was in the States, only he couldn't do anything about it."

"Why not?"

"The corporal was a swimming instructor at the post pool. She just took a sudden interest in swimming there and he couldn't stop that. They had just lost their first baby—one of those change of life things—and he thought . . . well, anyway, she went off the deep end, even began bringing the corporal home."

"And Mr. Wise just stood around looking silly?"

"No. He volunteered for here. Fregni seemed to know all about it. Said Mr. Wise didn't want to divorce her, but she got hysterical whenever he brought up the subject of the corporal . . . so he got out."

"And the corporal and the middle-aged woman live happily ever after."

"You're getting cynical, Warren," Rickley declared. "The woman wasn't stable, Mr. Wise was trying to keep her . . ."

"And the corporal?"

"How'd you like to be saddled with a middle-aged worshiper?" Rickley asked. "There's temporal punishment for you."

Warren caught a note of weariness in the voice. "It's good having you here," he said quickly. "Whose day is it, your family's or your girl's—Mary isn't it?"

"Mary," Rickley nodded affirmatively. "You mean for the letters?"

"Yes."

"I owe Mary a letter."

"Why don't you write it? You'll have lots of time here —unless Joe acts up."

"Yes." Rickley folded the leaflets methodically and set them aside. "I should do that. But first I want more practice on that gadget." He walked over to the machine and flicked it on.

"I think you've got it down," Warren declared.

"More practice wouldn't hurt." Rickley put the headphones over his blond hair and sat down on the battery box seat. His eye against the aperture, he began to rotate the wheel, while his finger turned the dial slowly.

Warren wandered out to the forward position. Lieutenant Sweet glanced up from his scope momentarily. "You're just in time," he said, returning to the instrument. "I've been watching them build a bunker out there," the lieutenant unbent from the telescope, "for three days. They're putting the finishing touches on it now. Take a peek," he waved his hand toward the instrument and raised the sound-power phone to his lips. "Are you ready, Sergeant?"

Through the scope Warren could see dark figures moving about a mound of earth on the skyline of a ridge.

"Fine. One round of H.E. Fire for effect."

Warren stepped away from the scope and the lieutenant, still holding the telephone near his face, bent to watch the rounds hit. The tank erupted and like a giant fist the high explosive shell pounded into the ridgeline. "Lovely shot!" Lieutenant Sweet announced to the tank crew. "Throw a few more in there." One after another, the blasts came, and the earth rolled with the punishment. "That's enough, Sergeant. They're through. Eight, Sergeant. They just flew apart, timbers and men. No, thank *you*, Sergeant. We must do it again sometime."

Warren left the bunker. Across the valley, splashed on

205

splintered timbers, were eight men—their blood, bones, and flesh commingling in the messy union of violent death.

On the phone the next day, Claypool—pleased to hear that Rickley was capable of manning the post alone for a day—instructed Warren to be at the turn-around point at noon.

Sometime before that, Warren followed the forward commo trench to the source of some disturbingly loud shouts. He found a group of men gaily screaming lewd suggestions to a woman who had dared to stand on the skyline of the opposite ridge to wash her hair. It was the first time Warren had seen one of the enemy's "comfort-girls." Excepting for her obviously long hair, which fell forward from her bowed head into a small basin, she looked just like any other brown-clad figure outlined against the murky sky. He stood beside the men who continued their excited invitations to obscenity. The woman continued with her toilet, once looking over and beckoning toward the men, but otherwise untroubled by their calls; then, finishing her task, she tossed the water from the basin down the forward slope of the hill in a broad gesture of defiance.

"Haw!" crowed one man happily, "she dropped the pan."

"Look at the damned thing roll."

Having slipped from her hand, the pan rolled down the forward slope of the hill and came to rest at a point about a hundred feet from the ridgeline on which the woman stood. She looked down at the pan and then disappeared behind the ridgeline. Warren turned and was leaving the trench when he heard exultant shouts.

"She's back! There she is!"

Returning, Warren watched the woman as she cautiously eased her way down the slope.

"She's going after it!"

"Some guts!"

206

Now the vocalizing began as the men bellowed out their biological needs. The woman picked her way carefully down the face of the ridge, her brown clothes light against the darker hillside.

"Watch this," a large man unslung his M-1.

"Don't shoot her," somebody pleaded.

"Aw, hell, I'm jest goin' to have a little fun with her."

"Leave her alone, Nick," an already defeated voice said. "She ain't doin' no harm."

But Nick was already pressing his heavy cheek against the stock of his weapon and squinting down the sights. The men, quiet now, looked from the rifleman to the woman who edged nearer the tin pan. Nick's finger squeezed the round off effortlessly and all eyes focused on the individual outlined against the slope. She straightened suddenly.

"You missed," one man cried.

"I didn't aim to hit," Nick replied.

"Boy, she's mad. Look at her curse you out."

The woman on the slope was shaking her fist violently against them. She stamped her foot, made a spitting gesture before stooping to pick up the round basin. The utensil firmly in her grasp, she shook it vigorously at them, then turned to ascend the hill.

Nick raised his weapon again. "Watch her scuttle her little ass up that ridge," he snickered. Again the men were silent as Nick leveled the weapon upon his target and applied pressure to the trigger. The rifle lurched against his cheek as the round exploded.

"Oh, my gawd."

"She's hit."

"Ya hit her, Nick."

The woman had sprawled on the hillside, arms outstretched, the pan still clutched in her hands.

"You killed her, Nick."

"Ah," Nick pulled his weapon back, "I didn't mean to. I was aimin' at her heels."

"But you killed her."

"Aw, shut up, will ya? I told ya, I didn't mean to." The hulk looked away from the figure on the hillside and, breaking through the ring of men, lurched down the trench. The others remained transfixed by the sight of the fallen woman.

"Wait! Is she moving or am I seeing things?"

Her hands clutching at every protrusion within reach, the woman had begun dragging her limp body up the slope of the hill.

"I'll go tell Nick." A small, smooth-faced boy ran down the trench.

Inch by inch, her legs like deadweights, her back straight, the woman pulled herself toward the top of the steep incline.

Nick, tagged by the runner, shoved his way to the front of the group. He thrust a strong jaw forward. "I told ya I didn't kill her."

"Ya hit her spine, I think," one timid voice said. "I saw a guy hit in the spine. He was just like that."

"Yeah. It paralyzes ya."

"Aw, shut up." Nick looked curiously at the struggling woman. After watching her tortuous movements, he turned to one of the men beside him. "Ya say she's paralyzed?"

"Yeah. Ya hit her spine. She can only move her arms. See? I knew a guy once—"

"Shut up!" Nick took his M-1 off his shoulder once more and flicked the safety catch off.

"What ya gonna do, Nick?" the little man asked.

"Ya think I'm gonna let her suffer? I'm gonna do what ya do to dogs." His thick neck bent as he looked down the barrel and focused the rifle on his target.

Warren grabbed the barrel of the rifle and pushed it upwards.

208

"Whatsamatter?" Nick glared him, his jowls flushing angrily.

"She's not a dog," Warren said, his hand still gripping the rifle barrel.

Nick's large face sagged, his dull eyes looked from Warren to the woman who was still hauling her stiff body up the muddy slope, then back to Warren again. "You gonna stop me?"

"She's not a dog," Warren repeated firmly and while he did not know what he would do, he knew that he would not permit Nick to fire again.

The large head dropped slightly. Nick glanced once more towards the paralyzed woman, then he turned. "Yeah," he decided, "you're right." Pushing the safety of his M-1 back, he slung his weapon. "I ain't killin' no woman." He glowered at the men about him. "And anyone else what gets funny around here answers to me." Turning his broad back on the men, Nick lumbered down the trench once more. The remaining men stood, their features marked by horror and pity, watching the fallen woman.

"This ain't no place for a woman," a voice groaned, but no one answered.

Before leaving the trench, Warren took another look at the woman fighting her agonizing struggle up the slope. She was still far from the ridgeline and no one had come to her assistance.

In the bunker, Rickley lay on his cot, as Warren finished his arrangements to go down.

"You'd better write that letter to Mary," Warren reminded him. The fact that Rickley had not opened his letter pad since his arrival the day before loomed large in Warren's mind.

"Yes," Rickley said wistfully. "Maybe today."

Warren was startled, a few minutes later, when Rickley lunged past him and dashed outside. Warren reached the

209

doorway in time to see Rickley bent double in a fit of vomiting.

"The food, eh?" Warren asked, putting his arm across the other's shoulders.

"No." Rickley shook his head from side to side, still gagging.

Warren gave him a handkerchief and he wiped his mouth before straightening up.

"Nervous, eh?"

"No," Rickley said. "I'm not nervous." He looked directly into Warren's eyes. "I'm scared."

Foggy had begun the climb up the hill lugging a battery on his back and was breathing heavily when Warren got down to him. "Here," Warren held out his own small pack. "I'll take that up for you." Grasping the pack straps, Warren swung the battery onto his own shoulders.

"Here's some mail for Rickley, forwarded from Baker." Folger smiled feebly and excused himself. "I'll go get the jeep turned around."

Warren plodded back up the road, the weight he carried forcing his feet deep into the sludgy earth. He was breathing heavily himself when he entered the bunker.

Rickley stood up. "Back again?"

"Got a battery for you. Forgot that I asked Claypool for it the other day. That one's low. Here's your mail." He handed Rickley the letters and squatted to ease the battery box from his shoulders. Disconnecting the cables from the battery they had been using, he connected up the new one. Rickley watched the entire procedure. Then Warren lashed the tired battery to the pack rack and, with Rickley's help, shouldered it. "Now you're set," he said. "They'll charge this one." In the bunker doorway, Warren turned around. "Mind if I ask what you were just praying for?"

"Courage," Rickley blushed. "I'm still scared."

"Order some for me, too."

At the base of the hill, Warren settled himself in the jeep. "I get my R and R next week," Folger announced.

"Good for you," Warren said. "Get a good case while you're there."

"Huh? I don't get you."

"Get a good dose of syphilis while you're about it."

"Yeah," Folger's voice weakened. "Ha, ha." His nervous attempt to laugh died into a silence that lasted the entire trip.

"I'm taking your word for that new guy Rickley." Sergeant Claypool spat a gob of brown juice. "He better know what's up."

"He does."

"Lieutenant Held says we get another new guy next week." The loose lips formed the words around the sticky cigar. "He's been promised it. Ya want to stay at Able company?" His tiny black eyes were demanding.

"Wouldn't mind at all."

"Okay." The cigar was plucked away from the wet lips by two fat fingers. "That's all right by me. I'm still trying to organize this damned outfit. It ain't no bed of roses when you ain't got no men."

That evening Lefevre announced that he had seen Rickley. "In fact, he stayed in this bunker the night before he went up," Lefevre said. "We stayed up half the night arguing. You told him what you told me, about your premonition, didn't you?"

"Yes."

Lefevre shook his head; his black hair fell forward over his forehead and he brushed it back, saying: "That wasn't a good idea."

"Why not?"

"Because he's . . . he's so damned innocent, so damned stupid, that's why not."

"I don't get you."

211

"He said someone else you both knew had a premonition of death and did die, a sergeant."

"Prevot."

"Yeah, and he said that he didn't want it to happen to you. He's all on fire with the thought that you might die and that you're not prepared to die . . ."

Warren shrugged. "I don't see how he can change matters anyway—"

"He's crazy, that's what he is! He's a pious little nut. He believes it all—every bit of it—and I just can't get through to him . . ." Lefevre paused, ran his hand through his hair once more, and reached for his cognac glass. "Why he even asked me to pray for the two of you. Me!" He lifted the glass to his lips. "Lot of good that'd do anybody." He drank and replaced the glass on the box beside him; now his gaze was serious, his tone very even: "Take care of him, Warren."

"What do you mean?"

"I mean look out for him, he's up to something. I'm sure of it."

"I still don't understand."

"I'm not sure if I know what he's up to myself, but I think . . . I got an impression from that talk he had with me that . . . well . . . oh, forget it. It wouldn't make sense to you."

There Lefevre dropped the subject of Rickley until later, when Warren had left the bunker and was beginning his descent down the hillside; then he heard Lefevre's voice break the darkness behind him. "Warren?"

He turned and looked up to see that Lefevre had left the bunker and was coming down the path after him. "Yes?"

Lefevre approached and the moonlight cast a strange pallor over his face, as of an actor powdered for a part, with faded lips and grayed hair. This trick of the moonlight, coupled with Lefevre's classical features, gave a mys-

212

terious, theatrical effect to his words. "Remember what I said."

"What?"

Lefevre's face came nearer his own, his deep eyes looked intensely into Warren's. "Take care of Rickley."

"I don't see what I can do," Warren shrugged.

In a moment the intensity was gone from Lefevre's eyes, his straight features seemed to sag and he turned away. "Yes," he said, "that's true. You can't do anything about it." He began to climb slowly back up to his bunker. Warren watched him for a few moments, then, deciding that there was nothing to be gained by following the other, continued his descent to the counterfire bunker.

The night brought a storm and at breakfast the rain was still heavy. Warren followed Sergeant Claypool from the chow area, carrying his food tray to the counterfire bunker. The toast was soggy with rain water and the cereal had more water than milk on it when he sat down in the shelter to eat.

"Gonna send you back up today." Claypool chomped at a mouthful of the rubbery scrambled eggs, gulping noisily. "So get your shower this morning." Poking a large finger into his toast, he grunted, "Damned rain. Don't count on comin' down next week. Foggy's goin' on R and R in a couple a days. Only gonna make essential trips in this muck."

"I thought he wasn't going until next week."

"Oh, he doesn't know which end is up." Claypool put his tray aside and swilled down his coffee. He looked into the bottom of the empty aluminum cup and put it down on the tray. His fist clutched at his pocket and, finding it empty, he turned to the workbench and scavenged a half-finished cigar from the ash tray. He eyed the dead cigar with a detached air, stuck it between his teeth. "Stale damned thing," he muttered pulling it from his teeth and looking at it again. "But it'll do." He popped the butt back between his brown teeth and lit it. "A good piece of ass might make a man of that weasel." He blew out a musty gray cloud. "A truckload is going to the showers in about an hour. You can get on that."

When Warren leaped down from the truck on his return from the shower point, he found Foggy waiting for him at the counterfire bunker.

"Mail," Folger handed an envelope to Warren. "Anytime you're ready."

Without looking at it, Warren put the envelope into his pocket. "I'll get my gear."

As the jeep cut through the downpour, Warren's thoughts centered on the ikon. Perhaps he would ask Rickley about it . . .

The rain pounded on the canvas top of the jeep, washed down the wide window in a steady flow that the wipers struggled in vain to erase. Folger was hunched over the wheel, attempting to catch a glimpse of the road through the thick watery lens.

Warren peered out the side aperture at the countryside suffering the beat of the rain. He was going again to the line, even as once with Zikowlsky, White, and Duke he had traveled there. On that day there had been a harsh clarity about the ridges and the road; impregnated by heat, pounded by the harsh glare of the sun, everything had seemed fuller, more real than lifesize, as though all things had been honed to a keen edge. Now, in a time just past midday, the world was like a blurred negative, and there were no sharp edges; even the sound of the motor was muffled by the rain. He sensed a change in himself—something lost or gained—somewhere between these two jeep rides, and he looked into himself to see a land as indeterminate as the storm-swept landscape without. The letter in his pocket was a closeted hope. Like the ikon, it too car-

214

ried a message—but its message could be read by opening the envelope.

When they reached the turn-around point, Warren regretted not having given some verbal recognition to the other's presence. As Folger handed him some mail for Rickley, Warren looked intently at the nervous, narrow face. "Come on, kid," he said. "Relax a little . . . You're going on R and R soon."

"Yeah." Folger beamed at him warmly, his thin lips loosening for the first time on the trip. "Yeah. Boy, am I gonna have fun." He was like a puppy, Warren thought, eager for affection. "Well, good luck," Folger said.

Fighting his way against the downpour, Warren waded up the roadway which streamed muddy water down against him. At one point, he stopped, straightened his shoulder pack and took off his helmet. Raising his face to the rain, he allowed it to wash over him. He stood that way for some time, feeling the stinging drops upon his face, eyelids, throat. The flesh awakened at the tiny shocks and the cool water, reaching his scalp, seemed to freshen his mind. He ran his long fingers through his hair, pressing the excess water away, and put on his helmet again to continue the climb. With Folger gone, he was eager to read the letter. He was actually relieved to be returning to the line, relieved and pleased at the prospect of seeing Rickley again. To catch his breath, he stopped again. Lefevre's solemn injunction disturbed that moment of pleasant anticipation. He could see no sense in it, but then he found Lefevre himself a puzzle; a man as disturbed, as restless, as the thoughts he expressed. Warren tossed off the recollection with a movement of his shoulders and looked up the road. Here and there smoke escaped from a chimney and was immediately dispersed by the rain. The bunkers which he could see were sodden, dismal-looking, but he approached them with growing eagerness. No one was in sight. Those not in their bunkers, he knew, were huddled in forward positions, trying to keep dry and warm while they watched over the melancholy terrain.

Rickley looked up in surprise when Warren entered the bunker. "Didn't expect you up today."

"Claypool didn't tell you?"

"Only contact I've had with him was the radio check yesterday. By the way, I got some Chinese squawks on that static-box."

"Normal." Warren pulled off his poncho and hung it on a peg near the doorway, where a pool of water immediately began to form beneath it. "Some mail for you." He took the letters from his field jacket and held them out to Rickley, who took them.

"All rested?" Rickley asked, only glancing at the envelopes.

"Restless would be a better word."

"Normal sort or different?"

"That ikon, for one thing."

"Yes?" Rickley looked up. "Where is it, by the way?"

"Here." Warren tapped his breast pocket.

"May I see it again?" Rickley asked, putting his mail beside him on his bunk.

Warren brought out the packet and handed it to the other before sitting on his bunk and removing his mud-covered boots. "Any action?" he asked.

"No," the other replied, slipping the velvet pouch out of its plastic covering. "I think the rain has bogged things down."

"White been over?"

"No." Rickley looked up from his task. "He was startled to find I was here, you know? He called over just after you left and he got a little upset."

"I can imagine."

"Wanted to know if I was competent enough to handle the machine by myself and then lectured about the

216

stupidity of leaving an untrained man, that's me, up here all alone." He opened the velvet pouch.

"Don't worry about him."

"I don't. Not about that side of him, anyway. Beautiful, isn't it?" Rickley now held the exposed ikon in his hand.

"Yes." Warren had not taken the ikon out since the days he had spent on C-ration hill.

Rickley gazed at it meditatively, seeming content merely to hold it and look upon it. "I mean truly beautiful," he said, "in the sense of mystery."

"Tell me about it."

"Tell you what?" Rickley looked up.

"What you think the girl meant when she gave it to Prevot."

"About understanding it?" Rickley's blue eyes rested upon Warren for a moment, then returned to the stylized faces of Virgin and Child once more. "That's in a way easy and in a way difficult," he spoke slowly, pausing after each phrase as though painstakingly selecting his words. "Easy to say, and difficult to understand. I've been thinking a lot about this." He looked over at Warren. "Personally, I believe she was trying to tell Prevot something about love. Maybe that marriage wouldn't be the end of the road, but the road itself—through human love to divine." He stopped, his blond head bent forward over the ikon in his hands. "She could've told him that, but it wouldn't have meant anything to him." He looked up. "There's a big difference between things we know intellectually and things we know spiritually."

"But the ikon," Warren insisted.

"God as a Child," Rickley said, looking again at the ikon. "God taking upon Himself a human nature that He might die for us. A supreme act of Love."

"Prevot didn't understand that?"

"Do you?" Rickley's eyes focused upon Warren's face. "Is this beauty to you—or Truth? For me, this," he lifted the ikon slightly, "is an expression of a basic truth, a mystery one could meditate on for a lifetime. Unless one accepts that truth, this is only so much art, some gold and precious stones, nothing more."

"Why do you believe it was meant for me?"

"Because nothing happens that is not God's will."

"War?"

"And just who," Rickley stood up, "do you think is responsible for war? Men make their own decisions." He walked to the shelf. "Okay to put this here?"

"Yes." Warren wanted to continue, but after removing a thermite grenade and placing the ikon in the center of the shelf, Rickley dropped to his bunk and opened a letter. Warren took his own piece of mail from his pocket and stretched out on his cot. The envelope was slightly crumpled, so he smoothed it against his knees before opening it.

Centered on a sheet of onion skin paper in dark lines was a single paragraph:

My Darling,

You know what is painful?—to be wise enough to know what is worthwhile, to know how it should be, to be able to tell, for instance, real love from all of those things commonly caught under that same word, love, yet to be unable, too young, too immature—or maybe too fearful—to achieve that which you know is love. That I love you, I'm certain. And that admission is a sign that I may be overcoming my fearfulness. This is my hope—let it be yours.

Jean

The next morning, two men had disappeared from the listening post in the valley. Their last contact with the C.P. had been at 0300 hours; at 0600 hours they had not come in as scheduled. When a small group of volunteers ventured out to the foxhole, nothing was found, not a sign; any tracks that might have been around the hole were washed away by the rain. After the initial buzz of the news, the company quieted. When Warren went to chow, he noticed the absence of the usual laughter and horseplay; there was a minimum of talking. The men, dull figures with gray faces, stood patiently in the murk. Rain sloshed down their ponchos and the mud sucked around their heavy boots as the chow line inched ahead. The company commander stood at the end of the serving line, greeting each man as he handed him an apple. Though a large man, the smile on his face was weak as he held out an apple to Warren and said, "An apple a day . . . you know the old rhyme." Warren took the apple and shuffled past the kitchen tent to the long slab table that had been erected so that the men could eat while standing. He ate hurriedly, as did the men about him, before the rain water saturated all the food on the tray. When he was through, he stuffed the apple in his pocket, disposed of his tray, and then started back to the bunker, unable to shake from his mind the silly phrase that kept returning to it: "An apple a day keeps the enemy away."

Two days later, Warren heard the company commander outside his bunker and looking out, he glimpsed the captain and one of the platoon lieutenants hurrying into the trench that led to their forward position. The rain had stopped during the night, the first real let-up in days.

"What's up?" Rickley asked.

"I don't know," Warren replied, pulling on his field jacket. "But I think I'll try to find out." His helmet he grabbed as he went out the door.

The forward position door was opening just as Warren reached it. "I'll have to call regiment," he heard the captain say and then the door swung wide and Warren stepped aside to let the two officers pass. "It's them all right," the captain said to the lieutenant.

"Not pretty," Sweet said in his quiet way as Warren entered. "Not pretty at all." He shook his head sadly. "You may look if you want." He indicated the scope. "Only don't move it, please. I was just scanning the area and I passed them. I couldn't believe it at first, but there they are."

Through the scope Warren made out the small grove of trees at the base of a ridge, just forward of the point on which Lieutenant Sweet had regularly called tank fire. He stared at the area for a full minute before he made out the figures. They were like two light X marks against the foliage.

"They've been stripped," Sweet murmured.

"But what have they done to them?" Warren asked, his eye still hard against the cold metal of the aperture.

"They've tied them up," Sweet clucked. "Tied them up, that's what they've done."

Warren studied the two X marks. The naked men had been spread-eagled, hung up by their wrists, and their legs tied down to stakes. He turned from the scope. "What will they do?"

"To them? They're dead."

"No. I mean the company commander?"

"Oh, he knows it's probably a trap, but he's calling regiment to see if he can bring them in."

"Lieutenant Held's coming up this afternoon," Rickley announced when Warren returned to his bunker. "He and Sergeant Claypool. The lieutenant has decided to inspect his positions. Also there's been a three-day artillery clam-up called, corps says no firing. The big boys have something up their sleeve, nobody knows what. Claypool just called to give me the scoop. What's up out there?"

"They've found the two men."

"They have? Where?"

"Hanging from trees."

"Oh, no! Who found them?"

"Lieutenant Sweet."

"They been brought in?"

"Not yet. They're way out there. Somebody'll have to go get them. Probably bait in a trap, the C.O. thinks, so he's calling regiment."

220

"You guys got any binoculars in here?" A strange head appeared in the doorway. "D'ya hear the news?"

"Yes, we heard the news," Warren replied. "No, we don't have any binoculars."

"Them bastards, eh?"

"Yeah," said Warren, remembering the woman on the slope. "Just like us."

The head disappeared, but not before the face registered a look of perplexity.

After chow that afternoon, Warren stopped by White's position.

"Of course they will go out and get them." White was cleaning his carbine. "They cannot let them rot before our eyes. It would demoralize the troops."

"I guess you're right," Warren admitted.

"I know I am right." White fitted the barrel of his weapon to the stock. "I am going. When the lieutenant gets here, I am going to ask him—but whether or not he gives permission, I am going."

"They think it's a trap."

"Of course it is a trap." White slapped a clip into his carbine and stood up. "More reason for going." He hung the weapon by its sling over a peg near the entrance. "You should come along, too." He turned, his short legs stiffly apart, his eyes bright and hard, a smile of contempt tinting his lips. "Or has Rickley converted you to praying for peace?" A dry laugh pushed its way out of the muscular face. " 'Give us this day our daily bread.' Oh, I know those prayers, I used to say them. But I was young then. Today chemistry is able to produce more bread than the market will bear; it goes stale to the pigs. Ha! Nor does man have to sweat any more to get it. Technology, the age of the machine, has abolished sweat in the West and the day is soon coming when it will be unknown for mankind. What else do you think the people of Asia struggle for? The fools believe that the Communists can deliver them from the bondage of sweat and the lack of food. Maybe they can. At any rate, it is better to try that than to sit around praying for what you want."

"Why do you despise Catholics so?"

"Oh, I am not so particular as that. It is the whole Christian network of lies. People, simple people, become content with their horrid lives of poverty and humiliation; they even become resigned to the thought of dying. How can the world progress if people are contented, like cows or sheep?"

"It's more than that, though. You say you prayed once. What happened?"

"Oh, the war, everything." White returned to his bunk. "But even before the war, I turned against the lies. While I was a boy, about fourteen, I saw through it all. We owned much property and on our land we had a small church for our people. Once, while I was away at the military academy, my mother's maid and a workman went to the priest to get married. The girl was pregnant. The priest would not marry them, so, frightened, they ran away. When I came home on a holiday, they had already been gone three days. My father told me what had happened. I saddled my horse and rode out looking for them. I knew that they could not go far, for they had no money and they were young—almost as young as myself. I had a thought about where they might have gone and I found them there —in a deserted woodsman's shack up in our hills. The boy was frightened and crying; the girl lay moaning on the floor of the dirty cabin. She had lost her baby in climbing the hills. I ordered the boy to wait and rode back at full gallop to our house to get help. On the way I passed the little church and the priest, an old man, was standing outside it. I rode up to him and leaped off my horse. 'You should have married them.' I shouted into his face. 'And I will make you marry them!' I beat him with my riding crop, slashing across one side of his face and then the other until

222

he fell weeping at my feet. Leaving him on the ground, I rode home and sent a wagon to bring the girl down. My father was in his study when I ran in. I told him that we must tear down the church, that we must send away the priest. He talked with me a little, but I demanded it. Then the priest came in to tell my father about what I had done, but I had already told my father and now, in front of the priest, I insisted that—at least—we must pay no more support for the church. Although the priest protested, my father said that when I was twenty-one, I would be able to do as I wished with the property anyway, so he would grant this request of mine now. When the bishop came, my father said the same thing, only now he was as convinced as I, for the girl—whom we had nursed in our home—had died. If the church was to continue to exist on our property, then it would have to do so without our support. The bishop even transferred that priest, but I would not relent. From that day to this I have not relented." White stood up and his strong, short body defied challenge. "And I will not relent."

"I don't know," Rickley said when Warren had repeated the story to him, "why the priest would have done such a thing." His head turned from side to side in a slow, melancholy movement. He was biting his lower lip, when he raised his face once more. "But still, isn't it strange how a man will react to a lack of charity? Instead of filling that lack of love, so many people turn and do the opposite— they boil with hatred."

"A vicious circle, eh?" Warren commented.

"It will be broken only when someone answers hatred with love. Then instead of a chain made of links of hate, you have a link of love and that link will have some effect upon those connected to it and—"

"And a chain reaction?" Warren smiled.

"Yes." Rickley stood up and walked over to the ikon, his

223

back turned toward Warren. "But I preach at you and, even if I were good at it, nothing is accomplished that way." He turned around abruptly. "If sermons did any good, then the past two thousand years of sermons would have accomplished something. If sermons did any good, we wouldn't be here."

"Tell me," Warren slipped the question in, "why are you here?" Rickley looked at him quizzically and Warren added, "I mean, why do you get involved in killing? Why aren't you a conscientious objector or something?"

"Because," Rickley hesitated, "because I want to help break the chain."

"How?"

Rickley clasped and unclasped his hands, watching his fingers as they interlocked. "I don't know if this will make any sense to you, but, well, take those two men out there. I try to make acts of love for the men who killed them."

"Sermon on the Mount and all that?"

"Never separate the Sermon on the Mount," Rickley warned, "from the cross on the mount."

"So this is it!" Lieutenant Held glanced around the bunker. "I tried to make it up here earlier, but something always came up." Behind him, a dead cigar clamped in the corner of his mouth, stood Sergeant Claypool who grunted his greetings to the two men and pushed their mail at them. Warren was surprised to see Folger with them, but Claypool made some remark about the climb doing him good. The three visitors strained the capacity of the bunker, and Folger was forced to stand in the doorway, a position he apparently did not relish for his wide, fear-filled eyes darted furtively outside every few minutes.

Glancing at the large envelope that Claypool had thrust at him, Warren noted that Jean's heavy nibbed pen had printed "Photograph" on it.

"The colonel's coming up, too," Lieutenant Held announced. "He wants those two men brought in. They're go-

224

ing to ask for volunteers. I've already asked to go. Claypool and Folger are coming."

Claypool grunted agreement, but Warren glimpsed distress in Folger's eyes before flicking his own to the envelope once again.

"Why don't you come, too?" Held's trim figure was moving about the bunker, as he glanced at the machine, picked up the map board and put it down again and scanned the desk top, neatly arranged for his approval. "Just down your alley," he looked at Warren, "isn't it?"

"Yes, sir," Warren replied. "I'll go with you."

"Thought you would. What's this?" Lieutenant Held lifted the ikon from the shelf. "Heavy." He weighed it in the palm of his hand.

"An ikon, sir," Warren answered.

"Yours?"

"Yes, sir."

"Hm." The lieutenant replaced the ikon. "Didn't know you were religious. Well, we'd better get over to White's position, eh, Sergeant?" Lieutenant Held began to move toward the door of the bunker, while Folger shifted his position further inside. "You've got a nice place here, men," Lieutenant Held said in routine fashion. "Keep up the good work."

"Ya want ta see the forward position, sir?" Sergeant Claypool growled. "It's here."

"Oh, yes. Let's look at it. One of you want to come along in case I have any questions?"

"Yes, sir." Rickley followed the two men outside. Folger did not budge but stood against the wall, his eyes darting everywhere as if seeking a place of safety.

"So you've volunteered? Glad to hear it," Warren said.

"I haven't!" The voice wailed upwards and cracked. "I haven't! Sergeant Claypool's forcing me. He says if I don't go out tonight, he'll get me transferred to a rifle company for good."

"Well? You wanted to experience everything. Just chalk it up . . ."

"He hates me!" Folger wailed. "I go on R and R tomorrow." His small body quaked. "He hates me."

"Why's he hate you?"

"I don't know," the words were a cry of anguish.

Outside, Warren heard the approach of the others. Rickley entered the bunker. "Sergeant Claypool says you're to come with them up to White's position," he said to Folger. "Says you need the exercise."

Folger cast one more despairing glance at the security of the bunker and flung himself out the door.

"Wouldn't expect him to volunteer for a patrol," Rickley mused, looking from the doorway to Warren. "Doesn't seem the type."

"Am I the type?" Warren opened the large envelope.

"You have your reasons," Rickley said, busying himself with his own assortment of letters.

"Him, too." Putting aside the protective pieces of cardboard, Warren opened the photograph. A newspaper clipping fell to the floor, but he looked at Jean's picture. Her clear face was tilted upwards, the lips were parted in the smile so familiar to him; he felt again the ache to see her, to walk beside her along darkened streets, her soft palm clasped against his, their arms moving in unison as they strolled along.

On the inside of the folder, facing the picture, Jean had written: "This is to remind you that days were once happy with adventures of the spirit and that your present condition will not last, but that *you* must last through . . ."

Warren's eyes moved back to the photograph; her face radiated a confidence he did not share. Her face was a reproach to his thoughts, her words a message from a world relinquished. If only he could believe that he would "last through"; but it was death that whispered to him, death

226

that he looked forward to, death for which he had again volunteered, not life.

He stooped, retrieved the fallen clipping, and focused his attention upon it.

First Lieutenant James J. Ordway, much decorated veteran of both WWII and the present Korean War, was found dead in his room in the Bachelor Officer Quarters, the Public Information Officer of Fort Dix announced today. The handsome officer, a native of Rhode Island, had shot himself through the head with his service pistol. Motive for the suicide is unknown. No notes were found. Lieutenant Ordway had served with distinction in the campaigns of . . .

Warren turned wearily from the newsprint and put the clipping on top of Jean's photo. The news item was anticlimactic, a too-much-delayed punch line to his talks with Ordway.

Rickley stood up and walked to the door, the pages of a letter still in his hand. "I thought so." He turned. "It's raining again."

So this was to be the night. And here he sat on the edge of a crude bunk, in the belly of an equally crude shelter, waiting. Jean had thrown her thread across the chasm, but her thread was too weak to have any effect upon the press of time mercilessly moving to the appointed hour. So this was what Prevot had felt on his last day. There was no escape. His head dropped to his hands and he dug his fingers into his scalp.

Warren heard Rickley walk in front of him, then the shuffle of papers and Rickley's steps as he moved toward the door once more. The sound of Rickley's rustling poncho caused Warren to look up. "Where are you going?"

The other adjusted his helmet over his blond hair and took his carbine from its peg. "Gotta test-fire this." His words suspended themselves in the crude doorway even as he disappeared through it.

Rapidly, Warren threw on his own poncho, clapped his helmet on, grabbed his carbine and went after Rickley.

Lieutenant Sweet was coming out of the F.O. position. "Hi," he said. "I'm out of a job. No firing for three days at least." He shook his head. "Corps must have its reasons," he went on, "but I'd sure like to give that patrol some support tonight."

"You mean you can't?"

"None." Sweet rolled his head again as if to some sad melody. "No artillery or mortars for anything except a major enemy attack." The thin, tall man eased his way down the trench. "Poor boys," he sighed as he moved out of sight.

Warren hurried along the wet trench to the point where Rickley was firing his carbine. Approaching him, Warren touched the weapon with his hand. Rickley turned on Warren quizzically.

"You're not going out there tonight," Warren stated.

"Oh?" The boy turned again to the front and fired another burst across the rain-swept valley.

"You heard me! You're not going out there tonight!"

Rickley shrugged. "You're mistaken. I've volunteered. Held was pleased to find his whole unit willing to go."

"But you've no right to go! It's a trap!"

"You're going."

"I've a reason."

"I know. Me, too."

"Be sensible. There'll be more than enough men volunteering. Don't risk it. You've got a girl."

"You've got a girl, too."

"And a family . . ."

"Most of us have."

Behind the frank blue eyes Warren sensed a will strong

228

in its determination. "For God's sake, why?" Already he felt he was losing to that will.

"Don't ask."

"I have asked."

"All right. But I don't have to answer."

"It's concerned somehow with me," Warren insisted. "You decided after I did—when you went out to the F.O. position. Why? What do you think you're going to accomplish?"

Rickley said, "You're sounding egotistical, Warren. I'm going for the walk."

"The hell you are! I'm going to tell Held."

Rickley laughed. "Won't you look foolish?" Drops of rain glistened on his face. He ejected the clip from his carbine and reached for another; it escaped his grasp and fell into the mud at his feet. He paused in his reach for another clip. "I haven't tried to stop you, have I?" He successfully slapped the new clip home and, turning his back on Warren, stepped a few paces down the trench and snapped off a few more rounds. Then he fired the whole clip in one continuous burst, the weapon rising upwards despite his grip. As the last shot was absorbed in the heavy wash of the rain, he slung the weapon and walked past Warren. "Better check yours, too," he said. "We may need them."

Later, White whistled over the sound power and Warren answered. "I hear you are both going," White announced happily. "Great news. It will be fun. More like a war should be. I am to tell you that the colonel will give us a briefing in about an hour. They have more volunteers than they need. They are weeding out some, those with wives and the old-timers due to rotate soon. We are all safe. See you there."

Rickley lay on his cot writing a letter, his boyish face a contradiction to the muddy boots which dangled over the end of the bunk and the garments of the soldier in which he was clothed.

Warren looked at Rickley a moment before speaking. "Briefing's in an hour."

The other turned from his letter only long enough to nod, then returned to the page before him.

Warren wanted to protest again, but the calm face aborted his desire. His hand touched Jean's photo; he opened it to read again her words and to scan her face. The world of her face was not his. She belonged to Rickley, to the confident joy of the monastery, to those who shared her vision and her hope . . . He closed the folder and set it aside. Had he found any meaning here? The ikon rested on its shelf, a mystery still. He, like Prevot, would leave it behind. Getting up, he put on his poncho.

"Early yet," Rickley said from behind his letter.

"I know." His helmet on his head, his weapon slung muzzle downwards, Warren stepped out into the rain. The gray drizzle harmonized with the hum in his ears, as if a seashell placed there whispered of secret worlds. Wearier than ever, weighted down by weapon, helmet and rain, his pace slowed by the muck, he moved along the road behind the sodden bunkers—temporary dwellings. Weren't all dwellings temporary? The world was shuddering, and perhaps it would end. It wasn't hard to believe. There was little reason for continuing this struggle—killing, waiting to be killed . . . Duke had run from the thought and saved his life by momentarily giving in to his deepest urges. Why didn't he run? His feet slogged heavily in the mud as if bound to the earth by strong elastic bonds. They rose against pressure and fell as if pulled down. He pushed against the gray sheets of rain; through them he could see the outlines of distant ridges, uneasily heaving against the sky. Folger's cry that he had not done everything yet echoed still. Warren looked at the black earth as his feet ploughed through it. He had done nothing. He had made a feeble motion toward love that had left him with a hollow ache; otherwise—nothing. He had plodded through life

230

even as now he plodded though this mud, fragments of it clinging to him, the rain of impressions washing off of him and into a soggy mass at his feet. But Folger meant sex, the feverish attempt to realize imagined orgies.

——"Man, oh, man, rolling in breasts, buried in breasts, tons of breasts, gobbling up them breasts . . ." The returnee from a rest leave had rolled his eyes in remembered delight, and Folger had sat openmouthed, listening. "Oh, man, oh, man, I ate that woman up, yum, yum, tasty woman flesh . . ." The returnee's lips smacked down as he chomped into an apple.——

Warren stopped, looked up; he was standing in front of White's bunker. He pounded on the door and heard White call, "Come in."

White was sitting on his bunk surrounded by hand grenades. He held one in his hand. "Ha!" he cried. "Friend Warren. We have fun tonight." He held the grenade aloft. "I am fixing the little morsels. See. One bends the cotter pin out just so and then one has no trouble pulling the pin swiftly." He put the grenade down. "Finished," he sighed, casting a satisfied glance at the grenades beside him. "Ah, Warren, for this I have waited a long time." He rubbed his hands together enthusiastically and his teeth appeared behind his heavy lips as he grinned. "Is it time to go?" He extended an arm, his thick wrist appeared from under the cuff of his fatigue jacket and he looked at his watch. "No, a few minutes yet."

Warren sat down on the battery box. "Have you ever been in love?"

A look of surprise crossed White's face, the grin disappeared for a moment, then he burst out in laughter. "Ah, I knew something was wrong," he chortled. "It is love. Yes. I should have known. You said it that night. I remember now, and here I have been wondering what had happened to my friend Warren." He shook his head in self-remonstrance. "I told you that night," he said, quickly serious. "It does not exist. I know." One solid fist thudded against his chest. "I have known many women who have said that they were in love with me. But love is a womanish fiction to keep men subservient. Nothing is more ignoble! Men crawl before women, begging, pleading, and for what? For relief from a physical urge. They become slaves to women—who are what? Just whores."

"You believe that?"

A smile crossed the thick lips again, an indulgent, fatherly smile. "Of course. Your trouble is that you still retain the old illusions about love and women. But love is outworn. It may have served its purpose once, but no more. Today it is a useless word, nothing more. Friend Warren, you are intelligent enough to see that. We can refashion the world when we remember that men are the masters of the earth, that men make all such concepts. We must junk the old illusions, the old delusions, then we start afresh."

"And you've never felt love?"

"Oh, maybe when I was a child. But as a man, no. It does not exist. The child dreams; the man must face reality."

"But—" Warren began.

"But nothing. As a man I need a woman's body occasionally, but that is no reason for me to become her slave. I take her body as I take an aspirin for a headache."

"You never feel anything toward them?"

"Feelings?" The broad hand caressed a grenade. "Oh, yes, sometimes I get carried away, but that is not love; that is passion. I despise the woman who causes me to be passionate." White looked at his watch again. "We must go." He rose, got his poncho and, bowing his thick neck, thrust his head through the opening. "I consider passion, too, a weakness. But," he smiled, "we are, none of us, free from it." He picked up his helmet. "The briefing is in the kitchen bunker, out of the rain." Warren arose and fol-

232

lowed White through the doorway into the rainy, already darkening evening.

The kitchen bunker was crowded with men. There were, Warren estimated, about twenty going on the patrol. Near the back of the room Sergeant Claypool sat glowering beside Folger whose face registered utter desolation, his eyes hidden behind his spectacles which mirrored the glare of the lanterns in such a way as to give him the appearance of having a pair of white saucers clamped to his gray cheeks.

Coleman lanterns, suspended from the ceiling, illuminated the kitchen and the light was reflected by the polished surfaces of the field stoves along one wall. The kitchen crew had completed its work for the day; the pots and pans glistened brightly. Men had pulled up orange crates and cartons of tinned food to sit on and at the front of the tent an area was left clear for the map board. Shortly after Warren and White had settled themselves on top of a full crate of apples, the colonel entered. Someone shouted the command and the men leaped to attention while the tall man strode to the center of the room. "As you were," the colonel said. From behind him the captain, Lieutenant Held, and Lieutenant Swiggart moved into the front row. Rickley entered and sat down near the front of the group as the colonel waited for the men to settle themselves once more.

"You may smoke, men," the colonel said. "That is if the cook will let us."

The men guffawed loudly. Cigarettes were produced and lighted while the colonel put a match to his own pipe.

Then the bunker was silent save for the breathing of twenty men waiting for the colonel to speak. "This is a nasty business," he said, looking soberly at the group, peering into each face in turn. "I do not like the looks of it and I want to leave plenty of opportunity for anyone who wishes

233

to, to leave. If you've changed your mind, just don't show up at the patrol formation at 2030 hours. No one will ask any questions. We've others who do want to go and they've been told to stand by. Now, with that said, let's look at the situation." He paused, glanced at the map, then turned his back on it once again. "There is little doubt that this is a trap; there is no other reason for them to do such a thing. As you all know, we have a corps directive down that says that we must have no heavy weapons or artillery firing for the next three days. I've checked and there's nothing I can do about it. Needless to say, it makes our job difficult; it means you men are going out there without the usual protective covering. You will take along a couple of grenade launchers which will give you some aid. Other than that you'll have to rely upon your own weapons and grenades. Carry as much ammo as you can without impeding movement. As for weapons, your patrol leader and I have worked out that: four BAR's and two light machine guns. The rest of you take your M-1's or carbines. I'm not going to give you any briefing. Your patrol leader, Lieutenant Swiggart, will do that. I simply wanted to commend you men upon your spirit, your willingness to take such a risk for the sake of your buddies. You have my respect. Now, Lieutenant Swiggart will give you the patrol briefing." The colonel turned towards the platoon lieutenant who had entered with him and nodded his head. The colonel took his seat alongside of the company commander as the lieutenant stepped to the map board.

Using the map board, Lieutenant Swiggart traced with his finger the routes the patrol would follow, out and back. He had marked the location of the bodies and the probable situation of the enemy. Intentness firmed the tired lines around his mouth and eyes. An informal drawling of the words, despite his serious, business-like manner, marked him as a southerner. At the end of each sentence, his eyes picked out those of one of his listeners for a moment be-

234

fore he continued. At check point two a squad under Lieutenant Held's leadership was to branch off and establish itself so that it could lay down a base of fire under which the rest of the patrol could withdraw if that was necessary. The machine guns, two grenade launchers, and a BAR would go with Lieutenant Held's squad. The main body of the patrol would proceed to the grove of trees to bring out the bodies on stretchers.

"We've got the rain on our side," Lieutenant Swiggart said. "It will cover our movements and it could cause the enemy to be careless." When he had finished his briefing, Lieutenant Swiggart glanced at the map board once more and then looked at the colonel. "Anything you'd like to add, sir?"

The men followed his eyes to the white-haired figure who rose to his feet and faced them. "No. I think you have covered the situation adequately. I do want to announce, though, that the regimental chaplain came up with me. The Padre asked me to say that Catholics desiring to go to confession should report to him at the C.P. now." Turning, the colonel sat down once again.

The company commander stood up. "I want to tell you men that this is the finest group I've ever served with. You were chosen out of many who asked to go. The others have been told to stand by in case you should . . . need a hand. That's all I have to say. Good luck. Attention!" The men leaped to their feet once more and the colonel put on his helmet and stood. The captain saluted him and the colonel left the bunker. "As you were, men," the captain said. "2030 hours—the company C.P. Those who don't have armored vests should get them at the supply room now. Dismissed!"

The men filed out of the bunker. There was little talk among them. A few, Rickley among them, turned abruptly to the left as they left the bunker and went in the direction of the company C.P. "Catholics," White spat. "Going to whisper their sins. See? Rickley, too. Going to protect themselves from hell." A short, explosive laugh came out of his throat. "There is but one hell and that is life on earth." He grasped Warren's arm in a strong grip. "Let us get our vests."

The two men got their vests and Warren picked up an additional supply of ammo for his carbine and six hand grenades. "Do what I have told you with them," White ordered. "Speed may make the difference. See you there, friend Warren." The stocky figure plodded off into the rain and Warren slogged back to his own bunker. The rain was coming down in a torrent. He carried the grenades in a small cardboard box that the supply clerk had given to him, and the box was soggy and falling apart by the time he reached the empty bunker.

Warren sat down on his cot, heedless of the water that drained from his poncho onto his bedding. He dropped the carton onto the bunk beside him and began to bend the pins, one by one, as White had shown him. Finishing that task, he slapped a fresh clip of ammunition into his carbine and hung it on the wall. He wiped his damp hands on the sleeping bag and picked up Jean's photograph. He did not look at it, but held it for a moment in his hand. Putting it down again, he sought for the envelope in which it had come. Finding it, he inserted the photograph; bringing her letter out of his breast pocket, he inserted that too. He closed the envelope, pressing down the little metal fastener where it penetrated the reinforced circle of the flap opening. On the front of the envelope he wrote: "Please return to sender," drawing an arrow to the corner where her name and address appeared.

While processing in Japan, he was asked about his insurance again. He had always had difficulty with that. The insurance was compulsory, but he had listed no beneficiaries. Then, in Japan, he had been asked again if he had any

236

changes to make in his designation of beneficiary. He had given them Jean's name and address.

"And secondly?"

"Secondly?"

"Yes, you should list two . . . in case one should die."

"She won't."

"You should list two, although I suppose you could leave it blank. It would just go to the government then."

"All right," he decided. "The Abbey of Solesmes, Solesmes, Sarthe, France."

The eyebrows had lifted, he had had to spell the names for the fellow, but he had put an end to the harassment.

It would be a shock for her. Maybe there should be an explanatory letter accompanying them. Anyway, it was good to think that she would get something out of having known him. The ikon caught his eye. He got up, took it from the shelf and stared at it. For him, as for Prevot, there was to be no solution to the enigma. Another question left unanswered. How much time did he have? He didn't have a watch. Somewhere he had the velvet bag and the plastic sack. He hurried to the desk and searched through the papers, then turned to his pack-sack, finding them there. Once he had the ikon safely in the bags, he wrapped it in a piece of writing paper and slipped a rubber band around the crude package. Grabbing another sheet of paper, he scrawled: "Send to . . ." and then printed plainly her name and address. He wanted no mistake. This, most of all, was hers. He slipped the note under the rubber band, and was rising from his pack-sack when Rickley entered.

"Just like Saturday night at home," Rickley announced, taking off his helmet. "A line." He sat down at the desk.

"Just time to end my brief note," he said casually. "Hello. You've put the ikon away. Carrying it with you?"

"No. Put it away for safekeeping."

"Should carry it with you."

237

"For luck?"

"Not exactly. Take it!" Then the head bowed to the desk as Rickley began to write rapidly.

Warren bent to his pack once again, but his motions were paralyzed. Rickley's abrupt words hung in the air . . .

The men shuffled about in a cluster near the C.P., waiting for the officers to appear. No one tried to smoke. Warren noticed Sergeant Claypool with a short, dead stub of a cigar between his teeth. Beside the skinny and pale Folger, he loomed large, the expression on his face impassive, almost sullen.

White came over. "It is well planned." His face beamed in the gray wetness. "The colonel must have planned it himself."

The two lieutenants came out. Lieutenant Held stood near the doorway and flashed a light at a piece of paper that he held in his hand. He read off a list of names.

"Good," White chortled. "Thought we might get stuck with Held's group."

Warren and White fell into the single file that Lieutenant Swiggart was forming.

Earlier, Warren had rediscovered the clipping about Ordway's suicide in his breast pocket. Wondering whether to give it to Lieutenant Held, he decided not to.

"Carbines?" Lieutenant Swiggart looked closely at them. "Up front. Where's the other BAR?" There was a shuffle of movement and the lieutenant nodded. "Stay at the rear of the column. You've got plenty of ammo, haven't you?"

"Yes, sir."

"All right. Just keep in contact." He moved along the line, forming the column. "Stretcher bearers?"

"Here, sir."

238

"Captain's sending out four more men to relieve you on the way back. Okay?"

"Right, sir."

"He'll send them out when he hears you're on your way in."

"Yes, sir."

"Now, whatever you men do," he whispered loudly to the whole patrol, "keep in contact. Stay on your toes. Be as quiet as possible. We might be able to make this without a hitch." He strode to the head of the line. "Radioman?"

"Here, sir."

"Good, let's move out . . ." Lieutenant Swiggart took the point position.

Into the gray night the men filed, silently climbing upwards in the face of the rain toward the top of the ridge, and then following a path down through the opening in the barbed wire, past the white, upturned faces of the men in the listening post, out into the valley where death lay buried in tin canisters and wooden boxes, awaiting the press of a foot, the tug on a wire, before springing up to show its ugly face.

——There was a song that Warren associated with Jean. Cycling through the Auvergne, through a lush valley where a golden dusk was stretching its fingers across the pastures, he had come upon a ruined castle. Only the remnants of walls remained, and a portion of a tower, on top of a hill between him and the setting sun. The jagged stones were softened by the golden hue and the castle stood, he thought, nobly, like an aged man surveying the domain of his trust for the last time. As he stopped his bicycle, Warren heard the song and, looking up the road, saw the first part of a herd of cows as it rounded a turn in the road. Behind the cows walked a girl, a smooth branch in her hand. She cast only the briefest glance at him even as the lovely sounds left her lips. Then she was only

239

a figure disappearing down the golden road behind a herd of golden cows, the lilt of her song fading into the evening. The words had been unintelligible to him, but the feeling had penetrated. He pushed his bicycle across the road, across the field and up the green slope and that night he had rested on the grass, in the center of the old castle, his arms under his head, and above him, vaulting the walls around him, were the stars of the clearest of nights. In his memory was the song.——

But this night was not clear, and there had been no stars during the rainy season. Ahead of him, through the rain, he could see the curve of White's steel helmet, and beyond that the shadow of another man. The rain obscured his vision, and he must keep his mind on his feet, his eyes to the ground or fixed on the figure ahead of him, the short bulging figure with the weapon held crosswise in front so that it appeared to pierce the body. There was a grunting sound, some confusion; somebody had slipped. As Warren approached, the line was again spacing itself, and he had to wait for White to move ahead again. A wind swept out at them suddenly, leaping down from some hidden place and swirling the rain about him more furiously. White's hand shot up and the men squatted. White scuttled back, still crouched, and whispered hoarsely, "Rest." Warren turned and waddled to the man back of him, putting his face close to the huddled form to whisper the word. The white face that turned to him was Folger's; his eyes were frozen in horror. "Rest," Warren repeated, then, seeing that Folger did not seem to comprehend, he added, "Pass it on." As he moved back to his own place, Warren could not shut out the sight of Folger's stricken eyes. He squatted on his haunches, his carbine locked in the crease of his body. Across his chest he had strung the grenades, hooking them to the bandoliers in which he carried his ammunition clips. Now the grenades pressed against his thighs uncomfortably. The wind was throwing rain against the back of his neck and the cold water ran down his back between his shoulder blades, along his spine.

He had remembered that song while with Jean; it seemed to express something he felt about her, but even as the words had been unintelligible to him, so the feeling had been inexpressible. He raised his head, trying to bring his helmet back over his neck so that it would stop the flow of water there. Out over the darkened valley he could see nothing. Had a girl ever sung in this valley? He had never seen any cows in Korea, but it was not hard to imagine that some girl had wandered here one afternoon as the sun was disappearing behind hills unscorched then by war and sung a song expressing her joy, her youth, her love.

White's hand lifted and then his body followed as if, grasping some invisible support, he had pulled himself up. Warren stood, turned, and motioned Folger forward. He had gone about ten feet when he heard the shout behind him. He swung about in time to hear the shot. Folger was not behind him. Warren heard a brief cry and other sounds muffled in the downpour as he hurried, crouched down, back along the path by which he had just come. A knot of men clustered where Folger had been squatting. Warren approached. "What's up?" he asked hoarsely, then saw Folger writhing at the center of the group.

"He froze." Sergeant Claypool's voice rasped with a quick intake of air. "I tried to budge him and he swung his carbine at me. I grabbed it and it went off."

"He's hit in the stomach," Rickley, kneeling beside the fallen man, raised his head to make the announcement.

"What in hell happened?" Lieutenant Swiggart's oval face broke the circle. He looked down at Folger who raised his knees slowly toward his stomach and then lengthened them into the mud again in a series of steady movements while his hands clutched at his stomach. "Oh,

241

my God." The lieutenant looked at the group. "How badly?"

"Stomach, sir," Warren said.

"You," the lieutenant shot a finger at Rickley. "Run back to the stretcher bearers. Get them up here." He looked at Sergeant Claypool. "What happened?"

Claypool told him.

"Why in hell did he volunteer?" the lieutenant asked in an anguished tone, glancing at the writhing form.

A gurgling sound came from Folger's throat. His face, smeared with mud by its constant twisting from side to side, contorted in a painful effort. The rain hammered down on his gray cheeks.

"Now we're really in for it," the lieutenant muttered. "Every Chink in Korea heard that shot."

The stretcher bearers came up and Lieutenant Swiggart urged them to step it up as they rolled Folger onto the canvas and strapped him down. "Take him to Lieutenant Held," he instructed. "I'll radio for the relief to come out and pick him up. Then get back here, fast!" He turned to Sergeant Claypool. "You'll have to make a full report, Sergeant. *If* we get back." Turning, he hurried toward the head of the patrol column again.

As the bearers raised the stretcher, Folger's arm lifted, wavered, and stretched toward Sergeant Claypool. The wide eyes did not change, the breath continued to come in quick gasps, and the hand curled feebly while one thin finger pointed to the thick face. The bearers moved off, but the hand still pointed out into the rain-filled sky.

Warren returned to his position. White was crouched in front of him. It seemed a long time before the patrol moved out again. The rest break had taken place at the halfway point, as announced at the briefing, so there was a chance that they were still far enough away from the enemy not to have attracted undue attention. The wind and rain helped, but they were nearer now to the enemy lines than they were

242

to their own. In another half hour or so they would be at the grove of trees. A half hour . . .

——The peasants were picking grapes, the women and the children, and the old men. A young man, basket slung over his shoulders, carried the grapes from the field to the horse-drawn rig at the roadside. There, he dumped them into great barrels. Another young man tamped them down, his strong arms and broad back stained blue with juice. In the field the women were singing and Warren nibbled at the grapes while listening to their song. One of the women smiled shyly at him; her eyes were brilliant brown, like polished wood. Another young man strolled through the field, talking to each person in turn, smiling at everyone and laughing happily. He approached Warren. "Three of the cows in that field are chickens, bread and butter. Watch that, invest your money wisely, wisely, invest your money. I've got it. Oh, all I need is a jug of paste and a coffee bean." The brown-eyed girl hurried over and took him by the arm. "He's my brother," she explained, gently shooing the babbler away. "It was the war . . ."——

Ahead, White's hand signaled Warren to halt once more and he squatted in the wet darkness to wait. The lieutenant would now be talking to the captain on the radio, whispering, "Check point two." It would be the last radio check, too close to the enemy to risk any more. Heading off to the left now, Lieutenant Held's squad would there set up a base for covering fire. Held's group had a sound-power phone connecting them with the men on line, while the rest of the patrol was cut loose from that world, isolated in the bowels of the night. Alone . . .

White's hand shot up and forward. Warren relayed the signal to Sergeant Claypool and, getting up, moved on. The column went more slowly, each forward step called for greater caution. As he had been taught in basic, Warren raised his foot carefully, set it down as carefully into the ooze of the paddy field, then lifted the other foot and set it down in the same way; it was a weird, slow-motion ballet performed by a line of adult men edging their way into fear.

There was a tension which had stretched life, as one would stretch a balloon, so far that it became transparent and one could see through it to the essentials. Yet the experience had anguished, not elevated him, for—like the balloon—he had found his life empty.

The patrol was entering a scrub area. Warren thought he heard a sound, but it might have been the wind in the brush. His body tensed even more, his legs were almost stiff as he brought them up and forward before placing them down. Then White dropped to his stomach. Warren fell immediately, clutching his carbine close. There was no sound but the ticking of the rain on his helmet—and wind. Then he heard it, or did he? A soft whistle off to the right and front came brokenly through the rain and wind. Had they been heard—or seen? Perhaps the enemy, whoever had whistled there to front and right, had heard Folger's shot and had been sitting in the rain, waiting for them to enter his field of fire. Then from the left and front came another whistle, broken, muted, but surely a reply. White did not move, he might have been a log, with the carbine like a protruding branch jutting out from him.

Warren's breath, short, rapid strokes of air, burned in his lungs. He tried to relax, took a long breath and deliberately slowed his exhalation. His face felt warm, but he could not tell if the moisture on it was rain or sweat. He dared not wipe it; his hand was glued to the wood of his weapon. The earth was beginning to feel good, warm and comfortable under him, when he saw White motion him forward and then, crouching, begin to move ahead. Reluctantly, Warren pulled his legs up under him, crouched, passed the signal on and moved forward.

At the head of the column something exploded. Warren flattened, lost sight of White and crawled forward on his

244

stomach, his grenades dragging against his chest; after a few minutes, still unable to see White, he crouched and ran forward. As he hurried, he felt a hand grasp his shoulder; his own forward momentum spun him around and he looked full into White's face.

"I almost killed you," White said sharply. "You surprised me." He dropped to one knee and fixed his bayonet to the barrel of his carbine.

"What was the blast?"

"Booby trap," White whispered. "Concussion grenade. Nobody hurt, but they are sure to hit us now."

Warren looked around, startled, noticing that they were only a short distance from the grove of trees. A bent figure ran toward them. "Pass the word back for the stretchers, then move up." The shadow spun about and ran the way it had come.

"You go," White ordered. "I'll stay here."

Warren hurried back, no need for precautions now. The booby trap had made enough noise to alert the whole sector. The suck of the mud at his boots, the lash of the grass and brush at his legs, were sounds left suspended in the darkness behind him as he rushed back to Sergeant Claypool. Upon hearing the message, Claypool grunted and left to carry the word to Rickley. Warren spun about and, breathing heavily, sloshed back to where White waited.

"Over there," White pointed to an extension of the larger ridge. "On that finger, I saw movement. Damn! I think our base of fire is too far away."

The stretcher bearers came by and White pointed toward the head of the patrol. "Only one?" White asked.

"Other's not back yet," Warren explained.

"Damn Folger," White snapped.

They heard the others moving up behind them as they moved out. Lieutenant Swiggart met them as they came up. "Over there," he directed White to a position to his right facing another ridge finger that stretched out toward

245

the grove. "You cover the finger on the left," he pointed, and Warren ran and dropped behind a bush. The grove of trees was about fifty yards away, to Warren's right. He faced the finger that White had been watching, peering at it through the rain, looking for any movement.

The enemy could not have built a trap as well as the one nature provided. This finger and the one White was covering were like two arms stretching out to encircle the grove that lay between and beneath them. Now men were on both flanks of the approach to the grove, others covered the center and rear. Through the center, the stretcher bearers crept toward the bodies. Behind them, "too far back," White had said, was Lieutenant Held's protective base of fire.

Warren could see nothing on the ridge above the grove. Once again he was enclosed in rain and dark so that everything appeared animate. Branches were gesturing men; shrubs crawled; the grass threatened to erupt into an enemy horde. He looked toward the dark grove, but could see nothing. For a moment he had the terrifying thought that the bodies had been removed. "Bastards," he murmured, then realized he was thinking of the corpses not the enemy. What right had they to demand rescue? The whole affair seemed insane; that twenty men should risk their lives for two dead bodies. He hated them, hated them with an intensity he had never felt before. He shook his head to dash away the passion. He had volunteered, he had chosen to come out—the bodies did not matter, the vision did—the vision on the train—that was why he was here—and Bernhardt's letter. He must remember these things. Why? Who was Bernhardt? What right had he to . . . ? And the vision . . . ? Had it really occurred? He groped for the truth of memory. The woman with the worn wedding band, the soldier, yes, the businessman, round-eyed, bald-headed, stooping for his papers . . . they were real. What about the other—the scene of himself being killed?

246

The pop of a flare refocused his mind. It would open in a . . . yes, there it was, a bright, small moon descending with the rain, dropping down over their heads. Another pop, another moon sputtering out its light through the dark. He pressed closer to the earth, his cheek upon its chilling surface, but he kept staring into the grove of trees. Then, through the flickering glow, he saw the two pale bodies. Arms and legs extended, heads dangling, the bodies showed like nightmare figures, an eerie glow seemed to permeate the flesh. He saw also darker shadows, the stretcher bearers, in the grass near them.

Instantly the firing began. The dark shadows near the bodies crawled into the grove. Rifles, carbines, and burp guns snapped at each other. The darkness returned and Warren looked up at the finger he had been assigned to cover; weapons flashed out, spurts of flame licking at the rain. He could make out four positions on the slope, four weapons firing from that angle. The carbine leaped against his cheek as he took aim on one of the flashes and fired.

A grenade exploded in the field in front, then another. Their *whumph, whumph* sounded mushy, but the shrapnel slashed near. The enemy had the advantage; they could practically roll their grenades down the slope of the finger, but he was not close enough to throw one himself. He raked the finger with slugs, ejected the clip, fired another clip without pause, hoping all the while that his weapon wouldn't jam. He crept forward and rolled to the right, expecting return fire. He slapped another clip into his weapon and fired three quick bursts. Again he rolled away rapidly and pulled himself forward. His grenades tugged at his chest. If he could get a little closer, he could use them. He heard grenades exploding on the finger. The grenade launcher with Lieutenant Held's group was at last throwing them in. Then suddenly the finger was quiet and dark again. Sporadic firing continued on the right flank of the patrol.

"Pull back," somebody from the right shouted. "Pull back, they've got 'em." Warren pushed himself up and turned to join other men falling back. They all dropped together as they heard the sound of the canister opening up above them. The flare cast its ivory glow over the rain-swept paddy. A machine gun began to fire down on them from the finger; somebody screamed, a long piercing scream that died slowly. The machine gun swept back across the area as the screaming began again.

The flare died out, but the machine gun continued to clatter down at them. Some of the patrol returned its fire, but another flare popped overhead and forced them to stop. From the rear, the grenade launcher began again to lob them in, the grenades crunching onto the finger. The machine gun was silent.

"They got it," somebody shouted. "They got it. Pull back."

But another flare erupted overhead, forcing them prostrate on the earth. The machine gun chattered flames and steel at them from a position lower down the finger.

"They moved it," Warren heard White's voice beside him.

"Why don't our own machine guns open up?" Rickley had crawled alongside of them. The piercing scream rose again, a demon struggling with the flesh. Warren felt the scream like a sharp ache in his bones. No one spoke until it whined out.

"Who knows?" White's face was ghostly pale under the light, the flesh like polished marble. "That damned grenade launcher better get to work."

As if in reply to his demand, two more grenades crunched into the finger, hurtling over their heads. The enemy machine gun continued to cut back and forth across the field, the slugs singing overhead. No more grenades came in, however, and the three men lay stretched on the ground, waiting for the diminishing flare to die. With the

248

darkness returned the long, skin-chilling scream. All around them, their weapons began to chop back at the machine gun.

"There's your machine gun now," Warren shouted to Rickley as tracers arced toward the enemy ridge.

"Too high," Rickley moaned, and the three men watched the tracers disappear into darkness high above the enemy position.

"All right," White commanded, "let's get him. He can keep us here all night, picking us off." He crouched. "Follow me." With incredible speed he darted in the direction of the enemy machine gun. Warren and Rickley followed as rapidly as they could. As another flare popped above them, they flattened again. The machine gun spattered the mud in front of them. "He's seen us," White called. "No sense keeping still now." He raised his carbine, answered the machine gun, crawled forward rapidly. Warren and Rickley, about five feet apart, followed. The flare went out, but the machine gun's lead punctured the air above their heads. Taking advantage of the darkness, they crouched, racing after White toward the gun. They fell again as another flare sounded above their heads. There was a pause in the firing as the flare opened the veil of darkness, then slugs thudded into the mud around them, prodding for their flesh.

"He's spotted us again," Warren grunted as he pushed forward, keeping his carbine out of the mud. White was a good fifteen feet ahead of them, almost to the base of the finger.

As the flare sputtered out, White leaped up, a dark splotch in the rain. Skirting the base of the slope, he ran a short distance up the end of the finger. The machine gun was still clattering over their heads when the grenade exploded along the edge of the ridge. Behind them, piercing the dark and the wet like the point of a needle, came the scream.

"Quick, he's attracted their attention." Warren thrust himself up and ran directly toward the hill, Rickley beside him. Another grenade exploded near the finger, and then the machine gun sent them sprawling in the mud again.

"White's hit," Rickley shouted.

"You sure?"

"Grenade. Saw him roll to the bottom of the hill." While speaking, Rickley began to crawl forward in the rain. He put his carbine at arm's length in front of his sprawled body, and then worked toward it. He repeated this motion several times, moving forward in a painful inching motion that reminded Warren of the woman who had dragged her shattered body toward the top of the ridge by the raw strength of her fingers. As Warren watched, Rickley repeated his movement again, but this time he pulled himself beyond his carbine, leaving it where it lay. He paused, unhooked a grenade from his bandolier and, clutching it in his hand, began to move forward again. The machine gun was silent, the dark mound ahead of them ominous as a giant watchdog. From the darkness behind them came the twisted shriek once more, but the inhuman sound ceased quickly: a short spurt of terror that shivered a moment in the dismal night. Warren stared, fascinated by Rickley's actions. Hypnotized, he watched Rickley bring his legs forward and thrust himself upwards, the grenade's pin yanked aside as the right arm shot back. The small object sputtered. Even as the machine gun flashed, Warren sprang toward Rickley, a yell clogged in his throat. As the hoarse cry left his lips, he was thrown back, a burning spear impaled in his chest. In his ears the sound of the machine gun, muffled by the rain, softened by the pressure against his ears, was a series of dull thuds. Sinking into blackness, he thought he heard the crumple of Rickley's grenade. He heard the sound again as deeper blackness smothered him.

250

Later, Warren heard other sounds: voices, shouts, indistinct commands, consultative whispers, grunts, all intermittent, chopped into fragments by blackness. On his body he felt strange pressures and movements. All things at a distance, he floated in a pool of darkness, his consciousness caught up in a strong rhythm which occasionally brought him near the surface world of sound and movement, only to spiral him away downwards in a gentle descent, back into warm darkness. When one upward thrust succeeded in pushing him above the rim of that dark world, he discovered he could not move; his arms were held to his sides, his legs were bound together. He looked up into the night; the rain pressed down against a glass, the droplets hit a few inches above his eyes, spread themselves out and were blown away as if by some giant mouth. He was aware of a noise, a rhythmic, grinding noise, which seemed connected with his body. The rain droplets above his face shimmered with the rhythm of the helicopter and he watched them for a time as if they were, of all created things, the most interesting. Then he fell under the spell of their dance and into darkness again.

The ikon leaned against a small vase full of fresh flowers. A chunky little army nurse, wearing lieutenant's bars and a business-only expression, brought the flowers from somewhere, changing them whenever they began to wilt, crossing herself whenever she finished arranging them. "It saved your life," she said the first morning he was allowed to sit up. "You should say a prayer of thanks to her." Then she swung about on her oxfords and was gone.

After the nurse had left, Warren reached out and took the ikon in his hand. A hole large enough for his finger to enter gaped on the side of the Infant Christ. On the back the metal cover was torn and jagged; the bullet had drilled through the half-inch thickness of metal and wood.

As he reached over to replace the ikon, Warren noticed

251

a piece of paper lying where the ikon normally rested. He picked it up. It was a small square of rice-paper, neatly trimmed, though one corner had been torn off. The words were written in a graceful hand: "Stand before the holy ikons, and gazing upon them, direct thy thoughts toward the invisible God."

"Nurse! Nurse!"

Someone at the end of the row of cots repeated his call and in a few moments the nurse was hurrying to his bedside.

"Where'd this come from?"

"Why, from your personal effects. What's wrong?"

"You didn't write it?"

"Of course not," she answered brusquely. "I thought it went with the picture there."

"What made you think that? I've never seen it before."

"You must have. It was in that little velvet sack that the picture came in . . . the picture that saved your life. You're just excited now, you calm down and you'll be all right in no time." Her voice was again professionally reassuring and he allowed her to ease him back to the pillow and pop a thermometer into his mouth.

"Lodged in front of your heart," the surgeon told him when he asked. The surgeon was a colonel about forty, with a thick crop of reddish-brown hair. "The armored vest wasn't made to stop machine gun slugs," he grinned, "nor was that," he nodded at the ikon. "But between the two they slowed the slug down enough to save your life. As it was, we had to dig it out from the fatty tissue around your heart."

It had been Rickley who had insisted that he carry the ikon. He recalled how he had thrust it into his breast pocket with mixed emotions, a last impulse. Warren asked the nurse about Rickley; she hadn't heard of him, nor had the surgeon any record of such a patient.

About White they were tight-lipped. "Ask the colonel

252

when he comes around," was all the nurse would say. The surgeon's bluff features had changed when he heard the name. "Yes," he said, shaking his large head, "he's here. Very serious, very serious, poor fellow." Then catching himself, he dropped his large freckled hand onto Warren's leg and said, "But we'll pull him through." He hung the clipboard on the foot of the bed and moved on to the next cot.

Each day the fresh flowers appeared in the vase in front of the ikon and each day the colonel strolled between the bunks to glance at the charts hanging at the foot of the beds. One day the nurse announced, "You have visitors." Warren looked up to see Lefevre and Lieutenant Held standing behind her. She tugged at his sheets, patting them down, and made a gesture at rearranging the flowers in the vase before leaving them alone. "No sitting on the bed," she said as she left.

"Thought I'd come down to check up on you." Lieutenant Held fidgeted nervously, his young face marked with a haggardness new to it. "Called and they said you'd be flown out of here tomorrow, so made it today."

"They didn't tell *me* I was going tomorrow."

"You don't have a lieutenant's bars," Lefevre grinned.

"Lefevre here is going on line to replace you," Lieutenant Held said, shaking his head. "Boy, will Ordway crow if he hears about what happened to us."

The mention of Ordway reminded Warren that the nurse had put the items found in his pocket in the drawer of the little table beside his bed. He reached for the knob.

"I've got some stuff for you," Lieutenant Held said, holding out a plastic bag in which Warren could see some of his personal possessions. "Thought I'd deliver them."

Warren took the bag. The brown envelope containing Jean's picture was visible. "And I'm searching for something I meant to show you," Warren said, feeling that the words were not right, but not knowing how to soften the

253

fact of Ordway's suicide. "I got this just before the patrol." He lifted the clipping out of the drawer. "Thought I'd wait until afterwards before I gave it to you."

"Well, let's have it." Warren handed over the clipping. Held, a quizzical expression on his face, glanced at it. "Oh, no. My God!"

Lefevre's own features altered as he saw the change coming over the lieutenant's face.

"But, but . . ." Lieutenant Held groped for words and stopped. He dropped to the edge of the cot, his eyes again on the clipping. When he looked up, his hurt face turned first to Warren, then to Lefevre. "I don't . . . Why . . . ?" He pressed his hands against his face. "And I just wrote him a letter." He stood. "I just don't understand it. That man could have been a general." He looked at the two men once again. "I'll wait in the jeep," he said to Lefevre.

"Sorry, sir," Warren said.

"Yes, yes, of course . . ." Held turned away, then paused a moment to add, "a general." He continued to shake his head as he walked down the rows of cots.

"Bad news, eh?" Lefevre asked.

"Yes. Someone we knew killed himself."

"Oh." Lefevre looked at the floor, his black hair tumbling over his forehead.

"Well," Warren shifted his position, "tell me, what happened?"

"Folger," Lefevre began.

"I know about him."

"Claypool, too?"

"Claypool?"

"Yes. Tracer in the stomach. It took him half an hour to die."

"White was wounded," Warren said. "They say seriously."

254

"Medic said that he got chewed up right along the thighs." Lefevre looked at the floor uneasily.

"You mean the groin?"

"That's what they say, but, of course," Lefevre looked up, "it always looks worse when it first happens."

"Yeah," Warren said. "Anybody else?"

"One other killed and two wounded. They were in the rifle company. Don't know their names. The KIA was a lieutenant."

"Swiggart."

"The patrol was successful, though. They got the bodies in and White got that machine gun."

"White did?"

"Yes. They'll probably give him a medal for it. After he got hit, he dragged himself up the slope and practically handed the machine gunner a grenade."

There was a long silence, painful for Warren. He turned to the ikon. "They say this saved my life," he pointed at the torn image. "Nurse says I should pray to her." He looked for a reaction from Lefevre, but the other remained silent. Finally, Warren braved the question.

"And Rickley?"

Lefevre's dark eyes met his. "I tried to warn you."

Their shared knowledge pulled them together in the silence that followed. It was as if language was an enemy to the mystery they confronted. When Lefevre raised his eyes, Warren followed his gaze to the golden image; the ripped metal heightened the sublime quiet of the portraits.

Lefevre touched Warren's hand in a gesture of going and murmured something, but his words went unheard. Long after he had gone, Warren, with considerable effort, stirred. With arm outstretched, he edged nearer the ikon until his extended finger touched and found its way, hesitantly, into the wound.